Other John Dickson Carr mysteries available from
Carroll & Graf:

John Dickson Carr
Scandal at High Chimneys

Carroll & Graf Publishers, Inc.
New York

For Joan Kahn

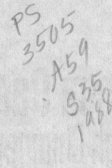

Published by arrangement with Harold Ober Associates, Inc

First Carroll & Graf edition 1988

Carroll & Graf Publishers, Inc.
260 Fifth Avenue
New York, NY 10001

ISBN: 0-88184-394-6

Manufactured in the United States of America

Contents

I.	Shapes of Dread	1
II.	The Bath-and-Bristol Express	9
III.	The Goblin on the Stairs	16
VI.	Two Sisters for a Valentine	23
V.	The Hanging of Harriet Pyke	31
VI.	Death with Patterned Trousers	39
VII.	How the Lamps Gathered Close Round a Witness	47
VIII.	The Masks of Georgette Damon	56
IX.	Encounter in Oxford Street	65
X.	The Moods of Kate Damon	75
XI.	Twilight in the Conservatory	84
XII.	"The World as I Find It"	92
XIII.	How a Dead Woman Waited for an Elopement	101
XIV.	Bewilderment in an Oyster-Shop	111
XV.	Cherry Ripe	121
XVI.	The Shadows of Scotland Yard	130
XVII.	The Hands of Celia Damon	138
XVIII.	Night-Life: The Alhambra	146
XIX.	Night-Life: At the Third Pillar	153
XX.	Night-Life: The Gas Burns High	161
	Notes for the Curious	177

I. SHAPES OF DREAD

It concerned Kate and Celia Damon, two sisters of whom people said that they did not seem at all like sisters. Kate was the dark one, Celia the fair. Kate inclined towards boldness and high spirits, Celia was demure but intense. That both were extremely pretty could not be denied.

"And, indeed, when they are married—" the second Mrs. Damon once remarked.

Mr. Matthew Damon turned in his stately way.

"They are too young for marriage," he said.

"Matthew, you astonish me. If I am correctly informed, Celia is twenty and Kate fully nineteen. How much older would you have them?"

"There is time in plenty to think of such matters. Meanwhile, let them be a credit to their upbringing and a comfort to our old age."

"Old age?" repeated the girls' stepmother, who herself was auburn-haired and handsome. "Speak for yourself, Mr. Damon!"

Then she cowered before the other's suppressed violence.

"Yet I do say it," he retorted. "Madam, I will hear no more of this; at least, not yet. Let them be a credit to us; that is enough. They are good girls, even in such fast times as ours."

Now this may have been exaggerated, perhaps as regards the times and certainly as regards one of the Damon sisters. But Matthew Damon, a man of the world and no fool, had much justification for what he said.

Rigid decorum ruled the drawing-room. No shock must be brought to the cheek or heart of a young lady in her crinoline and pork-pie hat. Few besides Miss Nightingale would have thought of seeing the Crimea. Yet on the fringes of their well-to-do world, for many hundred yards from the Regent Circus to the top of the Haymarket and then east-

1

wards to Leicester Square, brawled a night-life more vulgar than that of Paris because there was so little joy in it.

"Sparring snobs," wrote one who was no fool either, "and flashing satins, and sporting swells, and painted cheeks, and brandy-sparkling eyes, and bad tobacco, and hoarse horse-laughs, and long indecency. I can take personally an example from three quarters of the globe; but I have never anywhere witnessed such open ruffianism and wretched profligacy as rings along those Piccadilly flagstones any time after the gas is lighted."

That hardly mattered, it was true. We had prosperity to buttress us, and prove such conditions didn't exist.

We knew everything, or nearly everything. The railway, the steamship, the electric telegraph had abolished time and distance. Prosperity made a din like the noise of its own wheels and hammers, shrouding London in smoke and bringing darker fashions in clothes than did the death of the Prince Consort.

"We are proud of it," everyone said.

On the other hand, though we worshipped a sound money-changing God, we shivered pleasantly at the thought of outer darkness. Ghost stories had never been so popular. Of course, when murder entered the circle of Matthew Damon's family, with two violent deaths and a murderer who wasn't there, nobody at High Chimneys really believed in the supernatural. The problem was to account for the murderer's behaviour.

And this was the manner of it:

One night in October, during the full tide of Victorianism in the year 1865, a young man got out of a hansom at Bryce's Club in Dover Street.

His name was Clive Strickland, and he was a likeable fellow even if he appeared somewhat formal and conventional. The clocks had only just gone six; he knew he could get no dinner there until seven. But Clive Strickland only wanted to sit quietly, in an otherwise deserted smoking-room, and think about the new serial story he was writing for *All the Year Round.*

The foyer at Bryce's Club, a melancholy place of black and white tile flagstones, is haunted by an odour of damp greatcoats and boiled mutton. Pearson, the hall-porter, peered out of the glass cubicle as he heard Clive's footsteps.

"Good evening, sir. Gentleman to see you."

"Thank you, Pearson. Who is it?"

"I've shown him into the visitors' room, sir," said Pearson, craftily refusing to answer.

It was not necessary to answer. Victor Damon, in formal evening-clothes like Clive's own, hurried out of the visitors'

2

room and stopped short. Clive could not have been more surprised if Victor, the butterfly, had turned up in a bench of bishops.

"Got to see you, old boy," declared Victor, fingering his very broad white tie below the high collar. "It's rather important. In here, eh?"

And he bolted back into the visitors' room.

Only one hat and greatcoat, Victor's, hung amid many pegs on the wall of the foyer. Clive Strickland added his own to them and followed. Victor, his hands under his coattails and his back to the fire, stared out of gloom.

"Look here, Victor, what the devil is the matter with you?"

"Nothing," Victor assured him. "Nothing at all, give you my honour! Only—it's the governor."

"What about your father? Between ourselves, have you been getting into debt again?"

"Good God, no," said Victor, plainly startled.

"Then what is it?"

"You've met my two sisters, I think? Kate and Celia?"

"I have had that honour, yes."

"Well, old boy," said Victor, moving his neck, "I want you to do me a very great favour. I want you to go down to High Chimneys tomorrow, and ask for Celia's hand in marriage."

Silence.

Clive Strickland did not utter an exclamation or even show any surprise. But he was not sure he had heard properly.

The fire in the visitors' room was always poor and smoky, and its lights turned low to save expense. Stepping past Victor, Clive brightened the gas-jets in their flattish glass dishes on either side of the chimneypiece. Victor Damon's face, waveringly, sprang up at him.

Though Victor was not much more than twenty-one, slender and delicate-featured, he had grown a fairly heavy moustache like his heavy light-brown hair. His evening-clothes showed the most fashionable full-cut, his gold watch-chain was ponderous.

Clive would politely have claimed friendship with both the sisters, but in fact he had not seen them since they were in their early teens and hardly remembered either of them. It was the imaginative son he knew; Clive, having visited High Chimneys with his own parents in the old days, later became pretty well acquainted with Victor in London. Nor could he forget Victor's formidable father.

Matthew Damon, tall and tight-lipped, presented an enigma to any writer of fiction. And Mr. Damon, barrister-at-law, had no need of the law as a profession; he was very

3

wealthy in his own right. Clive judged him to be essentially a kindly man, though a terrifying prosecutor when he appeared for the Crown, and not too easy-mannered among his very few friends.

But still it seemed odd that Matthew Damon, who was also deeply religious in the old Evangelical way, should be followed everywhere by so many furtive speculations and half-whispers. It was not only that he had married again, after remaining a widower since Victor and Celia and Kate were small children. It was also . . .

"Well, old boy?" demanded Victor, suddenly moving away from the fire and turning round.

Clive woke up.

"I am forgetting myself, Victor," he said, and reached towards the bell. "What will you have to drink?"

"Nothing, I thank you," retorted Victor, even more surprisingly. "What d'ye say, old boy? About what *I* say?"

"It is a great honour, of course, to be asked to marry Miss Celia—"

"You?" exclaimed Victor. His hand went up to his moustache. "Damme, Clive, I didn't mean *you* were to marry her."

"You didn't?"

"No! You're a good feller, but you're no great catch. I mean to say: you're a lawyer, ain't you? You were a solicitor or something, before you began writing novels?"

"I was a barrister."

"That'll do. You're still empowered to arrange marriages, I daresay? You can go down and talk it over with the governor?"

"Arrange Celia's marriage? To whom?"

"To Tress."

"If you mean Lord Albert Tressider . . ."

Clive would have spoken at some length, but Victor cut him off.

"Sh-h!" he urged. No footstep creaked in the room, where gaslight shone on either side of the black chimneypiece. Victor craned his neck round to glance at the door. "Sh-h!" he repeated. "Don't speak so loudly! And Tress'll be here at any minute, so mind you call him 'my lord.'"

"Quite frankly, I'm damned if I will."

"You don't like Tress," Victor said in an accusing tone.

"No; I don't like him."

"But that's neither here nor there. His pa's a *marquess*. He's taken quite a fancy to little Celia, and he'll have her as neat as ninepence if we play our cards properly. How many girls get the chance to marry into the peerage? And my governor, bless him, is still rather a snob when all's said. Tomorrow afternoon you must go down and speak to him."

"Victor, I won't do it."

"But—!"

"In the first place," Clive raised his voice, "it's not a barrister's business. In the second place, even if it were, that's the very last commission I should care to undertake. It's a matter for Tress's own solicitor, if it's a matter for anybody at all. Why do you ask me?"

"Because the governor likes you. On my honour! Reads all your stories; says they're not half bad either. Besides, we keep it among friends."

"Tell me, now: does your father know anything whatever about this proposed marriage?"

"No! Not yet."

"Does Celia herself know anything about it?"

"Well—no."

"Victor," Clive said abruptly, "what's wrong at High Chimneys?"

His companion stood motionless, hand going again to his moustache. A boisterous autumn night, blowing all the waste-paper which is as thick as grit in London streets, whooped outside. Though the windows might be sealed with thick dingy-green curtains as all their lives (they hoped) were shrouded and sealed from view, the wind found loose frames; draughts carried away most scents except the pervasiveness of the damp greatcoats and the boiled mutton.

"Now don't tell me," insisted Clive, "that a match between Celia and Tress would be advantageous in the world's eyes. No doubt it would be. All the same! I always understood you were fond of Celia."

"So I am. Devil take it! So I am."

"But you sound as though you want to get Celia safely married, spirited away from your father's house and out of sight, as quickly and secretly as you can manage."

"It's not only a question of Celia. It's—it's a question of Kate too!"

"How?"

"Get *her* married," said Victor.

"That's what I mean. Do you want to pitch both your sisters into the matrimonial cart without so much as a by-your-leave to either? Why?"

Victor opened his mouth to speak, and shut it on the first word. In Clive's mind rose again the image of Matthew Damon: bedevilled, inflexibly honest, with a handsome young

5

wife and a fine country-house near Reading, yet his career clouded with whispers and a wonder among the initiated that all honours had passed him by.

There were even some who laughed when they spoke of him.

In another moment, Clive thought, Victor would have told him the whole story. Victor had begun, "You see—" when there were footsteps out in the foyer. A loud, cool voice rose above the obsequious tones of the hall-porter. Tress himself, escorted by the porter, appeared in the doorway and smiled in his agreeable way.

"Ah, Damon," he said by way of greeting.

"I say! Tress, old fellow! You're early, ain't you? The fact is, I hadn't—"

"Hadn't finished talking with the attorney?" inquired Tress, raising his eyebrows. "You should have, you know. I gave you plenty of time, and I don't like to be kept waiting. Perhaps it's just as well, though. To tell you the truth, Damon, I've half a mind to call it off."

"Call it off?"

"Cry quits, if you like," Tress said coolly. "Say Miss Celia Damon's too good for me, and here's my compliments and good-bye."

"But why?"

Tress laughed, a great deep laugh without much noise, and sauntered towards the fire.

Victor hastened to the door, closing it with a hollow slam which billowed its tasselled door-curtain, and then hurried after Tress.

"Why?" he insisted.

Tress spread out his hands to the fire. He was a burly young man, with stiffish dark-yellow hair and whiskers round a stolidly handsome face. He towered above Victor, diffusing animal vitality. Over his evening-clothes Tress wore a plum-blue greatcoat with an astrakhan collar, and carried a hat whose nap was a gossamer silk.

"The fact is, Damon, you haven't been very frank with me. I can't say I like that either. I've been hearing things, you know."

It was unwise to prod the mild-seeming Victor, whose head jerked up and back.

"If you've heard one word against Celia, it's a lie."

"Tush! Come, now! What a sputtering little Lucifer it is!" Tress grinned. Then his tone changed. "Not to do with your sister, Damon. It's to do with your governor-general."

"My father's never done anything he shouldn't have done!"

"Oh? He married an actress, didn't he?"

"It's no fault of Celia's if he did. Anyway, my stepmother is a dashed fine woman! I admire her!"

"We all admire 'em, Damon. But we don't receive 'em in our homes, you know."

Suddenly Victor lifted his hands and pressed them over his eyes.

"And that's not all, you know," Tress pointed out. "I talked to Serjeant Ballantine only yesterday. It seems your governor used to have uncommonly queer tastes. He enjoyed making up to women who'd committed murder."

Victor snatched his hands away from his eyes.

"Fact, you know," said Tress. "He would prosecute 'em, all as virtuous as an Old Testament prophet. Afterwards he'd go to Newgate and visit 'em any number of times before they were hanged three weeks later. Of course he pretended it was to pray with 'em and relieve his conscience, but Serjeant Ballantine says that's all my eye. Your governor-general was quite spooney about two or three of them, especially the young and pretty ones. It seems he couldn't resist 'em."

"God!" whispered Victor.

Wind whistled in Dover Street; the chimney growled under a cold sky.

"Tress, does this mean you won't have Celia?" Victor cried. "Does this mean you'll go back on your offer, Tress?"

Tress, after waiting for a moment or two, uttered his deep almost noiseless chuckle.

"Oh, come! Not a bit of it, my boy. I'm in something of a financial hole, you know; the younger son usually is; and your governor-general's money is as good as anybody else's. I offered my name; I'll stand by it."

There were those who called Clive Strickland a too-conventional young man, even by the standards of this year 1865. He was not. Clive, who had taken out his cigar-case, flung it into a padded chair near the fire.

"That's very generous of you," he said; and Tress, raising poised eyebrows, slowly looked him up and down.

"*You* said something, Strickland?"

"Yes. I did. Have you troubled to ask Miss Damon what she thinks of all this? Or thinks of you either?"

"Why, no. No, Mr. Attorney. I can't say I have."

"Has it also occurred to you, Tressider, that 'attorney' is a confoundedly offensive term?"

"Is it, now?" inquired Tress. " 'Pon my sang I don't know, and 'pon my sang I don't care."

Victor was in agony.

"Tress, don't antagonize him. For heaven's sake don't antagonize him, Tress. Clive don't like this business at all;

he don't for a fact; and he may not help me if you put his back up."

"Well, then, we'll find somebody else. Strickland might do worse than earn his keep; this book-writing, you know, isn't very much. However, I'll go along and leave you to it. If you care to stroll into the Argyll Rooms about eleven, I'll stand sam for a bottle to celebrate. Good evening, Damon."

And Tress, having derived some amusement from all this, put on his tall hat and patted it into place. After settling his shoulders, after examining his bristly chin-whisker in the looking-glass over the fireplace, he smiled agreeably and moved away like a tame tiger. Once more the heavy door, this time caught in a draught, closed with a slam that went echoing up through a club devoted to writers, painters, musicians, and other mountebanks.

Victor swallowed hard.

"I know what you're thinking of me," he said. "I know, and I can't blame you. But don't make a judgment too quickly."

"No?"

"No! Look here, old boy. There are any number of trains tomorrow, but your best is the Bath-and-Bristol Express. That leaves the depot in the afternoon and stops at Reading. I can write a telegram, d'ye see, so that Burbage will meet you with the carriage."

Clive, who had bent over to retrieve his cigar-case, straightened up.

"Victor, do you seriously imagine I mean to do that?"

"You must, old boy. Pray believe me!"

"For instance," said Clive, "you see no objection to having a sister of yours married to the gentleman who's just left us?"

"No; *I* can't see any objection." Victor's voice went high. "But that's not the point. You were right about one thing. I'd have Kate or Celia married to *anybody,* anybody at all reasonable or presentable, as long as they were safely away from High Chimneys and out of danger."

"Danger? For the last time, man, what's wrong at High Chimneys?"

The gaslight, vivid bluish-yellow, shone on a drop of sweat at Victor's temple. Whipping a handkerchief out of the tail-pocket of his coat, Victor mopped his forehead. Under the edges of that handkerchief, reflected in his companion's eyes, Clive Strickland sensed the shape of images ugly and unnatural and not well understood. Victor shut his eyes.

"I can't tell you," he answered. "I can't tell you."

8

II. THE BATH-AND-BRISTOL EXPRESS

The depot of the Great Western Railway, dim and sooty and hoarse with steam, rattled to a clamour of footsteps on wooden platforms. Dogs, as usual, barked frantically at the engine; small boys escaped from their mothers to stare at it. Also, as usual, there was the middleaged lady in the voluminous crinoline, who falls into a fit of megrims five minutes before train-time and cries out that she hasn't the courage to go.

At one o'clock on the following afternoon, a chilly day, the Bath-and-Bristol Express was 'getting a good head up.' Porters had finished piling heavy luggage on the roofs of the carriages. Though this terminus had been built of iron and glass like the Crystal Palace, you still groped and coughed in London smoke. Clive Strickland did.

'I am a fool,' he was thinking guiltily. 'Indeed, it were charitable to call me an outstanding jackass. People whose imaginations are kindled by the face of a damsel in distress, and who charge to her rescue without quite knowing what they are supposed to do, should be confined to the sort of fiction I write.'

"Fool!" he said aloud.

"Sir?" exclaimed the man carrying his portmanteau.

"I beg your pardon. First-class carriage number two, seat number six."

"Oh, yes, sir! Very good, sir."

This situation was not at all humorous. He had committed himself to a course he could neither approve nor justify.

Clive tried to put it out of his mind. A vigorous dark-haired young man, clean-shaven, in a short greatcoat and one of the new-style bowler hats, he strode towards the train. But the sense of impending disaster refused to leave him.

Whereupon, just ahead, he saw Mr. Matthew Damon.

Clive stopped short.

It was not so much the shock of seeing him there as shock at the change in Mr. Damon's appearance.

9

Victor had said his father seemed to have aged ten years in the past three or four months, and that he had hardly left High Chimneys during that time. Even so, Clive was not prepared for that change.

Matthew Damon, looking round uncertainly with one hand in the bosom of his frock coat, stood by the footboard of a first-class carriage with an open compartment-door behind him. Clive's first impulse was to turn and bolt. But he was within two yards of the other man; those sunken eyes had seen him.

"Mr. Strickland!"

Clive's head ached with all the drinking he had done the night before.

"Good afternoon, sir," he said.

Matthew Damon, at forty-eight, was still formidable. He wore all his old air of sombre power and authority; the deep voice was like a drum. He had been a handsome man and remained so. Though he had a somewhat old-fashioned appearance, wearing a hat of beaverskin rather than silk and a shawl round his shoulders, his clothes and linen were of the finest quality. But his cheeks had sunken badly between thick black side-whiskers turning grey-white; and the eyes seemed to have retreated into his head.

"Mr. Strickland," he repeated, and groped. "You—you travel by this train? Ah, yes. So do we. To what fortunate circumstance do we owe the pleasure of your company?"

"I imagine, sir, you did not receive my telegram?"

"Your telegram?"

"Yes, sir. I took the liberty of inviting myself to High Chimneys. It was a piece of insufferable impertinence, I'm afraid."

"Not at all. Not at all, I assure you! You are always welcome, young man, though I—I believe that for years I have not seen you except in London."

Then Matthew Damon pulled himself together, clenching the hand inside his coat. He spoke with sincerity, with a kind of awkward charm which was the other side of his nature.

"Indeed, you may be of great assistance to us in solving a troublesome and unpleasant mystery," he added, turning to the door behind him. "Is it not so, my dear?"

A pretty lady with auburn hair, standing in the open doorway of the compartment with her maid hovering behind her, made a grimace and cast up her eyes.

"Mr. Damon, for pity's sake!"

"Is it not so, madam?"

Before that quiet violence the pretty lady subsided. But

her wifely meekness carried other hints, like her broad if subdued charms.

"Hortense, pray do stop fussing!" she said to her maid. "And *I* believe, Mr. Strickland, that you and I met some while ago at Lady Tedworth's? I do hope you will join us in this compartment. We have it to ourselves, as you see, unless some horrid stranger should force his way in at the last moment."

And Georgette Damon, auburn hair brushed up into short curls at the back of a flat oval hat, glanced at Clive under her lowered eyelashes.

It was a perfunctory glance, a discreet glance. Yet in some extraordinary way it was as though she had pressed herself physically against him. It conveyed, embarrassingly, a sense of what lay under her dark-green Zouave jacket with its tight-fitting green-silk blouse. Her crinoline, grey-coloured and straight in front, stretched back in a balloon-like triangle according to the latest mode.

Damn the woman!

Clive Strickland felt his thoughts moving in a direction they shouldn't have moved, and he cursed himself too.

"My ticket-number is for a different carriage, Mrs. Damon, but I shall be honoured to join you. Do—do Miss Kate and Miss Celia accompany you?"

"No, no!" said Mr. Damon. "Kate and Celia are not with us; they are good girls," he added rather inexplicably. "My wife and I left Reading by a very early train; we have been in town only a few hours. You spoke of a telegram, young man?"

"Yes, sir. Victor was to have left one with the hall-porter at Bryce's Club last night, but I telegraphed first thing this morning."

Smoke and smudges drifted about them. Georgette Damon left off looking at Clive, and her husband's face had altered in an almost terrifying way.

"You were in Victor's company last night? For how long?"

"Well, sir, between six in the evening and about two o'clock in the morning."

"You are sure of that, Mr. Strickland? You are very sure?"

Clive had reason to be sure, and said so. Matthew Damon turned to his wife.

"Then it was *not* a prank," he declared, "and our visitor could not have been Victor. I should have trusted my instinct, madam. I should have paid a visit to that detective."

'Come, now!' thought Clive Strickland. 'What precisely is happening here?'

But he had no chance to consider it.

Already the bell was ringing for the imminent departure of the train. Hortense, Mrs. Damon's maid, slipped down with a graceful curtsey and hastened towards a second-class carriage at the rear. Clive found himself sitting in the corner seat against musty-smelling upholstery, his back to the engine and his portmanteau beside him, facing Georgette Damon with her husband at her right-hand side.

A guard with flag and whistle moved past outside, locking each compartment-door and taking away the key. The whistle blew soon afterwards.

There were cries and squeals of alarm from inside third-class carriages without glass in their windows. Amid fire-glare from the locomotive, with a chug and thud of steam shuddering through ten carriages of three compartments each, the great driving-wheels gripped and the train began to move.

'Gently!' thought Clive.

He was born in this railway age. He had no qualms about being locked up here, shut away beyond escape or communication with another compartment, in a train hurtling along at fifty miles an hour.

But the different looks on the faces of his companions, so far as he could see them in thick gloom, disturbed him not a little.

"Mr. Strickland," said Matthew Damon, in a harsh and troubled voice, "you will permit me to pursue this matter a little further. You are not moved, I hope, by any misguided sense of loyalty to my son? You are not shielding him?"

"Great Scott, no! Shielding him from what?"

"Be good enough, young man, to answer my question."

Wrath touched Clive, who sat up as straight as the other man.

"Then state your question, Mr. Damon."

"How did you and Victor employ last evening?"

"There's very little to tell."

There was very little, at least, that Clive cared to tell. Victor had dined with him at Bryce's Club, where Victor got tolerably drunk. There would have been no harm in mentioning this; Victor's father was addicted to brandy-and-soda and encouraged the old customs. But Victor, though always amiable in liquor, had made his usual announcement that he was going out to find female company of a more than dubious sort.

To have let him go out on his own would have been unthinkable. A man who strayed one step beyond the bright gaslight round the Regent Circus and the top of the Haymarket, especially alone and fuddled, might be set on for his money and beaten within an ace of death. Clive, himself none too sober but an able hand in a fight, had accompanied Victor to look after him.

But he couldn't tell this to the old man.

They had visited the Argyll Rooms, where there was dancing, though they did not encounter Tress. They looked in at three or four night-haunts, garish boozing-dens of mirrors and plush in which the best-dressed sirens strolled provocatively and champagne cost as much as twenty-five shillings a bottle.

"Victor," Clive had kept insisting, "what's wrong at High Chimneys?"

"Can't tell you, old boy."

"Then what's the danger to your sisters?"

"My goo' friend!" Victor said emotionally, and wept and collapsed.

Clive bundled him into a cab, drove home with him, and carried him upstairs to Victor's rooms near Portman Square. In the sitting-room, lighting a candle, he had first seen the painting.

It was a portrait in oils, of a girl's head and shoulders and bust, in a heavy gilt frame above the fireplace. Brown eyes looked back at him, wide open, under a broad forehead and glossy black hair. Intelligence, eagerness even to a touch of impatience, as at hearing nonsense once too often, animated the dark eyebrows and the full-lipped mouth. It showed litheness as well as delicacy, hand clenched at breast.

Victor, sprawled dead drunk on an ottoman, had been unable to speak. But a small metal plate at the foot of the frame was inscribed *Miss Kate Damon, 1865.*

Clive remembered all too well how the light of the candle had brought that face out of darkness like a warm and living presence.

"Yes, Mr. Strickland?" prompted Matthew Damon.

The rattle of the railway was in Clive's ears now. Through the cutting below Westbourne Park Villas, out the long stretch south of Alpert Road, the train gathered speed with a bone-shaking sway and jolt.

"There's very little to tell," Clive repeated. "Victor dined with me at my club, and afterwards I walked home with him."

"Come, young man! You stayed at your club until nearly two o'clock in the morning?"

"I did not say that, sir," Clive almost snapped. "Afterwards we sat in Victor's rooms, smoking and talking."

"Was my son drunk?"

"Yes. Would it not be better, perhaps, to address these questions to Victor himself?"

"I have already done so. That is why I went to London this morning. Victor was still drunk and incoherent."

Clive still could not understand.

"In any event, sir, he was with me the whole time. Should you doubt my presence in his rooms, I noticed a portrait of Miss Kate Damon which was not there when I called on him a week ago."

"*That* abominable painting?"

"If you'll excuse my saying so, it seemed to me a remarkably fine picture."

"No doubt. It was painted by Mr. Millais. But I had reference to its moral quality. I strongly disapproved of it, and Victor was free to carry it away. Mr. Millais wished to exhibit it at the Royal Academy, if you please, under the obnoxious title of 'Unfulfillment.' "

The London smoke-pall was clearing away. Quite suddenly, or so it seemed, autumn daylight penetrated through the grimy glass of the windows. Much mud had been trampled into the compartment, Clive saw, but then mud was trampled everywhere.

Matthew Damon sat bolt upright, clutching the shawl round his neck. His tall hat vibrated from the motion of the flying train.

"I have observed in Kate, Mr. Strickland," the deep voice continued, "a—a certain restlessness which is not present, perhaps surprisingly, in Celia. What do these young people want?"

Clive made no reply; none was expected.

"What do these young people want? Why are they not happy? I am not an unreasonable man, Mr. Strickland. Unlike some bigots, I see no objection to novel-reading or to attendance at the theatre for the best comedy or tragedy. But dancing, and loose talk, and unchaperoned intermingling of the sexes among those of immature years, I cannot and will not tolerate."

Mr. Damon lifted a powerful right fist and struck the padded arm of the chair.

His wife had been looking out of the window on her left. Her great dove-grey crinoline, on its collapsing framework of watch-spring wire, spread so far round her that her husband sat three or four feet away.

"Surely, Matthew," she cried, "you attach too much importance to all that? And in particular to what happened last night?"

"I think not, my love."

14

"But no harm was done!"

"Harm? What is harm?"

Each time he looked at her, it was with anger and self-distrust mingled with a fierce kind of hunger. Georgette gave him a coy glance, and he edged closer.

"You are all too ignorant of human evil, my love. But I am not. I have spent my life in meeting it and fighting it. I account myself a good judge of truth and falsehood. For instance," and Mr. Damon's head swung round, "I put it to you, Mr. Strickland, that you are concealing my son's behaviour last night because he had engaged himself with some unsavoury adventure in London?"

"I—"

"Yes or no, Mr. Strickland? Yes or no?"

"Let's say, sir, he might have *wished* for some such thing. But he had taken too much to drink, and he didn't."

"Ah! That is better. Will you give me your word as a gentleman that he could not have been at High Chimneys at eleven-thirty last night?"

"High Chimneys? At eleven-thirty Victor and I were just walking into . . . that is to say, I give you my word he wasn't within forty miles of High Chimneys."

"And I accept it," replied Mr. Damon, studying him during a hard-breathing pause. His fist clenched again. "Well! Such behaviour in a young man (a young man, mark you; not a young lady!) is reprehensible but not unpardonable. Well! I accept it."

"Look here, sir: why is it so necessary to prove Victor wasn't at High Chimneys?"

"I scarcely think, Mr. Damon," interposed Georgette in a lofty tone, "we need bore our guest with trivial domestic affairs."

"On the contrary, madam. Mr. Strickland, despite his youth, is a highly successful author. He occupies himself with what is called the novel of sensation, endeavouring to surprise us with what we may discover in the final chapters. It is a harmless amusement, and not uninstructive. I assume he will be interested, and I hope he may prove useful."

Matthew Damon bent forward, one hand gripping the chair-arm and the other holding his shawl.

"Mr. Strickland," he said, "do you believe in ghosts?"

III. THE GOBLIN ON
THE STAIRS

When he thought about it long afterwards, Clive knew he should have seen much evidence in what Matthew Damon said and did not say. But he could not guess that murder had already been planned, or even feel it.

He felt only the roar and jolt of the train, shaking them. Some veer in the wind brought a billow of black smoke and a swirl of sparks from the engine. High Chimneys, in Berkshire, was four miles from Reading; they would be at Reading in less than an hour.

If he saw anything at all, he saw Kate Damon's pictured face. Since last night it had drawn and fascinated him. He ached to rescue her from imagined dangers, after the fashion of the romances he wrote. But this particular danger he could not take very seriously.

"Believe in ghosts?" he repeated. "No."

"No! We are too sensible for that; we must look further afield."

Mr. Damon brooded for a moment, and seemed to shy back at what he imagined.

"The past three months, Mr. Strickland, have been no easy time for me. It is strange that a man may go on for years, almost decades, wilfully blinding himself to what must sooner or later be the result of his own folly. It was not sin; no. But assuredly it was folly. We postpone decisions, in the hope of we know not what. The mind tricks and befools us. And then we are lost."

He paused.

"Mine is the blame; so be it! Yet this is not to say all. Kate's restlessness (I call it no worse) and Celia's nervous state have combined with other circumstances to produce some *malaise*. My wife, good woman that she is—"

Here he stretched out his left hand to Georgette, who pressed it gently in both her hands and gazed out of the window.

16

"—my wife, being persuaded I must be ill, last week wrote to our London physician. Nonsense! I am not ill."

"Poor Matthew," murmured Georgette.

"I am not ill, I say! It would require a bullet to kill me. However, Mr. Strickland, all these remarks are not to our purpose. You may perhaps remember Burbage, my house-steward?"

"Yes; very well."

"You may also recall that Burbage has a daughter?"

"No, sir. Or, at least, I don't remember her."

"Well! Burbage has a daughter named Penelope. For some days she has been paying a visit to her father, being accommodated in a room among the servants on the top floor. Penelope, I should explain, is employed as a governess by a well-to-do family in Wiltshire. She is a young woman educated above her station in life, but well-conducted and sensible and trustworthy.

"Yesterday was Monday, the sixteenth of October. Penelope Burbage asked leave to attend a lecture at St. Thomas's Hall in Reading that night. She said that she would walk there and back, begging permission for Burbage to admit her if she should be late.

"The members of my household, Mr. Strickland, retire at ten-thirty. At ten-thirty Burbage is accustomed to close and bar all the shutters, and to lock and bar the doors. Such is my ruling; ordinarily I allow no one to be out after that time unless I myself am of the company.

"However!

"On this occasion I felt justified in making an exception. The young woman, of course, could not go unescorted. I instructed my coachman, an elderly married man whose living-quarters are over the stables, to drive Penelope to St. Thomas's Hall in the trap; to attend the lecture with her; and to drive her home.

"Further! I permitted Burbage to entrust his daughter with a key to the back door, telling him to leave it locked but unbarred. The young woman, I said, might let herself in and bar the door afterwards when she returned. No doubt this was foolish."

Again Matthew Damon leaned forward.

"Now mark well what I tell you. Ask any questions which may occur. It is of the most deadly importance, though my wife may call it trivial."

At the moment Georgette did not call it anything. Plump, uneasy, perhaps more mature than her youthful appearance indicated, she moved in her chair as though at some suspicion of which she was ashamed.

Her husband seemed to be fighting phantoms.

"For some time, Mr. Strickland, I have slept badly. The most sober of us may be visited by dreams of a frightening sort, and I have occupied a room apart from my wife. Last night I dozed amid such horrors, though I was wakeful enough to hear the noise of the horse-and-trap returning from Reading.

"You may recall the singular acoustic qualities at High Chimneys. The slightest noise indoors may be heard anywhere in the house with great distinctness. I thought I heard (correctly, as it proved) the sound of Penelope Burbage unlocking and opening the back door.

"I heard her close and lock this door on the inside. I heard her put up the bar and close it in its sockets, which cannot be managed without clatter. Very well. I was about to doze again when it occurred to me that I should have heard the young woman's footsteps going up the back stairs.

"They did not do this. The footsteps, *her* footsteps, went through the house into the main hall, where they moved about for a moment and grew louder as though approaching or ascending the main staircase at the front of the house.

"A trifle, you say? No doubt! But trifles become our preoccupation in the dark hours.

"I lit my bedside candle and opened my watch. The hour was just eleven-thirty, later than I had imagined.

"It was then I heard Penelope's voice say something. Next, distinctly, she cried, 'Who's there?' It could not have been three seconds afterwards that I heard—"

Mr. Damon stopped.

He lowered his head so that his chin rested on the fringes of the shawl and on a black satin necktie with a pearl pin. Clive, who had been watching a blue vein beat in the other's temple, spoke with unusual sharpness.

"Gently, sir! You heard what?"

Matthew Damon looked up.

"Screams," he said.

The Bath-and-Bristol Express had attained its fullest speed of fifty miles an hour. It swept round a curve, flinging Clive against the chair-arm.

"May God have mercy upon sinners! I have not heard such cries since Harriet Pyke, whom I visited so often in the condemned cell at Newgate, was carried to the gallows in '46. Do not think, I beg of you, that my conscience was troubled—"

"Why should it have been, sir?"

"—or that these screams put me in mind of Harriet Pyke. The woman was guilty. No: it put me in mind only of house-

18

breakers and thieves. I knew Penelope Burbage must have encountered one. In the shortest time it took to put on robe and slippers, I was at the head of the stairs with my candle held high.

"Burbage and the two footmen, I must confess, were not much longer in descending from the top floor. Penelope Burbage had not fainted, though she crouched at the foot of the staircase in a pitiable condition of shock.

"Her father would have run to her, but that I ordered him and the footmen to make an immediate search of the house and discover if we had been robbed. I myself lifted the young woman to her feet. Did I—did I mention that my physician, Dr. Thompson Bland, was our guest at the time and is still with us? Did I meniton that?"

Clive shook his head.

"No, sir. You said Mrs. Damon had written to him, that's all."

"Well! I was grateful for his presence. For some reason this young woman appeared to harbour extraordinary suspicions of me (of *me!*), shrinking away and screaming again. Dr. Thompson Bland descended soon afterwards and administered brandy. It was some time before Penelope could be persuaded to tell what happened."

"And what had happened?"

Silence.

"What *had* happened, sir?"

"As I surmised," continued Mr. Damon, calm and bleak once more, "Penelope had entered by the back door, which she locked and closely barred after her. Burbage had left her bedroom candle on a table by this door, but she could not light it. The kitchen fire had gone out, and there were no Lucifers at hand.

"Our rooms at High Chimneys, you may recall, are heavily curtained. However, it was not too difficult to grope her way through and light the candle by what little remained of the fire in the main hall. This being contrived, Penelope started up the front staircase. She did not go far.

"There was a man standing partway up the staircase, looking down at her.

"The man did not move or speak, nor did Penelope. After a moment Penelope said, 'Is that you, sir?' and lifted the light higher without being able to see his face. Still the figure did not move or speak. Penelope cried out, 'Who's there?' The man put out both hands and ran down at her to seize her, but his footsteps made no sound as he ran.

"Penelope stumbled backwards, throwing her arm across her face. The candle went out. Penelope screamed and continued to scream in the dark, though nothing touched her. By the time I myself appeared, she was alone."

Georgette Damon started as a head loomed up dark in silhouette outside the compartment-windows. It was only the guard, edging past on the footboard outside to collect tickets. Much dirt blew in; afterwards Clive closed the window hastily.

"She was alone?" he repeated. "What had happened to the man on the stairs?"

"Apparently he had disappeared."

"Could Penelope describe him?"

"After a fashion. She stated with some positiveness that he was wearing a frock-coat, a dark waistcoat, patterned trousers, and socks without shoes. Aside from the last point, which would account for the absence of sound, half the men in England must own such a costume."

"True; but . . ."

"Was he tall or short? Old or young? Fat or thin? Penelope, badly frightened, could not say. Nor did she see his face. She has an impression that the figure was gigantic; but this, she acknowledges, may have been because it stood well above her on the stairs."

"Did you learn anything else from her?"

The deep-set eyes gleamed.

"Only that Penelope told the truth. I have not spent half a lifetime at the Old Bailey for nothing. But it is ironical, Mr. Strickland, that the level-headed Penelope's story should have seemed so unconvincing to others. I can still see Dr. Thompson Bland turning to me and saying, 'My dear Damon, this young woman has been dreaming.' Apparently, I repeat, apparently, the mysterious prowler did not exist."

"Didn't exist? May I ask why you say that?"

"You may. When I had finished questioning Penelope, Burbage and the two footmen returned. They had searched every inch of the house from cellars to roof. No person was hidden there. And every door and window still securely locked and barred on the inside."

Clive sat up straight.

"But that's conclusive, isn't it?"

"I wonder!"

"Really, Matthew——!" began Georgette.

"My wife has an explanation, of course."

"Yes, to be sure I have," declared Georgette, with a trembling kind of dignity. "Much as I really and truly dislike to mention it——"

"Mention it, my dear. Pray mention it, by all means."

"Matthew, she invented the whole story! Despite her so-

called virtues your Penelope Burbage is a sly-boots, and anyone but a man would have seen it long ago."

"Indeed, my love?"

"Oh, whim-wham!" cried Georgette, not without vulgarity.
The auburn curls danced at the back of her flat oval hat.
"Who else saw this mysterious prowler? No one, I think.
Miss Penelope is too plain-faced and dowdy to attract men's
notice in any other way, and so she invents this fable to have
you all at her feet. *I* know her. You will at least allow the
possibility?"

"It is a possibility, let us grant. At the same time, since *I*
am familiar with the girl's character, it is a possibility I cannot credit."

"Just a moment, sir!" Clive intervened hastily, before the
other's temper should rise too far. "Was this the reason you
asked about Victor? Why should you think the prowler might
have been Victor?"

The question caught Matthew Damon in mid-flight, one
unsteady hand at his side-whisker, giving Clive an odd, indecipherable look.

"In my heart, Mr. Strickland, I could not credit that either.
My son has been addicted to pranks, stupid and indefen-
sible pranks. But the most ingenious young gentleman cannot leave a house locked and barred behind him; I have
never known the boy to be malicious; and I accept your
word that he was with you last night. Question for question,
Mr. Strickland! A moment ago you said the evidence of the
locked house was 'conclusive.' Conclusive of what?"

"Well, sir, that's fairly clear."

"Is it? Be good enough to explain."

"The prowler, if a prowler existed, must have been someone
at High Chimneys. For instance, how many menservants live
in the house?"

"Only Burbage and the two footmen. Do you suspect one
of those?"

Clive stared at him.

"Confound it, Mr. Damon, I don't suspect anybody! I only
said—"

"Apart from the fact that Burbage has the appearance and
mind of a non-conformist clergyman, not one of those three
could have frightened Penelope, run up to the top of the
house, doffed the prowler's costume, and descended again in
different clothes at the time each did descend. Am *I* under
suspicion, young man? Or is my friend Dr. Thompson Bland?
We were the only other men in the house."

"It must have been someone, you know. If you won't allow
a ghost, as I hope you won't, then where are we left?"

21

"We are left, it would seem, with a frock-coat, a dark waistcoat, and patterned trousers described as being of a red-and-white chequered design. Explain it how you can or will."

Patterned trousers of a red-and-white chequered design. Patterned trousers of a red-and-white chequered design. Those words droned in Clive's mind to the click and bump of wheels, creating grotesque images. All of a sudden he laughed.

"Do you find this so very amusing, Mr. Strickland?"

"No, I do not," said Clive, catching the mood and retorting in the same tone. "But it occurred to me that there might be one other explanation."

"I should be interested to hear it."

"Thank you, no. It's so absurd that I prefer to keep it to myself."

"For the last time, young man, I will not be trifled with. What is your explanation?"

Again Clive stared at him.

The whistle of the train screamed for a level-crossing. Far ahead of them, reflected back on a damp sky, fled the rolling fire-glare of the locomotive. Georgette, clearly much bewildered, had taken a flask of smelling-salts from her reticule.

"It has been remarked, Mr. Strickland," Matthew Damon said judicially, "that our younger generation have no manners. Hitherto I had considered you an exception. I see I was mistaken."

"That, sir, must be as you please."

"Mr. Strickland, for pity's sake!" cried Georgette.

But the others, unheeding, took on that air of stuffy, buttoned-up politeness which both generations so well knew how to assume.

"Since I am to be your host, Mr. Strickland, I may be forgiven for reminding you that you visit me at your own invitation."

"At my own invitation, sir, but not entirely at my own wish. In one respect I am here against my own wish, and in my capacity as a lawyer, because I promised as an act of friendship to put before you a certain matter concerning your daughter."

Mr. Damon's tone altered suddenly. "My daughter?"

"Yes, sir. The truth was bound to come out sooner or later—"

Despite the chattering floorboards, Matthew Damon rose to his feet. Clive stood up too.

"—and it had better come out now. A rather offensive

22

gentleman named Tressider wants to make an offer of marriage. That's one reason why I'm here, if it's not the only reason by a long way."

Georgette screamed. Her husband's face had already grown rigid with an emotion very like horror. He swayed, and might have fallen if the astounded Clive had not caught his arm. Then he sat down heavily, muttering to himself, with the top-hat trembling on his head and one big-knuckled hand shading his eyes.

IV. TWO SISTERS FOR A VALENTINE

Only a few minutes before Clive met Kate Damon, he had begun to wonder whether he would see her at all.

In the drawing-room at High Chimneys, where only one paraffin lamp was burning now, he glanced at the clock under its glass bell on the mantelpiece. It was five minutes past six. Very clearly Clive remembered Matthew Damon's words when they had left the train, and after he had visited the office of the Electric and International Telegraph Company at Reading.

"I must tell you everything, Mr. Strickland, whatever the consequences. Do not press me now! But I am resolved to be at peace before dinner this night."

Before dinner this night.

Clive had dressed for dinner in haste, impeded by a footman whose assistance he did not want. But nobody else seemed to have come downstairs. Except for hints of a storm gathering over the Berkshire hills, he heard little or nothing.

Soundlessly the pendulum switched back and forth on the gilt clock under glass, its image reflected in the mirror-panel behind the white-marble mantelpiece. Clive looked round; everything seemed new and strange in that dim light.

The drawing-room was not the shabby place he remembered from old years. Round him loomed rosewood furniture, much carved and at a high polish from vinegar and beeswax. The floor was muffled in a thick Turkish carpet of vivid pat-

23

tern, as the windows were muffled in thick new curtains. It showed the taste and hand of the second Mrs. Damon, to whom her husband could deny nothing.

You must not smoke a cigar here, Clive could well imagine. Behind the drawing-room lay the library, unlighted; and behind that, if he remembered correctly, was Matthew Damon's study.

Clive opened the door giving on the main hall. Just across the broad hall was the morning-room, used by the family as a sitting-room when there were no guests. Clive heard a girl's clear voice upraised beyond its open door.

"They—they brought a guest, I am told?" it asked in an off-hand way.

"Ah. That they did. A Mr. Strickland. You'd not remember him."

The second voice belonged to Mrs. Cavanagh, who remained in Clive's mind as a middle-aged straight-backed woman full of piety and unctuousness. Mrs. Cavanagh had risen to the post of housekeeper at High Chimneys after having been the children's nurse long ago.

"I remember Mr. Strickland quite well," the girl's voice replied straightforwardly. Then it grew charged with some kind of emotion. "But tell me, Cavvy. Why did my stepmother go to London this morning?"

"If you'd come down to breakfast at a Christian hour, you could have asked the madam yourself. Now couldn't you? Or, if you hadn't been gallivanting round the country on horseback, you could have asked this afternoon when she and your pa got back." Mrs. Cavanagh's tone changed. "But she didn't pay a call on a certain noble lord, *I'll* be bound. Not with your pa there."

Someone drew a quick, sharp breath.

"I don't understand you. What do you mean by that?"

"Maybe the same as you mean, ducky. Or maybe not. It's not my place to say. Why did your pa go to London, if it comes to that?"

"Well? Why did he?"

"Ask no questions," said Mrs. Cavanagh rather slyly, "and you'll be told no lies."

Clive, in the doorway of the morning-room with his hand raised to tap at the inside of the open door, remained motionless. The girl's face was that of the painting, but with every shade of its expression intensified.

Kate Damon had caught up a lamp in her left hand, and was holding it shoulder-high as though to study her companion. More clearly it illumined Kate herself: the black hair brushed back up into short curls, the vivid brown eyes. In an

24

evening-gown of heavy dull-yellow velvet, its waist tight-laced below a swelling bodice, she moved with a litheness and freedom young ladies did not usually permit themselves.

"What did my father want in London? I insist upon knowing!"

"Your pa don't confide in me, Miss Brimstone."

"Naturally not. Yet you always overhear—"

"Oh, shame!" breathed Mrs. Cavanagh, with shivering humility. Her rusty black dress, whose large crinoline resembled a hoop rather than a triangle, also shivered as she stepped backwards. "Shame, shame, shame to address your poor old Cavvy like that! *I* can't help it if housemaids gossip, more's the pity. I did hear your pa desired to see Mr. Victor—"

"Victor has always been your favourite, has he not?"

"But in the main it wasn't to see Mr. Victor, or even because he suspected the madam of carrying on with a certain noble lord. In the main it was to see an officer of the detective police.'"

"Indeed?"

"Leastways," said Mrs. Cavanagh, "this person Jonathan Whicher *was* an Inspector of the detective police, the sharpest and the cunningest of 'em."

" 'Was?' "

"To be sure. Your pa wouldn't have let you read of the Road-Hill House murder five years gone. Inspector Whicher found the murderer; that he did. 'I want you!' says he. But, lawk! Good people couldn't believe a well-brought-up young lady would cut the throat of her baby brother and dance for joy afterwards."

"Couldn't they? *I* could."

"I daresay. Inspector Whicher had to resign because they hissed him. Oh, ah. And then, only a year ago, the young lady ups and confesses she did it. Constance Kent, her name was."

"My father is concerned, then, about the identity of the man on the stairs?"

"That's for him to say. Or don't you believe there was a man in the house last night?"

"Oh, yes," Kate answered curtly and firmly. "There was a man in the house last night. He walked up and down, up and down, like an evil spirit."

"And attempted Penelope Burbage's virtue? Eh?"

" 'Attempted her virtue,' " mimicked Kate. "Dear God, what a term!"

"You mind your language, Miss Pert, or your pa'll wash your mouth out with soap."

About Kate, in the dull-yellow velvet, there was a repressed and smouldering quality which suggested Matthew Damon himself. She held the lamp higher. Her right hand was clenched at her breast, as in the painting, and her neck inclined forward.

"I am concerned," she said clearly, "with one thing only. My sister is not to be frightened by these bogey-tales. You will be good enough to obey me."

"Hoity-toity! I know my place, I hope."

"Do you?"

"Let your pa judge. As for Miss Celia—"

"Did someone call?" asked another voice.

The upheld lamp made an aureole in dusty air, against a morning-room of feminine gauds and knickknacks. Light also penetrated, from the long dining-room at the back, through strings of different-coloured beads forming a curtain across the archway between.

The bead curtain was pushed back. Another girl, in a heavily brocaded evening gown of dull purple, moved through with the crinoline swaying and cleaving. Less robust than the rather sensuous Kate, slender, with very large grey eyes fringed in black lashes, she wore her lustrous light-brown hair as her sister did.

Kate put down the white lamp on a table.

"Dear Celia!" she said with genuine affection.

"Dear Kate!" said Celia.

"Ah, 'tis all very well to be affectionate!" said Mrs. Cavanagh, folding big hands in front of her. "A husband is what you ought to have, both of you. The madam's in the right of it there, even if she only wants attention on her 'stead of you. But you'll never catch a husband, mark my words, if your pa goes on discouraging—"

The position of Clive Strickland, in the doorway to the hall, had already become embarrassing and was fast becoming intolerable.

A loud cough had failed to attract the attention of either Kate or Mrs. Cavanagh. It was Celia, nearly facing him, who glanced up. Her grey eyes dilated; her mouth opened. As three pairs of eyes turned towards him, a certain meekness descended on all of them.

Only the direct-seeming Kate advanced, after an appraising look which made her full lips tighten in an odd sort of way.

"You are Mr. Strickland, of course. And—and you have not seen Celia or myself since we were starchy little idiots in tartan dresses. *You* remember him, Celia?"

"Oh, no, I don't think so."

26

Kate gave her a look.

"Celia dear! I think you must. Shall we shake hands, Mr. Strickland? I suppose we must come to it sooner or later; and why not sooner? There! How stupid of Burbage not to have shown you into the drawing-room."

Kate had spoken rapidly. Now she raised her eyes to him. For perhaps ten seconds she and Clive looked at each other without moving. The realization, whether with prayers or an inward curse, had come to him several minutes ago. Whatever she herself might feel, he knew past doubt or denial that Kate Damon was the one woman on earth for him; and he meant 'woman,' with all that term implies; he did not mean 'girl' or sugar-candy doll.

"Burbage did show me into the drawing-room, Miss Damon," he told her in a loud voice. "Accept my apologies; I fear I intruded on you."

"*I* don't think you did!" said Kate. "Shall we go into the drawing-room now?"

"Yes; by all means."

Becoming aware that he was still holding Kate's hand, he pressed the fingers hard before releasing them. Kate did not look away. Celia, the delicate sugar-and-spice beauty, suddenly watched them with what might have been wonder.

"Good evening, sir," observed Mrs. Cavanagh, with all her old air of self-effacing humility. "If I may say so, sir, it's a great pleasure to see you again."

"Thank you, Mrs. Cavanagh," said Clive, still unable to take his eyes from Kate.

"If I might further make so bold, sir, would your presence have anything to do with marriage?"

"*Marriage?*"

"Or with a certain noble lord whose initials might be A. T.?"

Clive had stepped aside so that Kate and Celia could go past him into the hall. Both sisters stopped short in the hall, though without turning round. A glance darted between them, sending the emotional temperature up still further.

"Surely that is thunder I hear in the distance?" asked Celia, with a gesture of cupping her hand near her ear. "There will be a storm, I think?"

"Yes!" said Kate. "That is all, Cavvy. You may go."

Many petticoats rustled as two crinolines, several inches off the uncarpeted floor, moved across the hall and squeezed into the drawing-room. Celia, modestly pressing the skirt round her, glanced back once over her shoulder. In the drawing-room Kate swung round.

"Really, now, this is too provoking! Only one lamp here?

27

Only one lamp lighted, and the fire not yet properly made up?"

"Kate, dear!" said Celia, with gentle and puzzled remonstrance.

"Yes?"

"Whatever can be the matter with you?"

Kate did not reply. But her mouth and eyes expressed much.

"Do look at the clock!" begged Celia. She nodded towards the white-faced clock on the mantelpiece. "It is not yet a quarter past six, dear. No one is *ever* in this room until a quarter to seven at the very earliest. No one ever comes downstairs, even, except for father in his study."

Kate spoke abruptly. "Oh. Yes. I forgot."

"It would be most unjust to blame poor Burbage, would it not? Things seem to be all at sixes and sevens tonight. I could not help wondering why you yourself made ready so early."

"Made ready?"

"I mean . . ." And Celia nodded towards Kate's evening-gown.

"Well!" said Kate, after a quick-breathing pause. She stared at Celia's evening-gown. "For that matter, why did you do it?"

"Because *you* did, dear. I heard you in your room."

"Can it make any possible difference, Celia, that for once in this house someone is too punctual rather than too late?"

"No, dear, of course not." Celia looked a little shocked. "But I did not wish Mr. Strickland to gain the impression that we were in any way an odd or a strange household." Here Celia laughed, a deprecating laugh for which she apologized with a wry little mouth. "He must have thought Cavvy almost too outrageous and impertinent even for an old nurse. After all, it is most unlikely that Mr. Strickland should be here to discuss any such subject as—as Cavvy mentioned. That is *not* the reason for your visit, Mr. Strickland?"

Clive had been dreading the question.

"Well, yes," he admitted. "Yes, it is."

Kate and Celia exchanged glances.

"If you had asked me that question before I took the train from London," Clive went on, "I should have had to tell you the details. At the moment, as it happens, I can't. When I mentioned the matter to your father, I feared he would have a seizure. He made me promise to say no more until he had told me everything."

"About what?" Kate asked sharply.

"About one of you."

The effect of this statement was extraordinary. Both Kate and Celia regarded him with an expression that might have been incredulity, or bewilderment, or a sense that they could not have understood him, or some darker feeling in the depths of the heart.

"One of us?" cried Kate.

"Which one?" asked Celia.

"I don't know. Presumably—well, I don't know. Your father said he must tell me everything, whatever the consequences. He also said he would be at peace before dinner tonight."

Kate, about to speak, hesitated as there were footsteps in the main hall. Following the direction of her eyes, Clive saw Burbage in the doorway.

"Excuse me, sir," said the house-steward. "Mr. Damon's compliments, and could you find it convenient to join him in the study?"

"Yes; of course."

"At once, sir?"

"At once."

Impulsively Kate moved forward and put her hand on Clive's arm. The fingers tightened. Clive's impetuousness might be matched by Kate's scorn for conventions, but she was not perhaps as free from the conventions as she liked to think.

"I held you in high esteem," she said. "I have thought about you, if I must own it, more often than was good for me or for my own peace of mind." Despite herself, almost to her horror, colour flooded into Kate's cheeks. "No matter! At least I *esteemed* you. I never thought to find you the messenger in a sordid affair like this."

"Sordid, you call it?"

"Yes!"

"Well, you may be right. I am not proud of my behavior. But I came as an excuse to meet *you*, and at least no harm is done. If Tress wants to marry your sister, that is no reason for her to agree. She can always refuse."

Kate's hand dropped from his arm.

"Marry Celia? Marry *Celia*? What are you saying?"

"Just that. This is the nineteenth century; Miss Celia is under no compulsion to marry against her will."

"Dear God!" said Kate.

Burbage's voice rose up in the silence.

"If you will follow me, sir?"

Kate retreated a step, glancing at Burbage. Celia stood motionless. The fashionable lamp, its shade painted with blue

29

forget-me-nots against a background of red and white, threw cold shadows across both their faces.

"If you will follow me, sir?" repeated Burbage, more shocked than either Clive or Kate that they had blurted out personal matters in the presence of a servant.

The corner of Clive's eye caught the movement of the little gold pendulum on the clock. It was just fifteen minutes past six. Clive looked beyond it towards the archway, covered with another curtain of different-coloured beads, which gave on a dark library. Beyond that library was the closed door to Matthew Damon's study. Automatically Clive had taken a step in that direction when Burbage's restrained gesture corrected him.

"This way, sir, if you please."

Bowing to Kate and Celia, he followed the house-steward out into the hall.

If a disquiet haunted these airless rooms, even the solid Burbage felt it. Clive, walking after him towards the rear of the hall, could see only the man's back: an uncompromising back in a dark coat like a clergyman's; with something clerical, too, about his gaiters and even the cut of his thick sandy hair.

Nor did Burbage himself escape.

At the rear of the hall, facing front, a thick green-baize door cut off the kitchen and other servants' quarters from the rest of the house. A lamp in a wall-bracket, its flame turned very low, illumined the green-baize door. It also illumined a second door to Matthew Damon's study, in the wall towards their right.

It was the green-baize door which opened abruptly.

"Father—" began a woman's voice.

Burbage stopped. The back of his head showed as much, or as little, eloquence as his face.

"Your place is not here, Penelope."

"I ask your pardon, father, indeed I do. All daughters, one supposes, must keep a stock of apologies for existing at all."

Clive also stopped. The woman's voice, low and cultured and sweet, made so great a contrast with her face and figure that you looked twice to make sure it was she who had spoken. Intelligence and irony, too, tinged the eyes which were her one good feature against a heavy jowl and a snub nose. Short and dumpy, her hair severely bound round her head as was Mrs. Cavanagh's, she lurked under the dim lamp-flame.

"Your place is not here, Penelope. Even with your near-sightedness, you see this gentleman?"

"It is because I am near-sighted—"

30

"You see this gentleman?"

"I ask *his* pardon. I have remembered a fact, or at least an impression, about what I saw on the stairs."

For perhaps five seconds nobody spoke.

"May I not at least," said Penelope Burbage, "beg leave for a word with Mr. Damon?"

"No, you may not."

"Hang it all," Clive burst out, "why shouldn't she be here?"

"Allow me, sir. Allow me! Penelope, our meal is on the table. Be off."

Penelope Burbage made a small gesture which was at once hopeless and strangely pathetic. She looked past her father, beneath the oak staircase which dominated the hall as so many tall and top-heavy chimney-stacks dominated the roof of this house; and Penelope's expression altered again.

"You have barred the front door!" she said. "You have barred the front door on the inside."

"I have. At Mr. Damon's instructions, we are locked in for the night. Now be off."

The lamp-flame trembled amid weights of shadow as the green-baize barrier opened and closed. Burbage watched his daughter go. Then, austere and slow-moving and sandy-whiskered, he turned round.

"You must forgive her, sir. You really must try your best to forgive her. She has been under a great strain."

And he opened the door of Matthew Damon's study.

V. THE HANGING OF HARRIET PYKE

Austere, too, was Matthew Damon. He stood in starchy evening-clothes behind the flat-topped desk, with papers and a decanter of brandy in front of him. His height and bearing remained impressive. But on his sunken face, as the eyes moved round sideways towards Clive, was a look of illness which might even have showed a touch of madness.

"Come in, Mr. Strickland. Be seated."

"Mr. Damon, may I ask—?"

"No; one moment. Burbage!"

"Yes, sir?"

"You have looked to my instructions, Burbage?"

"Yes, sir. All of them."

"Thank you," said Matthew Damon, and dismissed Burbage with a gesture. He waited until the heavy door had closed, and footsteps moved away. "One moment, I say, before you sit down. This afternoon, you may recall, I sent a telegram from Reading."

"Yes?"

"I telegraphed to a Private Inquiry Bureau operated by a former officer in the Detective Branch of the Metropolitan Police. Forgive me for my secrecy about this. I shall visit Mr. Whicher at four o'clock tomorrow afternoon."

"Can't you ask him to come here?"

"I can, but I will not. This matter must be kept strictly secret, except in one event. If anything should happen to me in the meantime—"

Those deep-set eyes had already given Clive a shock. Mr. Damon raised his hand sharply, forestalling comment.

"If anything should happen to me, however," he went on, "you will visit him in my place and tell him what I propose to tell you. Do you understand?"

"I understand, yes."

"The address of the office," and Mr. Damon picked up a paper from the desk, "is given as '347 Oxford Street, beside the Pantheon.' You should find it without trouble."

"Yes; everybody knows the Pantheon."

This room, heavily curtained, smelt stuffy and musty. Clive still stood just inside the closed door. In the wall opposite him, between two windows, a fire burned between the bars of an arched grate under a low wooden mantelpiece. Matthew Damon, his back to the rear wall of the study, faced across towards a second closed door—the door to the library—in the front wall.

But he was not looking ahead of him. His eyes, turned sideways towards Clive, were kindled from underneath by the light of a student's lamp, a lamp with a green-glass shade, shining up from the desk.

"Number 347 Oxford Street!" repeated Mr. Damon, and dropped the paper. "As I have good reason to know, it is just across the road from the Princess's Theatre. Should it become necessary, will you promise to undertake this?"

"Look here, sir—!"

"Will you promise?"

"Very well; I promise. But whatever it is, whatever has

been troubling you for so long a time, it can't possibly be as bad as you think!"

"Perhaps not," agreed the other with sardonic courtesy. "Yet I think it bad enough, if I may state an example. You are not married, young man?"

"No; you know I'm not."

"Would *you* care to marry the daughter of a vicious murderess?"

"*Who* is the daughter of a vicious murderess?"

"Sit down, Mr. Strickland."

The fire crackled and popped amid shifting gleams. Matthew Damon indicated a padded armchair, covered with shabby red velvet, just in front of his desk. Clive sat down as his host stretched out a hand for the decanter of brandy.

"You are concerned with sensationalism, Mr. Strickland. You may read the law-reports. Are you familiar with the name of Harriet Pyke?"

"No, except that you mentioned it."

"*I* mentioned it? When?"

"In the train this afternoon."

"Ah, yes! Yes, I believe I did!" The barrister, after speaking almost at a shout, controlled himself and smiled agreeably. "But there were certain matters I could not possibly have discussed in the presence of my wife."

"Well, sir?"

"Well! It will be known to you that there are certain areas of London, St. John's Wood for instance, in which men of means and substance are accustomed to establish their kept women? Each in her own handsome villa? Or that there are thoroughfares north of Oxford Street (Berners Street, Newman Street for example?) where a pretty anonyma may be set up in her own expensive rooms? It is so now, and it was so nearly a generation ago. Harriet Pyke was such a woman."

Clive did not comment.

Lifting the decanter of brandy, his host removed the stopper and poured a tumbler about a quarter full. Perhaps it indicated his state of mind that he made no offer of drink to his guest, nor did he add soda-water from the small bottle.

There was a clock ticking somewhere in the study. Matthew Damon lifted the tumbler, drank, and then whacked down the empty glass on the desk.

"Mr. Strickland, do you think I don't know what they say of me?"

"Sir?"

"I am no stranger to the lusts of the flesh."

Outside in the hall, firm footsteps approached the door on

that side. Knuckles rapped lightly on the door. Matthew Damon broke off, twitching his head round, as the door was opened.

"I say, Damon—" began a man's voice, and also stopped.

In the doorway, altering both his tone and his bearing as he saw Clive, stood a portly gentleman with a short brown beard.

"Dr. Rollo Thompson Bland," said Matthew Damon in a repressed voice, "may I present Mr. Clive Strickland?"

"Your servant, sir," said the doctor with much formality.

"An honour, sir," replied Clive, rising and bowing.

Whereupon Clive, as his nerves crawled, became aware of two things.

Mr. Damon's eyes glittered with rage at the interruption. And, as Celia had said, there was a storm coming outside. Thunder shocked low down on the sky: not loudly, but as though approaching. A rising breeze swept round High Chimneys.

"Yes?" inquired Mr. Damon.

"My dear Damon," said Dr. Rollo Thompson Bland, "where is your wife?"

"My wife? So far as I am aware, my esteemed wife should be in her own sitting-room upstairs. That is where she usually is, at this time."

"The lady is not there."

"Then why not ask her maid? Or ask Burbage?"

"Tut, my dear sir! You seem to forget your own rigid rules and time-tables. The servants all have their evening meal together between six-fifteen and six-thirty. That's not much time, I have always said, when *we* begin at seven and take two hours. I scarcely like to disturb the poor devils."

"Indeed," said Mr. Damon, and snatched up his brandy-glass. "Let me applaud your consideration for others."

Thunder struck again.

With the door wide open, swinging inwards to the right as you entered from the hall, air prowled in the hall and a draught whipped through. The lamp-flame wavered; two papers fluttered up from the desk, and Matthew Damon struck them down with the flat of his left hand as though killing a fly.

Already Dr. Bland's eyes had narrowed. His manner, which combined the bluff good-nature of the general practitioner with the soothing stateliness of the specialist, congealed into medical watchfulness.

"Damon!" he said sharply.

"Since you are so familiar with my rules, sir, I might remind you of another. Even when I am not studying a brief,

34

it is my habit to occupy this room alone from tea-time until dinner-time."

"So I believe."

"I am on no account to be disturbed except at my own request. Is that clear?"

"Quite clear." Dr. Bland's colour was high; but his eyes, a very bright blue, watched the other with attention. "I shall beg leave for a word with you later."

A last draught whirled through. Heavy brown-rep curtains, on both the windows, swayed with it. Clive saw that more than doors had been locked and barred here; heavy wooden shutters, on full-length windows, were folded together and barred on the inside.

The door to the hall closed.

Matthew Damon, putting aside the brandy-glass, sat down in the chair behind his desk and closed his eyes.

"Mr. Strickland, I am growing old. What was I saying?"

"The lusts of the flesh," answered Clive. "And Harriet Pyke."

"Ah, yes."

Trees seethed in the wind outside. Mr. Damon opened his eyes.

"At the time I speak of, this woman was twenty-three. It will be unnecessary to mention the name of her latest protector. He had installed her, together with a maid and a private carriage, at a villa in St. John's Wood. Harriet Pyke was then at the height of her beauty and wantonness. But she had an unpredictable temper, especially in drink. Nor, for all her dainty appearance, could she conceal the strength of her arms and hands."

He looked at his own hands, and clenched them.

"One night towards the end of '46, after much amorousness at that villa, there was a quarrel, a threat, we cannot say what. Two murders were committed. Harriet Pyke's lover was shot through the abdomen with a revolving pistol, or so-called revolver. Afterwards the five remaining bullets were fired at him, though only one struck him. The villa was isolated; no person heard the shots except this woman's maid. But, because the maid might be a witness, she was seized and strangled to death."

Ugly images flowed out and filled the study.

Clive glanced over his shoulder at the other closed door, the door to the library, behind his back. Then he sat down again facing Mr. Damon.

"A revolving pistol?" said Clive. "Nineteen years ago?"

"Yes. Do you think the weapon is new?"

"Not new, it may be——"

35

"I do not refer, Mr. Strickland, to the revolver with metallic cartridges. *That* is new; that is most recent; I have one in my desk here, against would-be thieves."

"Steady!"

Matthew Damon had reached out towards a drawer, but he did not open it.

"The evidence seemed clear. The authorities wished an example to be made of this woman. I was briefed for the Crown. Her defence consisted only of a denial that she had been at the villa that night. Well, where had she been? She would not say. Brazenly she insisted that this protector of hers must also have seduced her maid-servant; that these two had quarrelled; that the maid had fired the bullets, and must have been strangled by the man before he died. An unspeakable tale, you must allow; the authorities would have none of it.

"It was not a happy time for me. My wife, my first wife, had recently died. But I was young then, as men of the law are accounted; my duty was to make the jury disbelieve Harriet Pyke's account of what happened; and I did so.

"It was only after the verdict . . .

"Had I exceeded my duty? Had I shown too much zeal? Had my grief for my wife been poured into the bitterness of the prosecution?

"When I went to visit this woman in the condemned cell, I do most firmly deny that I was in any way influenced by her physical charms. Throughout the trial she had watched me steadily, as though possessing some secret knowledge of me; I can still see her flaunting bonnet and her eyes in the dock.

"Later, in the condemned cell, she indeed proved to have some knowledge of me and my life. She professed to have read it. But there was little time to reflect on this. For she went down on her knees and told me a different story of the murders.

"Harriet Pyke had borne a child, of much the same age as my own babies: so much proved to be true. When her latest protector installed her in the villa, she left this child to be cared for by a sempstress and saw the child when she could: that also was true.

"On the night of the double murder, Harriet Pyke told me, she had been with her baby. The sempstress, she said, would confirm this. And yet, if she had stated as much in open court, there would be no chance for that child to grow up into a decent life.

"Now the accused was in mortal terror. The sempstress *did* confirm her story. But the sempstress was of dubious character, and a fallen woman too; the Secretary of State for Home Affairs would not believe her. And, when I failed to obtain a reprieve, Harriet Pyke was carried screaming to the gallows."

Matthew Damon paused.

He was sitting bolt upright, his hands flat on the desk, face almost without expression.

"Then what she told you was true!" said Clive.

"Oh, no," said Mr. Damon.

"It was *not* true?"

"Except for the points I have indicated, not one word," retorted the other. "But *I* believed it. Mark that! *I* believed it, and went on believing it for nearly two decades: until I learned the truth three months ago."

He stared at the green-glass shade of the lamp as emotion grew inside him.

"A daughter of Harriet Pyke would have been born to sin in any case. As it was, however, I hoped to avoid the worse eventuality. There would have been problems in any case; as, for instance, the necessity of telling the truth when *any* of the three married. None the less, if only she had been innocent . . ."

"Mr. Damon!"

"I beg your pardon?"

"Forgive me, but what are you talking about? And how does this concern your own daughter?"

Again Matthew Damon sat up straight, but his nostrils were dilated. Over his face went a look so richly sardonic that it seemed almost a sneer.

"Oh, come!" he said. "You are an intelligent man. Pray don't pretend you misunderstand?"

Clive did not misunderstand, but it was true he wished to misunderstand. Mentally he fought the images that crowded round.

"I should have questioned Whicher all those years ago," said Mr. Damon, "when he was a young sergeant of the Detective Branch. But no. It was my conscience, my conscience, my conscience! An innocent woman, or so I believed, had been hanged because of me. I have prosecuted many criminals since then; but never with the unscrupulous violence I used towards *her*. And I feared God's judgment unless I made atonement."

"You made atonement—how? By adopting Harriet's Pyke's child as one of your own?"

"Yes," said Matthew Damon.

He was silent for a moment.

"Oh, not a legal adoption! Every act had to be done in

secret. When my wife died, we were living in the north of England. I had dismissed all my household except the nurse of my two real children. Only one person shares my secret; the children themselves do not know. Friends? I have so few friends."

Clive looked at the carpet.

"All this I should have been happy to do (yes!), if Harriet Pyke had been innocent. But what is the result? Tainted blood! This very evening I have seen Harriet Pyke's eyes and Harriet Pyke's hands. 'The sins of the fathers—' "

"Or the mothers."

"Let us have no blasphemy, Mr. Strickland!"

"I meant no blasphemy, believe me."

" 'The sins of the fathers—' Need more be quoted?"

"No; I suppose not."

Thunder split its echoes round the house and vibrated amid roof-slates.

"Tell me, sir: was Harriet Pyke insane?"

"On the contrary, she was most calculatingly sane. She cared nothing at all for the offspring of an unknown father; she would have saved her life, could she have done so, by lies to strike at my conscience; she screamed and screamed only when she had failed. Why do you ask?"

"Because," answered Clive, with all the pressure of his ancestors' wisdom against him, "it's hard to believe that tainted blood, the certainty of brutality or theft or murder, can be handed down from father to son or mother to daughter. I have seen things in London streets . . ."

"Indeed. Do you doubt these facts?"

"No. Not really. It's rather more than that. In my heart, I suppose, I prefer to go on writing gingerbread romances about the best of all possible worlds."

"It is an evil world, young man. You have guessed, of course, who has inherited these criminal traits?"

"No."

"Then it is time for plain speaking.—*What was that?*"

"What was what?"

"That noise."

Matthew Damon rose to his feet. So did Clive.

"You mean the thunder?"

"No; I do not mean the thunder. Or the fire, or the clock."

Irrationally, as the mind will seize on trifles, Clive remembered that they faced each other now as they had faced each other in the train that afternoon, though in Clive's case at least with very different emotions.

Matthew Damon, his left hand on the desk-top and his right hand straying again towards that same desk-drawer, moved his eyes sharply to the right. He looked at the closed door to the hall. Then he looked behind Clive's back, at the closed door to the library some fifteen feet away.

"No, it was nothing. I was mistaken."

There *was* nothing. Clive had followed his glances, and looked back at the ravaged face.

"They complain of me, Mr. Strickland, that I do not show affection. But I have tried. I have tried to love a changeling as I should, and do, love my own. To all outward appearances, in any event, I believe I have succeeded. You can bear witness—"

Once more he broke off, his lower lip drawn down so that you could see the teeth. He was staring past Clive's shoulder.

Clive whipped round.

The door to the dark library had softly opened, with someone's left hand holding the knob. The figure standing in the library was partly shaded by the door; its face, at least, was in such fashion hidden that it seemed to have no head.

In the blur of dazed impressions following the shock when that shape lifted a weapon and fired, Clive could be sure only that he saw a man wearing a dark frock-coat, a dark waistcoat, and trousers of a patterned red-and-white design.

VI. DEATH WITH
PATTERNED TROUSERS

They ask you questions, and you are honest. But what did happen and what did you see?

A heavy explosion of thunder, close above all these unwieldy chimney-stacks piled into the sky, almost blotted out the explosion of the pistol-shot. The weight of a man's body, a man struck between the eyes as though by a sledgehammer, went back and over a chair behind the desk.

Clive heard this; he did not see it. Without knowledge of what he was doing, he ran straight at the library door.

The figure before him seemed to worm or dodge in a curious way. Clive himself instinctively dodged as something flew out towards him, catching the light, and landed with a thud on the carpet. The library door was pulled shut in his face; he heard a key turn from the other side. It was no use seizing at the knob and wrenching it. The door was locked.

He looked back over his shoulder, quickly, towards the chair behind Matthew Damon's desk. Then he looked away again.

" 'Will wash out rust-stains, mud-stains, blood-stains . . .' "

Clive ran to the door leading to the hall. That was locked too, and on the outside.

He could not believe this. After twisting at the knob, resisting the impulse to hammer at the upper panels, he had to go down on his knees and peer at the keyhole. A key, which had not been there a while ago, was turned in the lock.

Matthew Damon's right cuff twitched. Now you could hear his breathing.

Clive, averting his eyes from the place where the bullet had entered just above the bridge of the nose, was compelled to go to the man thrown back over the padded chair.

But it grew worse a moment later. Mr. Damon did not move for long, and he did not breathe ever again.

The rain began, a deluge, as Clive stood looking just past the edge of a limp arm. A reek of black powder stung the nostrils and made a palpable haze. He looked round at what lay on the carpet, a foot or two inside the study where it had been thrown.

Because he had seen a weapon just like it recently displayed at Stover's, the gunsmith's in Piccadilly, he knew it for metallic-cartridge revolving pistol, six-chambered, of the sort called rim-fire because the hammer struck the rim of the cartridge in exploding it.

They were manufactured by a French firm whose name he couldn't remember, and they were much lighter than the customary heavy and unwieldy revolving pistol. They—

Clive glanced back at Matthew Damon's desk.

There was a drawer on the right-hand side, a drawer his host had been about to open when the man could still move and speak. Not without an effort Clive touched the drawer and then pulled it open. He found nothing inside.

What was *that?*

Small noises darted out and struck at the nerves under the tumult of the storm. He imagined that a door, not one of these doors, had opened and closed in the direction of the hall. He was right. Hurrying towards the door to the hall, he heard outside certain stately footsteps which could belong only to one person.

"Burbage!"

The footsteps halted. "Sir?"

But Clive's voice, loud and hoarse in his own ears, would

40

never do. About to speak again, thinking of the tone he must achieve, he saw the clock which hitherto he had only heard. It stood on a low bookcase; its dial, white against black marble, swam out at him.

And the hands stood at only twenty-eight minutes to seven.

"Sir?" repeated Burbage's voice.

What he had heard, Clive knew, was Burbage returning from the servants' quarters at the back after the servants had finished their evening meal together.

"Burbage, this door is locked on the outside. Unlock it, if you will. Don't open it; simply unlock it."

A slight pause. "Very good, sir."

The key turned quietly, as though in an oiled lock. The other key had also turned in the same soft way when he was locked in.

"Now, Burbage, will you stand well to one side of the door?"

The footsteps outside complied. Unless Burbage stood well to one side, he would have a clear view of what lay inside. Clive opened the door, slipped out, and shut it behind him.

The wall-lamp shed its dim glimmer beside the green-baize door to the servants' quarters. To Clive all shapes and colours seemed unreal; he supposed he must be pale.

"Burbage, the questions I mean to ask may seem unusual. Bear up; we shall need to. Is a key usually kept in the lock of the study door here?"

"No, sir." Burbage's expression did not change.

"Or in the lock of the door between the study and the library?"

"No, sir. But a key from any door downstairs will fit them."

"Have you just come from having your dinner? I think you nodded? Good! Were all the other servants there?"

"Yes, sir. They are still there. That is," the house-steward amended, "all except Mrs. Cavanagh and my unhappy daughter. They were indisposed, and left the table."

The drive of the rain had deepened, making a hollow noise here in the hall. Clive glanced up and down the hall.

"Burbage, will you now go round and make sure that all the doors and windows are still fastened on the inside?"

"Very . . . yes, sir." Now Burbage's gaze did flicker.

"On the way, present my compliments to Mrs. Damon, and say—" Clive hesitated.

"Mrs. Damon, sir, is not in the house."

"Oh? Where is she?"

"I could not say, sir. About an hour ago Mrs. Damon ordered the landau, so that Hopper could drive her to Reading. Mrs. Damon took luggage, but not her maid. I re-locked and re-barred the front door when Mrs. Damon had gone."

"Did Mr. Damon know this?"

"I could not say, sir. It would be possible to ask him."

"It would not be possible, I fear. Mr. Damon is dead."

What Burbage said to this, or even what he thought as judged by his expression, Clive missed altogether. Other concerns had caught him.

About to add, "I must break the news gently to Miss Kate and Miss Celia," he saw in his imagination so clear a picture of Kate Damon's face (and, to a lesser degree, of Celia's too) that he began to understand the terrifying implications of that statement, "Mr. Damon is dead." He stopped feeling and began to think.

Burbage, a face of consternation between sandy whiskers, blurted out words of which he heard only the last few.

"No, it was not an accident," said Clive. "Stay a moment! I have remembered something. Come with me."

Turning the key and locking the study door, he removed the key and put it in his waistcoat pocket. Then he almost raced to the front of the hall.

When he left the drawing-room at six-fifteen, both Kate and Celia had been there. Now the room was empty.

Its thick carpet and curtains seemed a swathing for evil thoughts. The lamp, its shade painted in blue forget-me-nots against red and white, still stood on the circular centre-table. The curtain of different-coloured bead-strings, which shrouded the archway entrance to the library from this direction, glimmered as Clive took up the lamp.

He parted the curtain and held the lamp high inside the library. That was empty too.

"Sir!" protested Burbage behind him.

"Look there," said Clive, indicating a closed door just opposite at the far end. "That leads into the study, doesn't it?"

"Yes, sir."

Still another door, towards Clive's left now, opened from the library out into the hall.

"Mr. Damon was shot through the head. The—the person who did it was the same man who frightened your daughter on the stairs last night. He wasn't a figment of Penelope's imagination. She didn't dream him."

Burbage said nothing, though his tongue moistened his lips.

"The murderer opened that door to the study, *there*,"

42

Clive nodded opposite, "and fired a shot with what I think was Mr. Damon's own pistol. Then he locked me in and got away. He must have locked the hall-door beforehand. If you heard no shot—or did you?"

"No, sir. *No!*"

"Well! That was because he fired just at the beginning of a peal of thunder. Has the coachman returned from driving Mrs. Damon to Reading? No? When he does, I am afraid we can't avoid sending him back for the police. In the meantime, you might fetch that doctor: Dr. Rollo Thompson Bland. He can't help us, but we had better have him."

"Sir, which of all these things do you want me to do first?"

They were yelling at each other; even Burbage was yelling. Clive strode back and banged down the lamp on the centre-table.

"First of all, make sure the house is locked up. Then fetch the doctor."

Following Burbage out into the hall, he stopped and looked up. Kate Damon, a little out of breath, stood halfway down the heavy oak staircase, her fingers on the banister-rail.

Kate stood mainly in shadow, but he saw the shock in her eyes and the quick lift of her bodice in the dull-yellow gown with black trimmings. She gripped the banister-rail, swaying; for a second Clive thought she might faint. Then she ran down the stairs and across to him.

"You heard, did you not?" Clive asked bitterly. "You heard what I was saying to Burbage?"

"Yes. I heard. My father has been—"

She could not go on.

This was no longer the impatient, rebellious Kate, lashing out at things her intelligence would not accept. That aspect had disappeared. This was a warm-hearted and impulsive girl, perhaps a little too romantic-minded in her own way, and above all things physically desirable.

'Lock up your thoughts, fool!' Clive said to himself.

If in a manuscript he had so much as used the words 'physically desirable,' he could imagine what would be said by Mr. Wills of *All the Year Round;* not to mention the awesome Charles Dickens, its editor. You were not to think of such matters, let alone write of them. A man might keep a mistress or wallow among easy conquests; that could be tacitly ignored, so long as he did not intrude it into the sacred home circle. The fact that ladies in this circle themselves thought of such matters, and all too often, must not even be suspected.

Face it! Suppose *Kate* is the daughter of Harriet Pyke?

43

Well, even suppose she is? Suddenly Clive realized what astonishingly little difference it would make.

Now that Matthew Damon was dead, the secret was known only to Clive himself and one other person unnamed. Why shouldn't the secret be kept and never mentioned at all? Ah, but that was what he might not be able to manage. Jonathan Whicher knew much, perhaps everything.

He might be able to silence Whicher, or he might not. If Whicher chose to inform the police, when the news of this murder appeared in the press, the whole unsavoury scandal would blow up. It bore no relation to the murder; it was only a drab circumstance of parentage.

Wouldn't it be better to confide in Kate, and warn her?

"Miss Damon, listen to me."

Kate had gone rigid, and her eyes blurred with tears.

"Hear me!" insisted Clive. He caught her arms, bare under the short sleeves of the gown. "We must go—no, not to the drawing-room or the morning-room. That doctor will be here at any moment. What is the room across the hall from the study?"

"Across from the study? Where my father—?"

"Yes! What room is that?"

"It's a back parlour that—that opens into the conservatory at the side. *Why?*"

"Please to remain where you are for a moment."

Hurrying into the drawing-room, Clive again picked up the lamp and rejoined her. Holding Kate's elbow, he guided her towards the rear of the hall.

"The study is locked, and I have the key. No, don't look at the door!"

But Kate looked at it none the less, as he led her into the room opposite. The back-parlour, dark before Clive brought the lamp, was crowded with pictures in heavy frames and must also have been used as a breakfast-room.

Opposite them, as they entered, a glass door painted in a flower-design led out into an iron-ribbed conservatory with stained glass for its sides and an arch of clear glass for its roof. Someone had left the glass door partly open. A thick damp atmosphere of plants, artificially heated, crept out into the air of stale crumbs in the breakfast-room.

Kate, all of a flush and brightness, her lips drawn back over fine teeth, disturbed his judgment still more.

"Mr. Strickland, you must not mind what I say when I am upset. Especially you must not mind what I almost said to Cavvy. I think myself all very fine; and yet I am headstrong and stupid. I say so much that I don't mean!"

"We all do, I suppose. What I wished to tell you—"

And, now that he was about to take her into his confidence, Clive hesitated. Whoever might be the daughter of Harriet Pyke, would she so much enjoy hearing it?

"My father was *killed?*" Kate cried in a passion of incredulity. "And by the same man who was in the house last night?"

"I can only assume it. His clothes were the same as were made so much of. I was locked in the study, as you may have heard me tell Burbage. As soon as Burbage released me, I greatly feared for you and your sister."

"For Celia and me? Why?"

"This murderer," he said, and Kate flinched at the word, "approached from the library. The library was dark, true, and .there is another door from the library out into the hall. At the same time, when I went to your father's study, you and your sister were still in the drawing-room. If this man had run in there . . ."

"But Celia and I did not remain in the drawing-room! We went upstairs not a minute after you left us."

"You went upstairs together?"

"Yes. To Celia's room."

"Did you remain together the whole time? That is, until—?"

"Yes. Yes! The whole time. I can swear to Celia's presence."

Clive set down the lamp on the breakfast-table. The breath of relief that went through him was stronger than he would have cared to admit.

That afternoon, in the train, there had occurred to him a notion so grotesque that he would not even mention it to Matthew Damon. This notion, that the prowler on the stairs last night might have been a woman in man's clothes, was too nonsensical; it belonged to the stage rather than to human life.

And yet it had nagged at the back of his mind, turning fancies into ugly images. Now that he knew neither Kate nor Celia could have been concerned in a brutal murder, not only felt it but *knew* it . . .

Rain drummed on the glass roof of the conservatory. Kate had moved closer, her face tense and her lips parted.

"Well!" said Clive, and attempted a laugh that jarred against that close atmosphere. "It's hardly necessary to prove where either of you happened to be, though it may be just as well to make certain. I confess to having had a literal bad quarter of an hour. You may remember, when I left you and your sister, your father was going to tell me. . . ."

"Oh!" said Kate.

"What's the matter?"

"I forgot. I never thought I *could* forget, but I did. He was going to tell you everything. Did he tell you?"

"Not the full story, no. But enough to . . . Look here, Kate: do you know what your father was going to tell me?"

It was as though that first use of the Christian name broke a barrier between them.

"No, I don't!" said Kate. "I only know what Celia and I *thought* he was going to tell you. That has caused the whole misunderstanding; that's why you and Celia and I were speaking at cross-purposes just before my father called you into his study. We imagined it concerned my stepmother, and that dreary beast Lord Albert Tressider, and those two meeting in London whenever they can snatch an opportunity!"

Clive stared at her.

Georgette and Tress? The coy, auburn-haired Mrs. Damon, with her mature charms, and Tress like a tame tiger in Dundreary whiskers?

Whereupon, with memory returning, Clive could have cursed himself aloud as heartily as he cursed himself under his breath.

"Don't you remember?" cried Kate. "Cavvy did more than hint it; she said it, and you were there."

"Yes. I was there."

"It's been going on for a long time, and almost everybody knew except my father. Celia thinks Georgette and her noble lord wanted my father to divorce her (divorce, if you please!) so that those two can marry. I don't believe that. You catch our fine Lord Albert committing himself to marriage for anything except money!"

Kate's flush and brightness had again increased almost to tears.

"But it *was* possible," she said. "It *was* possible. Then, when you said you'd come to High Chimneys about a matter of marriage, and that my father all but had a seizure when you spoke to him of it—!"

"Kate, you didn't think—?"

"No; not for long! Because you said it concerned one of us, and that this oh-so-superior gentleman wanted to marry Celia. *That* was more like him, I allow: he would have the rich girl for his wife, and for his mistress (do I shock you?) a woman who played boys' parts in burlesque at the Gaiety Theatre and only raised herself to Shakespeare a few years before she married my father. Yes, that was like him! But it wasn't like *you* as I remembered you."

"Good God, Kate, what sort of man do you take me for?"

"I don't know. Or, at least—"

"Listen to me! Will you try to believe I never even dreamed there was anything at all between Tress and your stepmother? And that the person I came here to see was you?"

"I will believe anything you tell me," answered Kate, looking up at him and gripping her fingers together. "So please, *please* to tell me only what is true."

For the first time that night, through the glass roof of the conservatory, Clive saw the blaze of the lightning. A long peal of thunder rattled the glass with its concussion and fell in tumbling echoes down the sky.

What happened then, perhaps, should not have happened; and yet, in another sense, it was inevitable. A crinoline on watch-spring wires forms no obstruction when you take her in your arms and, far from being resisted, are welcomed with mouth and arms and body as well as eyes.

Even when another person entered the room and stopped short, Clive did not hear it. He roused himself only when a new voice, strident with authority, shouted, "Kate!"

VII. HOW THE LAMPS GATHERED CLOSE ROUND A WITNESS

"I think perhaps," observed Dr. Rollo Thompson Bland, in a tone of much significance, "I had best forget what I have seen. Don't you think so, Mr. Strickland?"

"Frankly," said Clive, with his arm round Kate and her warmth against him still exciting the senses, "I see no reason to forget it and I rather doubt that I could."

Dr. Bland, right thumb and forefinger in the pocket of his white waistcoat, looked him up and down.

"With the young lady's father," he asked politely, "lying dead across the hall?"

Kate cried out and wrenched away from Clive's arm.

"You will oblige me, my dear," continued Dr. Bland,

47

"by going upstairs and attending on your sister. Burbage was compelled to break this ghastly news none too gently, and Celia is not herself."

"Celia's not—?" cried Kate.

Whatever she had meant, Dr. Bland shook his head.

"N-o-o," he said, rounding out the syllable, "and we must always hope for the best, mustn't we? But you would be better employed, at an unhappy time like this, than in yielding to your baser nature and preparing to yield still further."

"Now by God," said Clive in a conversational tone, "but you have a happy gift for phrases."

"Mr. Strickland," said Dr. Bland, "mind your manners."

"Dr. Bland," said Clive, "mind your eye."

Kate ran out of the room. Dr. Bland, his face less florid and his good-nature less apparent, stood teetering with thumb and forefinger in waistcoat-pocket. But good-nature, expressed in bluff heartiness and soothing suavity, won him over despite his worry.

"Tut, my dear young man!" he said, with a smile twitching between grizzled brown moustache and grizzled brown beard. "I have no wish to be censorious—"

"And I have no wish to be offensive."

"Good! Then we understand each other. I merely say: put this matter out of your mind. Or are your intentions by any chance honourable?"

"They are."

"Then all the worse, I fear. Put this matter out of your mind. My old friend Damon wished neither of his daughters to marry—"

"Why?"

"I can't say." Exasperation crossed Dr. Bland's face. "But a father hasn't to give reasons for his wishes, you know."

"Oh? I think he has."

"The whole world differs from you; therefore the whole world is wrong. It's a habit of young people; I can make allowances. And I will give you a reason, if you like."

"May I hear it?"

"Murder," said Dr. Bland, opening his sharp, bright-blue eyes and fixing them on Clive with the effect of a blow. "You would agree that murder, and this murder in particular, is a horrible business? You would further agree that I, as a man somewhat older and more experienced than yourself, should be in charge here until the police arrive?"

"Yes, by all means!"

"Good," said Dr. Bland, suavely holding out his hand. "Then give me the key to the study, which Burbage tells me you have. We must go across there now. We must cast an eye over poor Damon. And we must see whether *your* story is at all probable."

"Whether *my* story is probable?"

"Yes," agreed Dr. Bland. "The key, if you will."

Somewhere upstairs, a woman screamed.

They heard it clearly above the driving of the rain. It went piercing up in terror. To Clive, whose flesh had gone hot-and-cold, it symbolized some force that prowled at High Chimneys, that frightened servants on the stairs, and that struck at last to kill: some force, hidden but malignant, peering round a corner.

Dr. Rollo Thompson Bland did not turn a hair.

"Tut!" he said in his bluff way. "So faint of heart, Mr. Strickland? That is only Celia. The young lady is not well, and we must expect these little *contretemps*. You give too great attention to shadows."

"Greater attention, it would seem, than you give to patients."

"Good, very good! But *I* am wanted *here*. You will see."

And in fact, as they crossed the hall and Dr. Bland unlocked the door of the study, that cry from upstairs seemed to have roused no one except Penelope Burbage. Penelope, standing near the back by the green-baize door, gave them only one look before she hastened away into the servants' quarters.

Dr. Bland left the study door open. Ignoring Clive, who remained in the doorway, he went over to examine the figure in the chair.

Nobody spoke. The ceaseless rain was bringing out an odour of old stone and of damp places behind the wallpaper. Then, sharp-eyed and portentous, something of a dandy, Dr. Bland walked round the room, glancing at both doors. After a time he picked up the revolver from the floor.

"Lefaucheux!" Clive said suddenly.

"I beg your pardon?"

"Lefaucheux!" repeated Clive. "That's the name of the French firm who manufactures those pistols."

"Just so," agreed the other, pulling out the pin which held the cylinder to the frame, and detaching the cylinder to examine it. "A double-action Lefaucheux: one shot fired, five chambers loaded." He replaced the cylinder. "Light to the hand, an easy trigger-pull when the hammer is drawn back to cock. Sportsman, Mr. Strickland?"

"Not much of one, I'm afraid."

"Ah. You don't appear to relish the sight of poor Damon."

"I don't. Do all dead men have open mouths?"

"Ah. Yes; a double-action Lefaucheux. I was with Damon when he bought this at Stover's in Piccadilly. What happened here when he was killed?"

Clive told what had happened: the facts, without a word of what had been said.

"Yes, yes, yes," the doctor said pleasantly. "But I understood from Burbage (correct me if I err!) that my old friend had something of great importance to tell you. Indeed, you appeared most engrossed when *I* looked in. What were you discussing?"

"I'm not at liberty to say."

"You must please yourself," smiled Dr. Bland, after a pause during which he looked very hard at Clive. "However, the police may perhaps be insistent. If I might instruct you in the law . . ."

"You need not. I was called to the bar four years ago."

"Ah." Thoughtful, holding the revolver in his left hand, Dr. Bland stroked the underside of his moustache with the little finger of his right. "You sat in *this* chair? Here?" He indicated it. "Facing Damon across the desk?"

"Yes."

"Like Penelope Burbage, you too saw this mysterious apparition which no one else has seen? Dear, dear, dear! I do hope," Dr. Bland added with great politeness, "you have no pressing engagement in London tomorrow?"

"Yes! I have a very pressing engagement in Oxford Street at four o'clock tomorrow afternoon!"

"That's a pity, you know. That's a very great pity. You won't keep your engagement, Mr. Strickland. No, I assure you! Tell this tale to the police, and you won't keep it. You will certainly be detained for questioning, and you may well be arrested for murder. No, don't speak! And we mustn't excite ourselves, must we? Excuse me for just one moment. One moment, my dear fellow!"

Still speaking with avuncular tenderness, Dr. Bland had turned the knob of the door to the library and found it locked from the other side.

And, repeating, "One moment!" while he made soothing gestures, he moved past Clive into the hall, where he disappeared into the library. He did this just as Burbage, carrying a small lamp, marched towards the rear of the hall.

"Sir, one moment!" urged Barbage, catching an echo of the doctor when Clive started to address him.

Into the back-parlour, through the back-parlour and into the conservatory, Burbage marched with great attention to every wall. The glow of his lamp sprang up amid greenery beneath rain-stinging glass.

"Ah!" continued Dr. Bland, unlocking the study-door to the library from the far side and appearing about where the murderer had stood. His tone changed. "The apparition, you say, was *here*?"

"Yes. Left hand on the far knob, right hand with the pistol."

"Like this? Good! Then this prowler *allowed* you to see him face to face in full light?"

"Yes."

"Criminals are fond of doing that, eh?"

"I can only tell you what happened."

"Can you see my face?"

"Yes."

"Could you see his?"

"No."

"Tut! To kill poor Damon, the prowler must have fired a bullet within an inch or two of your own head? Eh? Good. With so unpredictable a weapon as a hand-gun, would *you* attempt a shot like that and undertake not to hit a man standing between?"

"Look here, Doctor: the murderer was forced to risk it. Mr. Damon was just about to tell me—"

"Ah! To tell you what?"

"I don't know."

"If this prowler existed, why didn't he fire from the other door?"

"The other door?"

Briskly, with cat-footed steps, Dr. Bland crossed the study and stood beside Clive.

"The prowler, imagine, is here in the hall. He had been at this door, you maintain, since at some time he locked it from the outside. Be good enough to watch! If he stood behind this door, which opens inwards and to the right, you in your chair could not possibly have seen him behind the shield of the door. Agreed?"

"Oh, yes."

"He would have had a direct line of fire to the victim, at right angles, with nothing and no one between. Could he have been surprised here by someone from the servants' quarters? No! The servants are together at table between six-fifteen and six-thirty or a few minutes later. Could he have been surprised by any guest or member of the family? Likewise no. As a rule (I say as a rule!) no one comes downstairs until a quarter to seven at the earliest. Agreed?"

"Oh, yes," answered Clive. "I thought of that too."

Raindrops from the chimney hissed into the dying fire. Dr.

Bland, who had stalked back to the desk and put down the revolver there, wheeled round.

"*You* thought of it?"

"I did. Do you propose to accuse me, for instance, of killing an estimable gentleman who was scarcely more than an acquaintance?"

"Accuse? Oh, tut! You horrify me. At the same time, if you have any notion of going to London tomorrow, pray be quit of it. You will not go."

"Who is to stop me?"

"Why, as to that: means can be devised, if they are necessary. Meanwhile," and again the bright blue eyes struck across like a blow, "can you suggest why any murderer, any at all except one in your imagination, should have taken so much trouble in order to be seen?"

"Yes, I think I can," retorted Clive, with all the doubts and perplexities and bedevilments boiling up inside him. "You have just given the explanation."

"My dear sir . . . !"

"The murderer wanted to be seen," Clive interrupted, "because it was necessary for the clothes to be seen. And had to be seen and remarked because . . . well. Because nobody would suspect a woman of wearing them."

There was a stroke of silence, during which Dr. Bland's hand went up to his beard.

"A woman? That's impossible!"

"Oh, no," said Clive, advancing as the other advanced. "I dislike the idea. I hate the idea. In my heart I refuse to believe it. But it is the most likely supposition of all."

"Mr. Strickland, you are more quick-witted than I had imagined. And yet it won't do. I tell you it won't do! There is no—"

Dr. Bland stopped. That was the point at which both of them, each from the corner of his eye, caught a flicker of movement from inside the nearly dark library.

A man of Dr. Bland's portliness and dignity might move briskly, but he could not or did not move with speed. Clive, physically as hard as nails and in first-rate training, could and did. He was into the library within half a second, his shoulders cutting off the glow which penetrated there from the study lamp.

"Don't go in," he said gently to the person in front of him. "What you see there will only distress you."

"I had not intended to go in," answered Celia Damon.

He could not see her clearly, though he heard her breathe. Her gentle grey eyes, the lids puffy with weeping in a pretty face almost distorted from emotion, were fixed on him in a kind of horrified realization.

"You should not have come downstairs, Miss Damon. Permit me to take you into the drawing-room."

Only Celia's natural submissiveness prevented her from bursting out.

"Thank you," she said, and lowered her eyes. "But I have something to say, and I must say it."

"Celia!" cried Kate's voice in the distance.

Kate, carrying a lamp, ran into the drawing-room from the hall as Clive parted the bead curtain and escorted Celia there. Kate, as tempestuous of manner as Celia was quiet, stopped and watched them.

"Celia," she cried, "can't I leave you alone for one minute without . . .?"

"I am sorry, Kate dear, if I alarmed you. I would not do that for the world."

Dr. Bland, bringing the green-shaded study lamp, and Burbage with his own light, followed the others into the room. Shadows retreated, unveiling the big drawing-room to show its padded chairs, its Turkey carpet, its piano of carved rosewood with a brass candle-bracket on either side of the music-rack.

"I would not do that for the world, I do assure you," repeated Celia. "But I have something to say, and I must say it."

About Celia, slim and delicate in the purple-coloured gown, her back curls dishevelled, there was a quality of eeriness which held the others silent. She approached the centre-table, and hesitated.

Then her eyes, enormous, turned in the direction of the study. She went to the upright piano, opened its lid, and sat down on the padded stool. Kate's instinctive protest was checked by a gesture from Dr. Bland as Celia spread her fingers over the keys.

The famous hymn-tune, its beat emphasized by loneliness and storm, swelled up softly as though in a fervency of prayer. Celia had no music, but she needed none. A chill touched Clive Strickland. Celia's head was thrown back, and her eyes were squeezed nearly shut. No one else moved: perhaps no one thought of moving.

> Nearer, my God, to Thee,
> Nearer to Thee . . .
> E'en though it be a cross
> That raiseth me . . .

53

"Celia!" said Kate. That single word was swept away, lost, unheeded. Celia's fingers, strong and supple despite their delicacy, smote in a greater passion of dedication.

> Still all my song shall be,
> Nearer, my God, to Thee . . .

Dr. Bland stood with his head bowed. Burbage had also lowered his head, though the lamp trembled slightly.

> Nearer, my God, to Thee,
> Nearer to Thee.

The music died away; the fingers grew lifeless. Celia's own head bowed after she had finished playing. For perhaps twenty seconds she remained motionless before edging out the swell of the crinoline from under the keyboard and standing up to face them.

"You must forgive me if I speak now," she said. "I have guessed who killed my father—"

"Celia!"

"—and known it, I say known it, since Burbage told me who left this house while the rest of us were dressing for dinner."

"Oh!" said Kate, as though expecting something different.

"My dear young lady—" began Dr. Bland.

"I *will* speak," Celia said in white-faced quiet, "and you shall not stop me until I have done. It did not need Mr. Strickland to say this woman dressed as a man. She dressed in men's clothes often enough when she appeared with Charles Kean. But I should have known why she dressed like that when she killed my father. It was not to be mistaken for a man. No! Never in this world! It was to put the blame on Kate."

Three lamps, in three different hands, cast a wavering play of shadows above their heads.

"On Kate?" Clive blurted out.

"Dr. Bland knows it. Burbage knows it." Celia's tears blinded her. "I have heard so much—oh, so much!—about a girl named Constance Kent and a dreadful thing at Road-Hill House five years ago. Constance Kent, before she did a murder, once ran away from home in boy's clothes. Well! When Kate and I were much younger . . ."

Dr. Bland took two steps forward. Celia shrank back.

"*We* ran away from home," she said. "And Kate wore boy's clothes. Georgette Libbard, the woman my father married, has laughed and told that story ever since she heard it.

She even laughed when Kate slapped her face and said *she* had not the courage to be an honest prostitute."

"Celia," shouted Dr. Bland, "this is not seemly."

"*You* did not see her face when Kate slapped her. I did."

"Burbage," Dr. Bland said suddenly, and turned as though remembering, "you may go."

"Sir—" began the house-steward.

"Yes, Burbage?" interposed Clive. "*What is it?*"

"Sir, I—"

"Burbage," cried Dr. Bland, "you may go."

"No; stop!" said Kate, her brown eyes fixed and glittering. Clive had gone to her side and taken her hand, and the fingers were cold. "You have just finished making a—a tour to see whether all the ways in or out of this house are locked and barred on the inside. I heard Mr. Strickland tell you to do that. Are they all fastened on the inside?"

"Yes, Miss Kate."

"That's not true," cried Celia, fighting sobs.

Clive glanced from Kate to Celia and back again. Every lamp now trembled in a different hand.

"At half-past five or thereabouts, you said," Clive interposed again as Burbage's face turned towards him, "the coachman drove Mrs. Damon to Reading?"

"Yes, sir. To the railway station. Hopper has returned, and has—"

"Whether or not Mrs. Damon could have got back from the railway station, could she have got into the house?"

"No, sir."

The shadows swayed over curtains of purple velvet with gold cords and tassels. Though five faces were so clear under the light, you could not tell who exhaled a breath of relief.

"And at long last, Burbage," said Dr. Bland, "I think that will be all."

"No, Burbage," said Clive, as Kate's arm tightened in his, "that will not necessarily be all. Might we have a word with your daughter?"

"My daughter, sir?"

"Yes, if you will. Miss Burbage has remembered 'a fact, or at least an impression' about what she saw on the stairs. She wanted to speak to Mr. Damon, but he died before she could. May she speak to us instead?"

"Young man," snapped Dr. Bland, "take care what you do. To close the door of hell is not easy."

"I will fetch my daughter, sir," said Burbage.

He brought her within a matter of twenty seconds. Those in the drawing-room had hardly altered their positions, except that Kate put down her lamp on the centre-table beside a bowl of wax fruit, and Dr. Bland set his own lamp on the white-marble mantelpiece beside the clock, when Penelope entered.

Clive could have sworn Burbage had not prompted her. Yet she was far from being composed. The fine eyes shifted in the plain face; she smoothed at the straight front of her crinoline, and seemed very small beside her stately father.

Clive hesitated.

"Miss Burbage," he said, and saw her eager response to this formal address, "you told your father you had remembered 'a fact, or at least an impression' about the figure on the stairs last night. Is that so?"

"Yes, sir."

"You implied that this had something to do with your being near-sighted. Is that so too?"

"Yes, sir."

But the cultured voice hesitated.

"Penelope, please do tell us!" Kate burst out. "This figure in man's clothes: could it possibly have been a woman?"

Penelope's eyes widened; the cultured voice slurred away. 'And yet that's it!' Clive thought in astonishment. 'By the living jingo, that's what she was going to tell us.'

"Well, Penelope?" cried Celia. "What have you to say? It was a woman, was it not?"

Penelope steadied herself and said ten words. And the whole affair was in even worse darkness than it had been before.

VIII. THE MASKS OF
GEORGETTE DAMON

Along Oxford Street, towards noon of the following day, a hansom-cab rattled on uneven stones. The smoke of Oxford Street, the mud of Oxford Street, were equalled only by the volume of its noise and the slowness of its wheeled traffic.

Clive Strickland, in the hansom, left off arguing with his companion and looked at the north pavement.

They had driven across the Regent Circus, moving eastwards. The Pantheon, with Jonathan Whicher's office above an Easy Shaving Parlour beside it, was on the south side of Oxford Street between here and the evil squalor round St. Giles's. Against the movement of the crowd on the pavement one figure caught Clive's attention.

A bearded police-constable, in a greatcoat and the domed helmet which had replaced the top-hat of past years, paced by at his unhurrying tread.

Policemen! Beards!

More than a little bitterness rose in Clive's soul.

He was not unduly worried that the Berkshire County Constabulary must be asking sharp questions about his absence; Clive believed he could always return to High Chimneys in good time. But other doubts and worries obsessed him.

"The girl was lying," he declared. "Penelope Burbage was lying, and I'd stake my life on it."

"That may be, old boy," said Victor Damon, making a fussed gesture; "but what did she say?"

"Beards!"

"What did the dashed gel *say?*" insisted Victor. "And who killed my governor?"

"I don't know, Victor. Penelope has confused matters still more. You hardly seem very cut up about your father's death."

"If you mean I don't wear the proper clothes, or a crape band round my hat, that's because they're not ready yet. I only got Dr. Bland's telegram two hours ago."

"I was not referring to mourning."

"No more was I. I mean I can't shed tears simply because it's the fashion to weep buckets of 'em. There's too much of that."

A crashing of wheeled vehicles, the profanity of ill-temper from drivers, rose under a damp, cold sky. Victor gritted his teeth. His eyes, clear grey above the straight nose and heavy light-brown moustache, remained steady.

"You couldn't call my governor a free-and-easy sort. But there was more in him than in most people. He let me live in town; he pardoned in me what he wouldn't have pardoned in anyone else; it won't be so simple to stand on my own now."

"Cheerfully selfish, as usual. You're going to answer a few straight questions, my lad. When you said Kate and Celia were in danger, did you mean somebody hated them and would do anything to get level with them?"

"Yes! In particular I meant Kate. But two nights ago, Monday night it was, you kept running on about Celia, Celia, Celia; I had to pull you up and say I meant Kate too."

"And the person who hates them is your stepmother?"

"My stepmother? Georgette?" Victor, about to push his silk 'goss' to the back of his head, sat up straight in the hansom. "God Almighty, no!"

"You didn't mean your stepmother?"

"No! I've always admired Georgette, and I've told you so. Actress or no actress, I think she was good for the governor."

"Then whom did you mean?"

"When I said I couldn't tell you, I meant that and no more. I don't know! If I had known, I needn't have persuaded you into this at all."

"Then one more straight question," said Clive, seizing the lapel of the other's greatcoat, "and mind you give me a straight answer. Did you know our friend Tress was having an affair with your stepmother?"

"No, I did not," retorted Victor, spacing his words and with something like horror behind his astonishment. "That's going too far, old boy, even for me. To get my sister married to a cove who's been making up to my stepmother: no, curse it, that's not done. Mind you, though! I don't say, in a way, that Tress mightn't still be a good match for Celia or for Kate either—"

"Damn your soul, leave Kate out of this!"

Mud splashed up as the hansom swayed.

"Here!" said Victor, blinking at him. "Here!"

"You're a snob, Victor. . . ."

"Thanks very much. I thought you were a friend of mine."

"I am. You get yourself into these fixes and expect me to solve your difficulties because I am all of six years older; and you're deeply impressed by Tress because he sports a crest on his note-paper. But he's been making a fool of you and me and everybody else; he had better be told so."

"Then *you* tell him, old boy. Tress ain't the man you can talk to like that."

"You think not?"

"I know it. Take care he don't make a fool of you still more."

"Tress! Georgette! She was supposed to take a train for London. If only we knew whether she did, and where she met Tress if she did meet him—!"

"Devil take it, you don't think the old gel killed my governor?"

"Victor, she can't have done. But why did she go and where did she go? According to what Penelope Burbage said . . ."

To Clive, brooding, returned all the frustration of last night's questioning in the stuffy drawing-room with the purple curtains and the Turkey carpet. He was in a different atmosphere now: nearly half the men striding along Oxford Street, it seemed to him, wore the Dundreary whiskers made fashionable by E. A. Sothern four years before.

"Victor, do you know what anti-climax is?"

"Hey?"

"We fetched in Burbage's daughter, as I was telling you. I had begun to question her as gently as possible, when both Kate and Celia were too impatient; they walloped out with what lawyers call a leading question. 'This figure in man's clothes: could it possibly have been a woman?' And, 'Was it a woman, or was it not?' I don't think I can ever forget Penelope's answer. She looked at Celia and said, *'No, miss, it was a man. He had a beard.'* "

"A beard?" exclaimed Victor.

"Yes."

"Do you think she was lying?"

"Victor, I'm certain of it."

Just ahead, the driver of a dray cursed luridly in the slow lurch of vehicles. A street-urchin of nine or ten, standing at the kerb and seeing Clive's expression, retaliated by thrusting his thumbs into his ears, wriggling the fingers, and making a hideous face with outthrust tongue.

"Penelope saw a woman on those stairs," Clive insisted. "She meant to tell us so. Whereupon, for some reason, she blurted out that statement about a man with a beard. I refuse to believe there were two different persons in the famous costume: one on the night of Monday, the sixteenth, and one who killed your father on the night of Tuesday, the seventeenth. Does that seem likely?"

"No. Not on your life!"

"Up to the time Penelope said that, I wouldn't believe the murderer could be a woman. Now I'm not sure. There are too many women in this affair."

"Yes!" said Victor thoughtfully. "You mull 'em over, old boy. Yes."

"Following Penelope's remark, there was the very devil of an uproar. I decided I had better leave before the police arrived."

"Last night, you mean?" demanded Victor, with one eyebrow travelling above the other. "You left High Chimneys last night? Why?"

"Don't you understand even yet? That doctor was determined to prevent me from meeting Whicher; he as good as said so. He might, just might, have persuaded the police to hold me. I couldn't risk that."

"Damme, Clive, you couldn't have locked yourself in the study with the key on the other side of both doors!"

"Yes, I could have; there's a way to do it. And I repeat that I couldn't risk being held. The only person who knows what I did is Kate. I don't have to tell you Reading is a big railway junction; I walked there and found a train. And I was at Whicher's office by eight o'clock this morning."

"Oh? You saw him?"

"No. There was nobody there; door locked; no message on it. The London Directory doesn't list any address except that one. I waited for two and a half hours. Then I wrote a note; I explained the situation and said I should return at noon; and I pushed the note under the door. If Whicher's not there now . . ."

"You're dished, ain't you?"

"No; but all I can do is take the Bath-and-Bristol Express back to Reading before the police really lose their tempers."

Clive glanced up, past the reins of an ambling horse which had almost ambled too far. On the south side of the street loomed the Pantheon, now falling into bankruptcy as a bazaar and picture-gallery as it had gone bankrupt when it was a concert and lecture hall. Clive threw his head back.

"Cabby!"

The trap in the roof of the hansom opened; the driver's face appeared, in its customary rather startling fashion, upside down.

"Cabby, pull up here! We must cross the road."

Pushing up the flaps of the hansom, Clive climbed down to the north pavement with Victor following him.

An east wind whipped the smoke. Two fashionable ladies on a shopping expedition, the wind carrying out their crinolines like ships under sail, veered past the front of the Princess's Theatre. In a row of dun-coloured houses that theatre stood out only because the Royal Arms were displayed against its facade. The board beside the entrance announced an original drama in four acts, *It Is Never Too Late to Mend*, taken by Charles Reade, Esq., from his own popular novel and preceded by a farce called *Quiet Lodgings*: the drama itself to begin at a quarter to eight with carriages for eleven o'clock.

Clive, paying the cabman, would never have looked twice at it if he had not seen who was just going in by the front entrance.

Georgette Damon.

She did not see him, though she glanced quickly left and right before slipping into the foyer. Georgette's mature charms were enhanced by a short fur jacket and a blue silk gown. She wore another of the modish hats, flat and oval against auburn hair, and she carried a very large brown-paper parcel.

Victor, who had clipped a cigar and was trying to light it against the wind, did not see Georgette any more than she saw Clive. Clive jabbed his companion in the ribs.

"Stay where you are and don't move. I'm going in here."

"But we can't go to the theatre at this hour, old boy."

"Victor, stop playing the E. A. Sothern silly-ass when you're anything but that! Stay there and don't move!"

The foyer lay hushed and almost dark. Clive, following Georgette, heard her hurry through into the pit. Then he saw her dimly, going down the left-hand aisle past the boxes. He did not trouble to conceal his footsteps on bare, echoing boards, but she was too preoccupied to notice.

The theatre, haunted by a smell of gas and orange-peel, seemed deserted. One gas-jet, feebly burning somewhere beyond the wings, touched a stage set for the scene of prison-life in *It Is Never Too Late to Mend* whose brutally real details, especially in the punishment of the treadmill, had provoked cries of protest from the squeamish on opening night.

Georgette stopped in gloom. She was not now either arch or coy. Plump, rather imperious, she spoke softly but clearly.

"Mr. Vining!"

Clive stopped too. Mr. Vining had been the owner of the Princess's Theatre for many years. And, up to 1859, it had housed Charles Kean's company of Shakespearean players. Though this was before the days of Clive's acquaintance with theatrical people, he should have guessed why Matthew Damon had made such special mention of it.

"Mr. Vining!" Georgette repeated.

"I am here, Miss Libbard," said a man standing in the aisle in front of her.

"My name is Mrs. Damon. Call me that."

"As you please, Mrs. Damon. But you might have—"

"Might have entered by the stage-door?" Georgette inquired sweetly. "Oh, no! No, Mr. Vining. Not *ever* again."

"Well, well! That also is as you please."

"I have brought the clothes," said Georgette. Brown paper crackled on the large parcel. "And I hold you to your promise."

"Where did you find these clothes?"

"Where I knew I should find them. Hidden among a certain young woman's belongings in her bedroom at High Chimneys."

Clive, about to move forward and speak, checked himself beside the red-plush rail of a box. The prison-scene was grey and brown and black. Mr. Vining made a short gesture of disquiet or even anger.

"Mrs. Damon, I know little of your affairs in these later days. What do you want me to do?"

"Why, keep your promise, to be sure! You can't deny you made it. Hide these things; or, rather, give them to the wardrobe mistress. They will go all unnoticed in a theatre until . . . well! *If* I have need of them to denounce someone."

"You should have hidden these clothes yourself."

"And have my maid find a man's clothes among *my* possessions? Don't be ridiculous!"

"The answer to that is simple. Tell your husband."

"I can't! I won't!" Georgette's voice had grown breathless. "You see that treadmill on the stage?"

"I see it," answered the other, though he was not looking at it.

"I can't conceal from *you*," said Georgette, "that I know a vast deal of prisons from my own two parents' experience. There is somebody who deserves the treadmill, and the irons, and the whip lashing and lashing; yes! And will get it, too, if things go on as they go now. But my husband has been kind to me, in his own way. I can't hurt him. He must cherish at least one illusion."

"Including the illusion," Mr. Vining asked dryly, "that his wife is Caesar's wife?"

"Oh, don't be so virtuous! What I do harms no one except myself. All this fuss and botheration about accepting some cast-off clothes?"

"Mrs. Damon, will you swear to me there is nothing that might embroil me with the law?"

"There is nothing yet. I swear to it."

"Very well. For the sake of old times, then, give me the parcel. I still say, though, that you would hurt your husband far less by telling him whatever is the truth."

"You may be right."

"Trust me, Mrs. Damon: I know I am right."

Against the gas-glimmer across the stage, a red-haired silhouette, Georgette raised both arms in a tragic gesture which might or might not have been sincere. Clive could not see her face; he could not be certain of anything.

"I am going to Laurier's now," she said, "for an appointment that may be fateful in the future. Not my future, I thank you, though I have risked much in coming to London. But it may be fateful to the wretch who has been abusing our confidence at High Chimneys. I will think of what you suggest, Mr. Vining. Good day."

Gracefully Georgette inclined her head and turned round.

Laurier's, eh?

As soon as Clive heard that name, he was on his way out of the theatre with as much anxiety to walk without noise as he had been careless of it when he entered. At least, he did not think Georgette had seen or heard him. Victor, waiting outside and smoking a cigar, he hauled to one side towards a shop-window.

"Well, old boy," Victor asked with somewhat sardonic inflection, "did you see the play?"

"A kind of one. I saw your stepmother.—Keep your head turned away from the theatre, and don't look in the direction of St. Giles's."

"Well, carry me out!" said Victor. "You saw Georgette? In daylight? What was she doing there?"

"Meeting an old friend. What else she was doing remains to be seen. She's going to Laurier's now, and I mean to follow her."

"What about this detective?"

"It won't take fifteen minutes, unless something unforeseen turns up. You go across to Whicher's; it's there, above the sign that says EASY SHAVING; and I'll join you."

"Look here Clive: if a woman goes to Laurier's, that don't mean she's no lady. It only means she's a bit fast."

"Fast! I'm concerned with something more serious. Off you go, now."

Victor dodged out amid the traffic. Clive, affecting to be fascinated by a stationer's shop-window, watched from the corner of his eye as Georgette Damon came out of the theatre. Still she did not observe him, or seem to observe him. After looking round vainly for a cab, the pretty lady made a pouting mouth and set off to walk eastwards.

Clive walked twenty feet behind her.

"'In polite society,'" he remembered reading in a book published during that same year, "'a FAST young lady is one who affects mannish habits or makes herself conspicuous by some unfeminine accomplishment—talks slang, drives about in London, smokes cigarettes, is knowing in dogs, horses, etc.'"

At Laurier's, which had some status between a restaurant and a very luxurious public-house, you found little talk of dogs and horses. The book did not define feminine correctness in the matter of drink. Such correctness went without saying. Provided she sipped genteelly, a lady or her mother or stepmother might put away enough Burgundy or Marsala to float a ship of the line.

But a parcel of men's clothes? The costume which could only be that of a prowler and a murderer?

63

"Where did you find these clothes?"

"Where I knew I should find them. Hidden among a certain young woman's belongings in her bedroom at High Chimneys."

Kate's, for instance?

Along the north pavement of Oxford Street, amid foot-traffic moving sedately past dun-coloured buildings and long solemn lines of street-lamps, Georgette's words came back to him with a ring of outrage and sincerity. She really hadn't seemed to know her husband was dead.

On the other hand, if Celia Damon had been right and, every move of the murderer were directed towards putting the blame on Kate, the clothes would have been found among Kate's possessions because Georgette (or somebody!) had put them there to be found. It was a logical step, an inevitable one.

Granted a certain set of circumstances, Georgette could just possibly have been the murderer.

Matthew Damon had not been killed when he was alone, shut up in his study behind barred doors and windows. On the contrary! Only the house was locked up on the inside. Suppose she had some accomplice inside High Chimneys itself?

Georgette makes a spectacular exit, flaunting bag and baggage, at about half-past five. Burbage bars the front door after her. Shortly before the time of the murder, then, this accomplice opens a door or a full-length window, admits Georgette for her masquerade, and locks up again after she has gone.

'Nonsense!' said his common sense. 'What accomplice? Can you really credit this?'

'No, I cannot,' replied the same. 'But all things are possible in the nightmare. And it *is* just feasible.'

Clive, raging, wished to all gods he could make up his mind about her.

There she walked, in blue gown and short fur jacket, with the smoky wind whooping round her. At times she was coy and shrinking, at other times angry and imperious, at still others fearful and racked by conscience, precisely like all the other women he had ever known. Was Georgette, unlike most women, unduly preoccupied with thoughts and dreams of sensuality? Well, so was his own Kate. And Clive, who was damned if he would be a hypocrite, refused to condemn in Georgette what he found so agreeable in Kate.

Steady!

Georgette walked a little faster. So did Clive.

Berners Street, full of expensive shops and kept women, went by on their left. So did Newman Street, ditto. They were approaching Rathbone Place, with Laurier's round the corner. Straight ahead, beyond the other side of Tottenham Court Road, lay the odorous slums and thieves' kitchens which were not supposed to exist.

Georgette had crossed Rathbone Place. A four-wheeler, whisking out of the Place just after she crossed, momentarily obscured Clive's view of discreet windows in arabesques of frosted glass below the curly gilded letters *Laurier*.

On the far pavement she did not turn left in the direction of Laurier's. Instead she pressed on towards the intersection of Tottenham Court Road with Crown Street and St. Giles's High Street.

Then, unexpectedly, as Clive quickened his step, trouble was upon him.

IX. ENCOUNTER IN OXFORD STREET

"I don't know you, sir," said Georgette, suddenly stopping and turning round. "Why are you following me?"

"And yet, Mrs. Damon, I had the honour of making your acquaintance yesterday. It was for the second time, you said."

"My name is certainly Mrs. Damon. But you are either mistaken or mad. Why are you following me, sir? Do you mean to molest me?"

Her actress's voice again rose up clearly.

This was the one weapon, Clive thought with an inner curse, that you could never meet.

Wind blew the sparks from a pieman's fire. A pavement artist, hunched against the wall in the last stretch of Oxford Street, looked up in blear-eyed glee from a coloured-chalk drawing of Napoleon Bonaparte and a couple of herrings.

"Mrs. Damon, let me assure you—!"

"And *I* assure *you*, sir, that if you have made a mistake I shall be glad to excuse you. If you continue to molest me, I shall be obliged to call a policeman."

The word policeman rang out with peculiar effect above all other noises.

Hitherto there had been any number of well-dressed and stately passers-by. Now the pavement, for yards round Georgette and Clive, was cleared of them as though by magic. They did not hurry; they kept their eyes fixed ahead; they simply vanished. But the word acted with equal magic to whistle up others.

That was where Georgette's expression changed.

Head raised, innocent blue eyes fixed on Clive, beaded reticule clasped against her breast, she had been poised in an air of martyrdom. Now she looked past him.

"No!" Georgette cried. "No!"

"Oh, yes," said a heavy, pleased voice Clive recognized only too well. "*I* don't excuse him."

A self-confident figure, as tall as Clive but more burly, came padding round the corner of Rathbone Place with a wickedly pleased smile and the step of a tame tiger. Tress's glossy hat was stuck on the back of his head; his chest swelled under a plum-blue greatcoat with an astrakhan collar.

In his right hand, grey-gloved, Tress gripped a thick walking-stick with a silver head. He looked Clive up and down.

"Well, well," Tress said agreeably, as though just recognizing him. "So it's Strickland, is it?"

"Now look here, Tress—!"

"Up to your old tricks, eh?"

"No!" cried Georgette, clasping both hands on the reticule. Something honest, something deeply human and likeable, flashed in her blue eyes.

"Got anything to say for yourself, Strickland?"

"Yes. Keep off. I warn you."

"Oh, you warn me? Why?"

"Do you want a public scene? Here in the street?"

"*You* don't, I'll be bound."

"Now look here—"

Tress's wide-spaced teeth, framed in yellowish Dundreary whiskers with beard-like hair under the chin, appeared in a smile.

"*You* don't want a public thrashing, Strickland. But that's what you deserve. And that's what you're going to get."

With a lightning-like motion Tress shifted his grip on the walking-stick, lifted it, and slashed it down at the other's face. Clive's temper blew to pieces. He slipped aside, swinging his weight to drive his left fist into the middle of Tress's stomach, at the same moment that powerful hands locked his arms at both sides and flung his weight back again.

A roar of delight from spectators almost drowned two other voices.

"Now, then!" said a bearded police-constable at Clive's left side. "None of that, you!"

"Now, then!" said a bearded police-constable at Clive's right side. "What's all this?"

"*Was* you molesting the lady, sir?"

"No," said Clive.

"Oh, yes," said Tress, unruffled and grinning.

"Ask the lady," shouted Clive.

The lady was not there.

"*Was* you molesting the lady, sir?"

"Heard her say so, didn't you?" inquired Tress.

"That's right," agreed Police-Constable Number One. "Quiet, you!" he added to Clive. "Station-house, Tom."

"Make way, there!" interrupted a new voice. "Make way, there!"

Both constables stiffened to salute-position without relaxing their hold on Clive. Into the nightmarish group of spectators, who had begun to whistle and caper, pushed a shortish thick-set man, his face somewhat pock-marked, with an unmistakable air of authority despite his shabby plain clothes.

"Indecently molesting a lady, sir," Police-Constable Number One announced importantly. "Lady's fainted, most likely. Anyways, she ain't here."

"I heard it, I heard it!" The pock-marked newcomer, after studying Clive for an instant with a bland, shrewd eye, turned to Tress. "Do you give this man in charge, sir?"

"I do," said Tress, unbuttoning his greatcoat. "Here's my card."

"Ah. That'll do, sir. All right, my lads: St. Giles's Station-House. Take him along."

There are times when it is just as well not to speak, because the extent of your rage would make you sound foolish. Two noises most affected Clive Strickland then. One was the first note of the clock at St. Giles's Church, banging out the hour of noon when he should have been elsewhere. The other was Tress's deep, almost noiseless laugh.

Clive's shoulders opened and heaved with a sudden wrench that threw Police Constable Number Two off his feet before both officers fastened on him again.

"You'd better be quiet, Strickland," Tress said maliciously. "*You've* got nothing to say."

"I've got something to do, Tressider, the next time you and I meet."

Tress, not impressed, turned away.

"Quiet!" snapped the pock-marked man, and swung to the crowd round the prisoner. "That's all," he said. "Stall your mugs, the lot of you! Hook it!"

Most of these obediently hooked it and faded away. But some few, the more nightmarish from the slums, trailed after the fighting group as Clive was borne across towards St. Giles's High Street.

"All right, my lad," the pock-marked man told him loudly. "If you've got anything to say, get it off your chest now."

"As a matter of fact," panted Clive, making the others stop when he stopped, "I have quite a few things to say. The fact that I did follow Mrs. Damon may make it partly my own fault. But that's as far as it goes. At this minute I ought to be talking to a man named Whicher about a murder that was committed in Berkshire last night. Why the hell don't you go the whole hog and arrest me for that too?"

The pock-marked man got in front of him.

Shortish and thick-set, in one of the new-style bowler hats and new-style suits with the short coat, yet shabby and great-coatless, he had a manner which was not quite that of the gentleman yet far from being that of the lout.

"Let drive all you please, sir," he urged in an apologetic whisper, "but for God's sake stop fighting until we get you to the police-station so they won't know it's not a real arrest. I *am* Whicher."

A dray loaded with beer-barrels went over ruts with a rumble and crash. Clive, still panting, looked down at the other man.

Then the little group, with Clive offering only a token resistance, staggered through an offensively foul street to the station-house in the shadow of the church. Inside the charge-room the policemen dropped their hands; both beards were split with grins.

"Sorry, sir," said Police-Constable Number Two, setting out a chair by the fire.

"Sorry, sir," said Police-Constable Number One. "Ex-Inspector Whicher is an old pal of ours. He thought the gent with the Dundreary whiskers was out to make trouble for you, and we'd best handle it like this. Good thing the sergeant's not here, though."

"Well, I'll be so-and-so'd," observed Clive, and sat down in the chair.

"Ah!" breathed Mr. Whicher, in a more cheerful tone. "That's all right, then."

But Jonathan Whicher was far from being cheerful at the back of it.

Always with a reserved and thoughtful air, as though turning over some deep arithmetical calculation in his mind, he regarded Clive with his head on one side.

"I ask your pardon, sir," he apologized, "for putting you to this inconvenience. You must think I am foolish, like; ay, and more than foolish. But I heard this gentleman,"—and he held up Tress's card—"shouting your name. My little game might have had a different ending if I could have talked to the lady. I never thought Mrs. Damon would hook it too."

Clive jumped up from his chair.

"Inspector . . ." he began.

"Stop!" said Mr. Whicher, holding up his hand. "If you don't mind, sir, I'd rather you didn't call me Inspector. Charley Field got into trouble for calling himself that; and *he* retired from the Force in good order. He wasn't forced to resign like me."

"Then what do I call you?"

"Well, sir, that's as you like. Mr. Dickens, when he wrote some pieces about us in *Household Words* fifteen years ago, called me Witchem. The swell mob spelled Witchem with a B. I'll answer to any name that allows I've got wits in my head."

"Anyway!" said Clive, sweeping this aside. "Are you acquainted with Mrs. Matthew Damon?"

"You might say I am. In a way."

"And you know my name too. So you got the note I left at your office?"

"Yes, I got it." A grim look crossed the pock-marked face. "Pity I wasn't there. But I knew Mr. Damon had been shot before I read your note. That's why I wasn't there; the electric telegraph sent the news to Scotland Yard this morning, and a friend of mine thought I might be interested."

"You *were* interested, I hope?"

"More than interested," said Jonathan Whicher, removing his bowler hat to show scanty greyish hair. "You mightn't believe it, sir, but that gentleman was one of the kindest-hearted men I ever knew. I'd hate to think I was partly responsible for his death."

"You told him something, didn't you? Three months ago?"

"Yes!" said Mr. Whicher, putting on his hat again.

"And you know which one of his daughters is really the daughter of Harriet Pyke?"

It was only afterwards, long afterwards, that Clive interpreted the strange look on the other man's face. But the riddle, the doubts and all the weighing of possibilities, had come back with a kind of anguish.

Police-Constable Number One spoke up heartily.

"Well, Mr. Whicher, Tom and I are on duty. Look sharp, Tom! You and this gentleman stay here, Mr. Whicher, until the last of them curious 'uns clear away from the station-house." He turned to Clive. "No offence taken, sir?"

"No, no, of course not!"

Far from offence being taken, money changed hands. The two constables saluted and marched out with hoarse chuckles. The only other person left with Clive and Whicher was a third policeman, bearded but helmetless, who sat on a kitchen chair near the entrance to the cells, smoking a clay pipe and reading the *Morning Post*.

"Tell me!" Clive insisted. "You know whether Harriet Pyke's daughter is Celia or Kate?"

"No, sir, I don't know," answered Whicher. "And I'd hardly have to tell Mr. Damon, now would I? He knew it already. But there's somebody else at High Chimneys who knows it too."

The air in the station-house, never very clean, had grown choking to Clive's lungs.

"Inspector . . . I beg your pardon. I explained in my note, Mr. Whicher, why I'm here today."

"That's right, sir. You did."

"Mr. Damon had an appointment with you for four o'clock this afternoon. At least, I suppose you got his telegram?"

"Again very true. I did."

"Mr. Damon made me promise, if anything happened to him—"

"Stop!" said Jonathan Whicher. "Did he expect something to happen to him?"

"Yes. He had a revolver, *the* revolver, in his desk-drawer. According to a witness named Dr. Bland, Mr. Damon bought the weapon a fortnight ago. If he armed himself like that, it doesn't seem to indicate he suspected a member of his own family."

Throughout this Mr. Whicher's gaze, thoughtful and deprecating and fixed, had never left Clive's face. With one hand he jingled coppers in his pocket; with the other he ticked his thumb against Tress's visiting-card.

"Mr. Damon made me promise, then," Clive went on, "that if anything happened to him I was to be here in his place. *I* want to engage you to find the murderer. And you may name any fee you like."

"Thank you kindly. I'll take your fee, sir, and I won't deny I need it. But finding the murderer may not be as hard a job as it looks."

"Oh? Why not?"

"Because I think I can guess already."

A little reflection of firelight climbed the wall in the fusty room.

"Oh, not from police-work!" said the pock-marked man, making a face and jingling coins. "Not from brain-work, more's the pity! It's a guess from information received by accident only last August."

"Then who killed him?"

"No!" said Mr. Whicher. He took a turn up and down the room. "If you don't mind, I'll keep that to myself for the moment, specially as I may be wrong and specially as I've not heard one word except what came over the wires to Scotland Yard. I made one mistake, the tomfool's mistake of my life, in the Road-Hill House murder in '60. I arrested Constance Kent before I'd got enough evidence; and it finished me. The King might have backed me up, and stood by me. . . ."

"The King? What king?"

" 'King' Mayne. Sir Richard Mayne, the Commissioner of Police. He's a very old man, I grant you. He's been commissioner since there were two commissioners when the Metropolitan Police was founded in '29. Howsoever! He didn't stand by me, and that's that. The girl was guilty then. It may be, sir, another girl is guilty now."

"Damn and blast the air in this place," said Clive, tugging at his collar.

The third police-constable, who was sitting by the entrance to the cells, took the clay pipe out of his mouth and spoke with passion.

"It's no warse o' flowers," he said. "Not in St. Giles's it ain't."

"Sorry," muttered Clive.

Jonathan Whicher studied him without seeming to do so.

"Howsoever! By your leave, sir, I won't intrude *my* troubles when I can see *you've* got 'em about a young lady."

"You are mistaken, Mr. Whicher. I have no troubles or doubts at all."

The other drew a deep breath, still ticking his thumb against Tress's card.

"Then if you'll just come along with me to my office, sir, I'd like to know what did happen last night. That's before, with your permission, we go down to High Chimneys and hammer the one person who *can* tell us the truth. There's nothing more been happening today, has there?"

"Not at High Chimneys, no. Purely by accident I did follow Mrs. Damon into the Princess's Theatre a while ago. I saw how a certain set of clothes, the murderer's clothes, are to be hidden until needed; I heard a reference to a young woman, unnamed, who will be condemned to the treadmill if she's caught."

You couldn't tell what would go unremarked and what might cause an explosion.

Whicher, it is true, never exploded; and he seldom raised his voice above that courteous, insistent, worry-away tone. But, at this reference to a treadmill, he gave so obvious a start that Clive became even more disquieted.

"Now, sir, if you don't mind," he suggested, tapping his finger lightly on Clive's chest, "you might begin this story of yours *now*, and tell it to me as we walk along. No! Not the part about the Princess's Theatre. At the beginning and from the beginning, if you will."

Their departure was hastened by an elderly woman, suffering the horrors from drink in one of the cells, who at this point began to scream. An angry pickpocket, and a thin young mother with a child at her breast (arrested for begging) added complaints to the din.

Clive also could have sworn he saw, outside a half-smashed window giving on the refuse-piles of the lane behind, the shadow of a side-whiskered man who might have been the late Matthew Damon.

He almost bolted back in the direction of Oxford Street, with Whicher tut-tutting and trotting on short legs beside him.

In Oxford Street, while they walked, Clive began to speak. The scenes at High Chimneys built themselves up round him; he gave conversations just as they had taken place, together with such of his own theories he considered worthy of mention at all.

The pock-marked face had grown more and more grave.

"Ah! There's no denying, sir, I'm a good deal responsible for this death."

"How? What did you tell Mr. Damon three months ago?"

"If you don't mind, sir, just you go on."

They were within a few steps of the Pantheon when Whicher touched his arm at the entrance to a public-house advertising midday dinners. In a damp cellar like a dungeon, with the gas lighted, they ate a bad meal while Clive drank anything in sight and Whicher sipped a weak brandy-and-water.

"Come, sir! You'd not maintain this is *exactly* what the gentleman told you? Word for word?"

"I do maintain so. It is."

The former Inspector's bowler hat lay beside his plate. He drank from a great dropsical tumbler with one leg.

"—and that," Clive concluded, when the glass was empty

72

and the plates had been removed, "is every word about the murder spoken in my presence at High Chimneys yesterday evening. You can't say whether Harriet Pyke's child is Celia or Kate. I hold it doesn't matter a curse *who* the child is."

"Ah!" murmured his companion.

"Apart from insanity, I won't believe murders are done because of tainted blood. Bring up any child in starvation and brutality and horrors; that child may well turn prostitute for bread or murderer for cakes and ale. Bring up the same child in a well-to-do home, and you need never have a dream of it."

"Just between ourselves, sir, I agree with you. Though there are always exceptions."

"In the second place," continued Clive, striking his fist on the table, "I mean to marry Kate Damon if she'll have me. Whoever committed this murder, I'm certain she didn't."

"And again, between ourselves, I agree."

"By God! Thanks for that!"

"Mark me, now!" said Whicher, wagging his finger. "We may have to change our minds about that. You can't expect the doctor (not that I'm an educated man like a doctor), but still! You can't expect the doctor to say what the disease is until he's seen the patient. Meanwhiles, I agree."

"Well, then! Mr. Damon, being a lawyer, must undoubtedly have made a will; he may speak of the adopted child in that. There are always such things as birth-registrations or even records in a family Bible. . . ."

"I wonder."

"Otherwise," said Clive, with a dryness in his throat, "is there any reason to mention this matter to Kate or Celia either? I thought of telling Kate, and confiding in her. But I couldn't force myself to give her a shock like that, and Celia is not at all strong. If the police don't discover it, why shouldn't we keep it to ourselves?"

"We can, sir. I think we should."

"Thanks again. Very many thanks."

"Now, sir, you take it easy and don't be all upset! We can keep it to ourselves, ay, provided we get the proper answers from the one other person who knows the truth."

"Mr. Whicher, who *is* this person?"

"Can't you guess?"

Shabby and troubled, with his sparse greyish hair and his pock-marked countenance looming against the cellar wall, Whicher fell to ruminating.

"No, I'm not what you'd call an educated man. But I pick up what I can; and, in the old days, a Peeler had to sound pretty genteel if he had his eye on the swell mob. Tell me, sir. Are you the same Mr. Clive Strickland who wrote a serial story called 'If Death Should Keep a Tippling-House . . .'? I read it in *All the Year Round*. Did you write that?"

"Yes." Clive was a little taken aback. "Why do you ask?"

"It's rum, you know. It's uncommonly rum. Those words didn't seem to have much to do with your story, and yet blow me if I could forget 'em. 'If Death Should Keep a Tippling-House . . .' They haunted me, as you might say."

"They haunted me too. That's why I chose the title. It's the first line of some verses from the Roxburghe Ballads. But I don't see how this concerns us."

"Quite right, too. It hasn't a blessed thing to do with Mr. Damon's murder."

Clive looked at him.

"The point, howsoever," pursued Whicher, and leaned forward, "is there all the same. I judged by that tale you'd have made a pretty fair detective-officer yourself; and now I'm sure of it. For instance: you'd like to know who killed Mr. Damon?"

"Yes." Clive restrained himself. "I think I've indicated that."

"Ah! But Mr. Damon told you who was going to kill him, or thought he'd told you. Only he was half out of his mind and near demented, as you described him; he loved to quote examples, like all the lawyer gentlemen; bang went the example, and he wasn't too helpful about the main fact."

"Mr. Damon didn't have time to tell me the main fact!"

"Sir, at least three people have all told you the main fact."

Clive rose to his feet, seizing hat and greatcoat.

The cost of the meals at the pub was sixpence apiece, with an additional shilling for what they had both taken to drink. Dropping half a crown on the table, Clive struggled into his coat and spoke formally.

"Mr. Whicher, if you want to be cautious about making any statement before you have talked to this witness at High Chimneys, very well. Use caution! But don't talk hocus-pocus. I only ask you to say something, or else say nothing."

"Now, now, sir, there's no call to be excited."

"On the contrary," shouted Clive, "there is every call to be excited. Come with me."

Still striding ahead, he led the way upstairs, past the window of the Easy Shaving Parlour, and up a dirty staircase in the house beside the Pantheon. A gas-jet was burning on the landing outside the locked door of Jonathan Whicher's office.

"I've just remembered," Clive continued, as he heard footsteps pacing the landing, "that it's well past one o'clock. I have had a leisurely meal and left a friend of mine stranded outside your door since before twelve. But I never thought he would wait."

Victor had not waited.

Instead, as Clive reached the landing, he met Dr. Rollo Thompson Bland and one other person. All his anger left him.

"Kate," he said. "What are *you* doing here?"

X. THE MOODS OF
KATE DAMON

For over an hour he had experienced a series of strong, varying emotions. This was the strongest if not the last of them.

The house had been built in the third decade of the eighteenth century, when Oxford Street was little more than the road to Tyburn gallows amid fields and flowers. And, though the house had gone to seed, its graceful lines and fanlight windows survived all grime of a utilitarian age.

Kate, on the landing under a bright gas-jet and against an arched window, wore a black-and-red costume which heightened her vivid colouring. Her boat-shaped hat with the short flat plume fitted closely against the dark hair.

"Kate. What are *you* doing here?"

"I am here because—"

"She is here," interrupted Dr. Bland with some exasperation, "because I verily believe she would have come alone if I had not escorted her. That a young lady should go unchaperoned to London, and to meet you, and on the very day after her father's death, did not even seem to strike her as outrageous."

Kate closed her eyes.

"Tut, now!" said Dr. Bland, shaking his portly figure as though to add the emphasis of the watch-chain. "I am a man of the world, but this would not have met with my dead friend's wishes. However, some good at least has come of today. Penelope Burbage has confessed."

Clive stopped short on the landing.

"Confessed?"

"Oh, to nothing sinister. The poor girl now swears the figure she saw on the stairs on Monday night was a woman in man's clothes."

Here the doctor uttered his bluff, common-sense laugh.

"That is absurd, I know. Still more absurd than Penelope's claim to have seen a man with a beard. It gives us only further evidence that this unhappy girl was dreaming."

Kate had extended a black-gloved hand to Clive; they talked intimately with their eyes before he spoke aloud.

"How are you, Kate?"

"Better, at least, now that I have seen you. But, if you had not told me where you were going . . . ! Please, please! You must return to High Chimneys without delay. They are making themselves very unpleasant, especially that police-superintendent."

"Can you blame the superintendent, my dear?" inquired Dr. Bland.

"Yes, I can. And I do."

"Heaven knows," said the doctor, "he is not very intelligent. But he must accept facts as they are. According to Kate, Mr. Strickland, you ran away because you wished to engage this particular private inquiry agent. May I ask why? Was it because Penelope changed her story?"

"No," retorted Clive, without looking at him. "And Penelope, I tell you again, was not dreaming. I saw the figure too."

"My dear sir, *your* account would have been more credible if you had given any description at all. Height, weight, any kind of detail!"

Clive dropped Kate's hand and returned to meet this always-badgering attack.

"I couldn't tell you that. I still can't. I saw the figure too briefly, when a pistol was fired almost in my face. There was little more than a kind of impression."

"Ah. An impression. Should you have said, for instance, it was the figure of a man with a beard?"

"No," Clive answered honestly.

"Very well, then! Should you have said it was a woman?"

"No."

They looked at each other. Dr. Bland, in a sartorial splendour of greatcoat, frock-coat, white waistcoat, and black-and-white chequered trousers, shook his fist in the air.

"Perhaps it is just as well," he observed, controlling himself, "you have sought out an inquiry agent whom we can altogether control. Confound it, sir, *someone* killed my old friend. Who killed him? And who can tell us?"

A very faint throat-clearing, on the stairs behind Clive, reminded him of what had been undertaken for good or for ill.

"Former Detective-Inspector Whicher," he said, "may I present you to Miss Kate Damon and Dr. Thompson Bland?"

Whicher, seen against the elegance of those two, might have seemed no very impressive symbol of the social graces. And yet, for a combination of reasons Clive would have found hard to define, he did inspire confidence.

"I am honoured, ma'am," said Mr. Whicher, removing his hat. "And your name, sir," he bowed to Dr. Bland, "is also familiar. You've not been waiting too long, I hope."

"No, not long," replied Kate. Then she addressed Clive, with an intensity near tears. "Long enough, though, to learn something more of my stepmother and to be terribly frightened for you. Will you look at this? And forgive us for reading it because your name was on it? It was pushed partway under the door there."

Kate held out a piece of shaving-paper borrowed from the barber downstairs. Across one side the words, CLIVE STRICK-LAND, ESQ. were printed large in pencil; across the other side was scrawled a written message. Victor, once intended for a brilliant Army career, had gone to Harrow and spent two years at Sandhurst without learning either to punctuate or spell.

Waited 5 mins. old boy and followed you. Met Georgette running back along Oxford S. Said you were arrested and it was all her fault in tears, asked her did she not know the gov. was dead and she screamed and wept it was awful. Said she could kill Tress ? ? ? ? Am takeing her to train Bath-and-Bristol Express, then back to get you out of gaol if you are still there and if not hope you get this and excuse hastey note. Yours sincerely V.

Up to that moment Clive had not realized how Kate's concern troubled and hurt her.

"It's a mistake, that's all. I haven't been arrested, as you can see for yourself." Then he broke off. "Stop: what were you thinking? You didn't believe I had been arrested for *murder*, did you?"

"I don't know what I thought."

"Nor I," snapped Dr. Bland.

Jonathan Whicher unlocked the door of his office and opened it.

"Will you give yourselves the trouble of walking in?"

Kate hesitated only briefly.

About to speak, she thought better of it before entering a chilly room with three straight chairs, a kneehole desk, an oak wardrobe, and a sofa clearly used as a bed. Dr. Bland and Clive followed her. Whicher, after taking the piece of paper from Clive and glancing at it, closed the door.

"Yes, this is best," said Kate. She looked at Whicher. "Mr. Strickland told me yesterday evening he was going to bring you, and that my father desired it."

"Damon wished this?" exclaimed Dr. Bland, his colour higher. "May I ask why?"

"I can't say." Kate lifted one shoulder. "Nor do I think it matters. Mr. Whicher, there is a train at two-thirty; not so fast as the Bath-and-Bristol Express, but it will do. Can you take that train with us?"

"Yes, ma'am. I can do just that. There's someone at High Chimneys I'm bound to seek. Meanwhile, you know, it would help a great deal if I might ask a few questions of you and the doctor here."

Whicher had pushed out a chair for her, but Kate did not sit down.

"Ask!" she said.

"Well, ma'am, it's like this. Mr. Strickland's told me everything that was said at High Chimneys last night. About the murder, that's to say," Whicher added quickly and smoothly, as Kate's eyes shifted. "Tell me, now. Do you share your sister's suspicions of your stepmother?"

"About what?"

"Begging your pardon for putting it so bluntly: do you think Mrs. Damon killed your father?"

"No, I do not."

"Ah!" murmured Whicher.

"Kate, my dear—" began Dr. Bland.

"Ask!" repeated Kate, and moistened her lips. The brown eyes, intensely luminous, were turned sideways as though regarding him past a barrier.

"From a number of things I'd heard, you know," Whicher told her in an apologetic tone, "it didn't seem you thought it was your stepmother. But I might have been wrong. It seems (forgive me again!) you didn't get on too well with Mrs. Damon?"

"I slapped her face. Now I wish I hadn't. It was because I hate to be treated as a child, and because I won't have anyone accuse me of . . ."

"Yes, ma'am? Of what?"

"Of being unfeminine. Unfeminine! I!" Kate changed colour. "I have never particularly liked her. She married my father for his position and nothing else. And yet it horrified me to learn Celia thought she might be capable of—of murder. I am sorry I lost my temper with Georgette Libbard.

There are times when I think she has a better heart than anyone ever suspects."

"Then, ma'am, if someone should be trying to put the blame for this crime on you . . ."

Kate gave a little cry of protest.

"Do you think that's probable, ma'am?"

"How can I say? It's possible, perhaps."

"If that's so, Miss Damon, you don't believe the person would be Mrs. Damon?"

"No. I don't."

"But you might be able to guess who it is?"

"No! Certainly not!"

"Still! When Mr. Strickland here visited High Chimneys with a proposal of marriage for your sister from Lord Albert Tressider, I understand neither you nor Miss Celia took very kindly to it?"

Dr. Bland, drawn up with his silk hat cradled over his arm, opened his eyes in an astonishment near outrage.

"My dear Kate," he said, "I must interrupt very firmly. What is this about marriage for Celia? I have heard nothing whatever of it."

"No, to be sure you haven't!" cried Kate. "I wasn't likely to mention it, under the circumstances, nor was Celia." She looked at Clive. "Have you told anyone else except Celia and me?"

"Not a soul," replied Clive. At Dr. Bland's insistence, while Whicher watched both of them, he explained the situation to the doctor.

"Celia, I may tell you," added Kate, addressing Whicher, "has no more fondness for that conceited lout than I have myself."

"In that case, ma'am, I won't trouble you with questions any longer." The former Inspector turned to Dr. Bland. "And I needn't trouble you, sir," he added with subdued heartiness, "if I may just hear something from you as a matter of form. You don't honestly think it was Mr. Strickland who committed the murder, now do you?"

"My good man! I have never said I did think so!"

"Still and all, sir, it's hard to see what else you could have meant. Just between ourselves, now; I take it you're afraid the murderer might be somebody it oughtn't to have been?"

"I fail to understand you, my friend. No person 'ought' to be a murderer."

"True for you, sir, true for you! But somebody is. For instance, Doctor! You were an old friend of the late Mr. Damon, you said?"

"Indeed I was."

"Just so. You'd been his doctor for a long time? Attended his first wife in her last illness, I daresay? Brought his children into the world?"

"No. I was not his medical adviser for so long a time as all that." Dr. Bland, waving the silk hat, spoke with some vehemence. "If you refer to any suggestion that there is mental instability in poor Damon's family . . ."

Kate, her mouth open, swung round from the desk.

"Uncle Rollo," she asked, "who on earth has ever made such a suggestion?"

"Not I, my dear! And it is utterly absurd. Dismiss it."

"But you said—"

"Dismiss it, Kate!"

Whicher, who had taken Tress's visiting-card from his waistcoat pocket, made a deprecating gesture with the card.

"One last question, Doctor, if I might trouble you. Last night, shortly before the murder, why were you so eager to find her?"

"Find her? Find whom?"

"Mrs. Matthew Damon. As I understand it, sir, you were looking for Mrs. Damon and were so concerned to find the lady that you even disturbed Mr. Damon in his study. Was it anything in particular?"

Dr. Bland looked him up and down.

"If it was, Mr. Whicher," he answered politely, "I can't recall it now. In any event, Mrs. Damon had already left the house."

"Yes, sir. We know she had left the house."

"The matter was so trivial, whatever it may have been—"

"Stop!" said Jonathan Whicher.

Replacing Tress's card in his waistcoat pocket, he took out a cheap watch and opened its case.

"You'll all forgive me, I'm sure," he declared, "if I remind you of the time. Two-thirty-train, eh? If we're to take that train, you know, we'll need at least half an hour to go from here to the station. And that's by cab, to say nothing of an omnibus. Miss Damon, ma'am! Is there a public-house near your home, by any chance, where I could put up if necessary?"

"But you have no need to go to a public-house! You will stay with us, of course!"

Whicher almost crowed.

"Now that's very kind of you, ma'am, if you have no objection to a rough fellow like me. I appreciate it. Then could you and Dr. Bland, maybe, go along to the station now? And Mr. Strickland and I will follow in time for the train?"

Kate, suddenly uncertain, looked at Clive.

"You *are* coming with us?" she asked.

"I am coming with you, Kate. Be sure of that."

"Then couldn't you . . . ?"

"Now, ma'am," Whicher interposed heartily, "I'm obliged to pack a carpet-bag, for one thing." He nodded towards the wardrobe. "And for another, to be quite frank with you, I want a word with Mr. Strickland in private. But he won't miss the train, I promise you. Trust me, ma'am!"

('I hope to God *I* can trust you,' thought Clive Strickland.)

Again Kate hesitated.

She made no more secret of her feelings towards Clive than he made of his feelings towards her. An arbiter of the age would have called her 'fast' if not very much worse. But the presence of Dr. Bland, that symbol of correctitude, was like a barrier between.

"Allow me, my dear," intoned the doctor, extending his arm.

"But—!"

"Allow me, Kate," Dr. Bland said firmly.

The door of the office closed after them. Whicher, his pock-marked countenance harassed and a wiry energy suffusing him, went up and down the room like a terrier.

"Find the lady!" he said. "Find the lady! Sounds like a three-card man at a race-track, now don't it? But this is devilish damned bad, sir; this is even worse than I'd thought. So I'd better tell you what I had to tell Mr. Damon in August."

"Well?"

"Since there's somebody at High Chimneys who knows the secret of Harriet Pyke's child, and that's the person we're bound to question—"

"In case it has escaped your attention," yelled Clive, "you've mentioned the matter several times already. You also said I ought to have guessed who it was, from what Mr. Damon told me."

"He told you, didn't he, there *was* another person who knew the secret?"

"Yes. I thought he meant you."

"Ah!" said the other, biting his forefinger and then shaking it in the air. "That's excusable enough, mind you! And yet, even if you include me, there's certain to be someone else. Suppose you're Mr. Damon, nineteen years ago, and you want to take an ugly duckling into the family without anybody being the wiser?

"That's not easy, sir, but it can be done. It can be done provided the young 'uns are babies within a year of each other's age. You move from the north of England to the west

81

of England, as Mr. Damon said he did. You haven't many friends to begin with, and you drop those you have. It's not a legal adoption, so there's no record. Your wife is dead. You've dismissed all the servants; all, that is, except one.

"Let me quote Mr. Damon's words, sir, as you quoted 'em to me. 'I had dismissed all my household,' says he, 'except the nurse of the two real children.' Thunderation, now! Think of it! Who's the one person on all this green earth who's still certain sure to know?"

Clive opened his mouth, and shut it again.

"The nurse," he answered presently. "This Mrs. Cavanagh! The woman they call Cavvy!"

"That's right. Got it in one. Did you think at all about her?"

"I wondered about her, if that's what you mean," snapped Clive. "But I didn't set eyes on the woman at any time after Mr. Damon was killed. To tell you the truth, I completely forgot her."

"Don't ever forget anybody in a murder case, sir. It's not safe."

"But you're not thinking . . . wait! Just because Mrs. Cavanagh knows the secret, it can't make her a suspicious character! It doesn't provide her with a motive for murder."

"Oh, yes, it does," said Jonathan Whicher.

"Why?"

"Because of what I discovered, slap-bang by accident, in August of this year."

"I still ask why! That vinegar-faced, unctuous, respectable old woman—"

Clive stopped.

"Vinegar-faced, unctuous, respectable old woman, eh?" inquired Whicher, in the manner of one who hears what pleases him. "Oh, ah! That's what she'd like to be thought. Don't forget it. And don't forget Mr. Damon told you something else too."

"About what?"

"About the hanging of Harriet Pyke."

Along the pavement of Oxford Street, below the soot-grimed windows, thumping music from brass horns approached and brayed. A street-band, composed of those earnest Germans who usually disturb only the quietest streets and squares, now marched past and blew hard for stray pennies.

For an instant it drowned Whicher's voice.

"Hark'ee, sir! Before Mr. Damon prosecuted the Pyke girl for murder, he'd never seen her in his life. And yet, all through the trial, though she couldn't testify in her own defence, she stood in the dock and watched him as though she'd got some secret knowledge about him. Isn't that what Mr. Damon told you?"

"Yes! But if he meant it in a figurative way . . ."

"Figurative my foot, if you'll pardon the liberty. She *did* have real knowledge of Mr. Damon and his life. He couldn't understand it when he talked to her in the condemned cell. He knew she couldn't have learned it just from reading about him. He told you that, didn't he?"

"Yes."

"He also said Harriet Pyke was calculatingly sane?"

"Yes; but—"

"You bet she was, Mr. Strickland. That girl was as guilty as hell. She emptied a revolver at her lover and then strangled the maid-servant in a craze of fury. But she was clever too. She had a trick left even in the condemned cell."

Under the windows, thumping with brassy blare, the music surged in a blattering and cheerful way. Whicher raised his voice.

"She knew she could prey on Mr. Damon's conscience if he visited her at Newgate. Which he did, and she did. It wasn't to save her child. It was to save her own neck and the other charms she had. And she very nearly managed it. But it still won't help us, unless I can get some proof about—"

Now it was Whicher who hesitated, seeming to listen to the band-music.

"Proof," he repeated, staring at some memory. "Princess's Theatre! Alhambra! Thunderation! I might just be able to lay some kind of trap. Listen, sir. You forget what I've said, for the moment. You go after Miss Damon and Dr. Bland; you take that train at half-past two. I'll stay in London for an hour or two, to have a word with a young magsman in St. Giles's, and I'll join you when I can."

"But look here . . . !"

"Will you trust me, sir?"

"If you tell me what's so very suspicious about Mrs. Cavanagh: yes, I will."

"Ah!" murmured Whicher, with a kind of pounce. "There's reasons why Mary Jane Cavanagh was mentioned more than once in the letter Harriet Pyke wrote from the condemned cell. Are you aware who 'Mrs. Cavanagh' really is?"

"No, naturally I'm not. Who is she?"

Whicher told him. Clive stared at the door, informed but still not entirely enlightened. Outside, under a smoky sky, passed the rolling inanity of the band.

Up and down the City Road,
In and out The Eagle—
That's the way the money goes:
Pop goes the weasel.

XI. TWILIGHT IN THE CONSERVATORY

Late afternoon sunlight in Berkshire, clear though chilly, rippled with a wind outside the full-length windows of Matthew Damon's study.

Superintendent Muswell of the Berkshire County Constabulary, a large bull of a man who restrained choleric temper with some difficulty, stood behind Matthew Damon's desk and breathed hard.

"Mr. Clive Strickland or whatever your name is, you're the only one who could 'a' done this murder. Ain't you?"

"No."

"*I* say you are. And I'd be within my rights if I took you into custody this minute."

"Then why don't you arrest me, Superintendent?"

"You're feeling pretty bobbish, ain't you?"

"Frankly, yes," replied Clive, who had just spent some time alone in the conservatory with Kate Damon.

All the same, he was not too easy in his mind. Nor was his disquiet caused alone by the atmosphere of tension and hysterics, which had infected even the police. Mr. Superintendent Muswell, whose small eyes and thick-whiskered jowls seemed fixed in a kind of bloated hypnosis, made noises of menace behind the desk.

"I'll go over it," said Superintendent Muswell, "just once more. Just once more," repeated Superintendent Muswell, "I'll go over it. Am I right, Peters?"

"You're right, Superintendent," hastily agreed a uniformed constable.

"This murder," Superintendent Muswell declared with passion, "ain't a woman's murder. No woman would 'a' done it. You see this pistol here on the desk?"

84

"I see it," said Clive.

"No woman on earth would 'a' done it. Because for why? Because there's no woman who wouldn't be frightened even to pick up that pistol and pull the trigger. Can you think of any woman who wouldn't be frightened to do that?"

"Yes, I can."

"Any respectable, genteel, well-brought-up woman?"

"Yes. Mrs. Garrett Anderson, Mrs. John Stuart Mill, Miss Florence Nightingale—"

Superintendent Muswell made a strangled noise.

"And stood in that door fifteen feet behind you? And scored a bull through the poor gentleman's head when he stood where I'm standing now? Miss Nightingale done that, did she?"

"I never said . . ."

"We *know* it wasn't a woman. Because for why? I'll tell you."

Superintendent Muswell illustrated the points on his fingers.

"This murder was done last night about half-past six, maybe a minute or so later. All the women servants, bar two, were having their supper together in the servants' hall between six fifteen and twenty-eight minutes to seven. That puts 'em out. O-u-t, out. The two as weren't there, Mrs. Cavanagh and Penelope Burbage, they're out too. They were together, and they swear to it."

Mrs. Cavanagh, eh?

The sly and unctuous Mary Jane Cavanagh, her hands folded, in a circular crinoline and an odour of sanctity, her hair bound tightly round her head and an alibi supplied by Penelope Burbage.

Clive had not seen the housekeeper since he returned to High Chimneys with Kate Damon and Dr. Bland. But then he had seen nobody except Kate, and Burbage, and the police who faced him in the study now.

The sun was setting over ten acres of parkland. Rooks cawed homewards heavily. Clive could hear the black-marble clock ticking in the study; it was twenty-five minutes to six.

"Miss Celia Damon and Miss Kate Damon, they were together too. Not that I'd ever suspect young ladies like them. No!" said Superintendent Muswell. "But they were together and that's flat. Mrs. Georgette Damon, she was miles away and couldn't have got into a locked-up house no more'n anybody else. If you keep going on about a woman . . ."

"Superintendent, I never said one word about a woman!"

"Ho! Then you admit it was a man?"

"I don't know."

"The menservants are accounted for: servants' hall and supper. Who's left?"

"Yes, I can understand that. There's—"

"There's the doctor, and there's you. Was it the doctor?"

"I don't think so. I can't say why, but I don't think so."

"Neither do I. Dr. Bland couldn't 'a' got at the weapon, and you could. Besides! An elegant gent like the doctor? What was his reason?"

"What was mine?"

"That might be easy, me bucko, if you told me what you and Mr. Damon were quarrelling about just before the murder."

"We were not quarrelling. And I've told you all I propose to tell about that conversation. Mr. Damon believed someone was threatening him; he died before he had time to say who it was."

"Now you listen to me! Look here at the upper right-hand drawer of the desk!"

"I'm looking."

"Mr. Damon bought this pistol a fortnight ago; Dr. Bland says so. He kept it in the drawer here; everybody says so. We found the drawer open, and you admit you opened it yourself. *You* say it was after the murder. But why'd you open it?"

"To see whether he had been killed with his own pistol, naturally."

"Ho, now! If he bought this barker a fortnight ago, and you've not been at High Chimneys for years, how'd you know it was in the drawer?"

"I told you. Mr. Damon made a move towards it while we were talking."

"And that was when you was threatening him, wasn't it?"

"I had no occasion to threaten him. Why should I?"

"Burn my body if I know. There's *some* flummoxing; I know that. The gentleman's will is gone, for one thing. Mr. What's-his-name Burbage says he made a will, a holo-something will in his own writing that don't need witnesses. But we've been all through this desk and everything else. There's nothing but a lot of papers and some photographs of his wife and children. What's more! When I twig it how you shot Mr. Damon and locked yourself in here with both keys on the outside . . ."

"If that's all that troubles you, Superintendent, I can tell you how."

"What's that?"

"I can tell you how I might have done it," Clive explained. "See Mayhew, extra volume, 1862, page two-eighty-eight."

"See who?"

"Henry Mayhew's work, *London Life and the London Poor,* published by Griffin, Bohn, and Company. In the fourth volume, dealing with thieves and prostitutes, it's shown how hotel-thieves rifle a locked bedroom and still leave it locked. They turn the stem of the key from outside with what is described as a 'peculiar instrument'; then they turn it back again after the robbery."

"Hey, ecod! So you're confessing you—"

"No, not at all. I only said that's how I might have done it. Now why don't you arrest me?"

Outside, over lawns still drenched from last night's storm, the pale sunlight faded. A yellow leaf or two spun past. Clive rose to his feet from the same chair, with shabby red-velvet covering, he had occupied yesterday evening.

"Easy does it, Superintendent!" cried an alarmed Police-Constable Peters. "You hadn't ought to be took so. Easy!"

"I don't want to be offensive, Superintendent," insisted Clive, "but I received this telegram half an hour ago," and he took a crumpled piece of paper from his pocket. "You won't let me say a word about it. May I read you the telegram again?"

Superintendent Muswell spoke in a hoarse, furred voice. "No, my lad, you may not."

Clive's own temper was going up out of control.

"I will read you the telegram again. It says, 'Regret I am unable to join you today as promised. Occupied with magsman.'—By the way, what's a magsman?"

"Ho! I thought everybody knowed a magsman is a sharper. Might be a horse-couper, might be a confidence man, might be anything."

"I see. Or, rather, I don't see. The telegram concludes, 'Do not worry. Am arranging to trap culprit at High Chimneys.' It is signed, 'Whicher.' "

"Whicher," said Superintendent Muswell, unable to get his breath. *"Whicher."*

"No, Whicher's name is not popular in rural districts. During the Constance Kent case, you may remember, he was right when everybody else was wrong. He proved Superintendent Foley, of the Wiltshire County Constabulary, was the stupidest police-officer who ever wanted to arrest the wrong murderer. Wiltshire is not so very far from here."

"Superintendent," yelled the alarmed Peters.

"I've had enough o' this," said Superintendent Muswell,

beginning to pound his fist on the desk. "Fair's fair; I've had enough. Mr. Clive Ruddy Strickland, what do you *want?*"

"An answer, that's all."

"Ho!"

"Nothing would please me better than to stop at High Chimneys indefinitely," said Clive, who was thinking vividly of Kate. "But I ought to be in London discovering what Jonathan Whicher means to do. How long do you propose to detain me here?"

"It might be till tomorrow, it might be for a year. If I'm so minded, me bucko, I'll detain you till the Kennet freezes over."

"No, I don't think you will."

"Superintendent!" cried Peters.

"Either take me into custody, as you've been threatening to do, or else allow me to come and go within reasonable limits. Which is it to be?"

"Get out," said Superintendent Muswell, pointing dramatically at the door to the hall.

"You're not stupid, Superintendent. In your heart you don't believe I'm guilty. But you can't make up your mind what to do, and that's why you've lost your temper."

"Get out."

"What's the answer? May I come and go under reasonable supervision?"

"I'll think about it," breathed the Superintendent. "I say I'll think about it. Meanwhiles, if you set one foot outside this house before I give you leave: so help me, I'll have you in the Bridewell and chance it. Now get out. Sling your hook!"

Clive hesitated.

For an instant he seriously thought Superintendent Muswell would pick up a double handful of papers and hurl them into the air.

Only West-Country stolidity on Muswell's side, and long public-school training on Clive's, prevented an outburst. Clive went out into the hall. But he could not escape that atmosphere of tension and hysterics, creeping again through High Chimneys as the shadows gathered on the evening of Wednesday, October 18.

A mental picture of Mary Jane Cavanagh, now that he knew who Mrs. Cavanagh really was, haunted every corner round him.

If only he could leave High Chimneys tonight! Yes, and if only he could take Kate Damon with him when he left . . .

'Come, now!' he thought to himself; 'this will never do.' Though in his own heart he might know himself for as unconventional as most of his literary friends in the *All the Year Round* coterie, and though certain endearments of a fairly intimate kind had passed between himself and Kate before Superintendent Muswell summoned him to the study, Clive could not help thinking of Kate as an Eminently Proper young lady.

All the same . . .

The house seemed utterly deserted. There was not a sound in the main hall.

Clive walked straight through the back-parlour, with its heavy-framed pictures and its breakfast-table, towards the conservatory where he had sat with Kate.

Everything, tonight, seemed unreal; not alone from the presence of murder and devilry, but as though they moved and groped towards a new age. When he and Kate and Dr. Bland took the two-thirty train at Paddington, talk had buzzed round the carriages.

Lord Palmerston, somebody said, was dying at Brocket Hall in Hertfordshire; bets were made in clubs as to whether the veteran statesman, so often Prime Minister as he was Prime Minister now, would attain his eighty-first birthday in two days' time.

If Pam died, Clive was thinking, it would snap almost the last strand stretching back from the roaring years of the Regency through "progress" to the Crimea and the Indian Mutiny.

Crimea. Indian Mutiny. Revolving pistols . . .

Never mind!

Clive strode through the back-parlour. It was not yet quite time to light the lamps, but a lamp burned amid exotic greenery in the conservatory. Clive saw a woman's gown; he imagined Kate must still be there.

But it was not Kate who sat in the middle of the conservatory, on a bench of iron filigree under an Indian azalea.

Georgette Damon, who had changed her blue gown for one of unrelieved black, had her hands pressed over her eyes. Hearing his footsteps on the gravel, she sat up straight.

"Oh!" she said in complete stupefaction.

"Good evening, Mrs. Damon."

"Oh! I thought—"

Clive's impulse was to inquire with some bitterness whether she recognized him this time, or whether she thought he was still locked up at St. Giles's station-house. Behind her, in imagination, loomed Tress's sneering face and all Tress stood for.

But he could not say it.

Georgette's eyelids were puffed and reddish from weeping. Grief, and rage, and a kind of helplessness breathed from her as palpably as the hot damp air of the conservatory.

"Mr. Strickland, you must forgive me."

"There is nothing to forgive, Mrs. Damon. I understand."

"Oh, no! You don't. Nobody understands."

"Well . . ."

"I attempted to hide the fact," said Georgette, "that I was meeting a certain gentleman at Laurier's. I could have spared myself the trouble, it seems. Everyone knows of my affair with this man. Mark you!" The blue eyes overflowed again as she widened them. "I say to you, as I would say to all the world if I dared, that I did no harm to my husband. Bah! Is it of any importance to give one's body? True importance?"

"I am no preacher of morals, madam. If you happen to love Tress, however inconceivable that seems . . ."

"Love him?" Georgette echoed incredulously. "Love him?"

"Yes. And it's certainly of far less importance than another matter. Mrs. Damon, what young woman deserves to be condemned to the treadmill? What young woman will be condemned to the treadmill if things go on as they are?"

Georgette did not reply.

Her face, deathly pale against the auburn hair and a background of ferns, had grown rigid with still more incredulity. Tears splashed down on the bodice of the black gown. And, though Georgette clutched a damp handkerchief, she did not put it to her eyes.

"Yes!" Clive told her. "I was skulking and spying. I saw you go into the Princess's Theatre; I followed you there."

"You heard—?"

"Yes."

"Your parents were never in prison, I suppose? You don't know, Mr. Strickland, that no woman is ever condemned to the treadmill?"

"Then what . . . ?"

Georgette ran her tongue round her lips.

"Yesterday, when you and Matthew and I were in the train to Reading, I tried to divert suspicion from the right person. I said Penelope Burbage was telling lies about seeing someone on the stairs; but I knew full well Penelope was not telling lies. Matthew knew! Matthew was too clever not to guess. And then, when I found the clothes hidden in someone's room where they were meant to be found . . ."

"In whose room? Can you tell me who the murderer is?"

"Yes, I can. When I am a little more composed, I will tell the police."

90

Somewhere in the conservatory there was a faint noise as though someone, moving stealthily, had brushed past leaves and then stopped.

Clive glanced over his shoulder.

The lamp here at the heart of greenery, its shade of the same stained-glass pattern as the walls of the conservatory, stood on a spindly iron table beside the bench. Its glow mingled with the last glimmer of daylight through a clear-glass roof, so that they swam in tinted twilight.

"But before I do—" began Georgette.

"Wait!"

Clive caught up the lamp. Holding it high, he looked slowly round.

Georgette, fighting back sobs, hardly saw him. She made a pettish gesture like a child. In her left hand she held a gold-topped bottle of smelling salts, and she put this down on the bench.

"Before I do—"

"Wait! Did you hear someone moving just now?"

"No. Before I do, Mr. Strickland, let us be clear about my —my relations with Lord Albert Tressider. Yes! Pray look at me! I am not what the world would call a virtuous woman. Except to Matthew, who set such store by it, I have never pretended to be. If a man has taken my fancy, I have seen no reason to resist him."

"Mrs. Damon, these are not confidences for me to receive."

"They are confidences for me to give, if I choose!" Georgette stamped her foot on the gravel. "For all of this, your friend Tress . . ."

"He is no friend of mine."

"Well! He is no fancy of mine, you may be sure. Do you imagine I should have risked so much if I had not been forced?"

Clive swung back fully to face her, the stealthy movement in the leaves forgotten.

"Forced?"

"What else? It was the choice of becoming his blowen, and running to him whenever he cared to whistle for me, or of having my husband learn the whole story of my past life."

Silence.

Then Clive, waking up, set down the lamp on the iron table with a crash that almost smashed the lamp-base. Georgette cried out.

"For pity's sake, take care! What is wrong?"

"Nothing."

"What is wrong?"

"Well, let us say a personal matter. At noon today, Mrs. Damon, I promised Tress something the next time we should meet. Now I do more than promise. I swear."

"And as for Kate . . ."

"Why do you mention Kate?"

"Kate is human," said Georgette, closing her eyes. "Kate is all too human. I will tell you something, though you don't know it and Kate herself is unaware *I* know it. She has been in love with a certain man, yourself, since she was fourteen years old; and she will never change. You may not have said ten words to her; you may not even have noticed her. But someone is trying horribly hard to get her hanged. If you have any pity at all, try to help her!"

Clive nodded.

"I promise that too," he said. "Now, then! Who is the murderer?"

XII. "THE WORLD AS I FIND IT"

"The murderer," said Georgette. "Poor Kate! And this prized commodity of female virtue!"

Through an ironic grimace of tears Georgette began to laugh.

"Kate thought I mocked her. She struck me across the cheek, here, and said I had not the courage to be an honest prostitute. And I laughed again; I liked her; I admired her spirit; I mocked only at her innocence.

"Go to London, Mr. Strickland! Ask the hundred thousand women of the town how they might earn a living at all if they did not take to the streets. Some are the daughters of poor tradesmen. Most were brought up, as I was, in a family of fifteen crammed into one room for hunger and cholera to kill. They think very little of a 'virtue' they lose as a matter of course when they are eleven or twelve years old. Merciful God, how unutterably stupid men are!"

The laughter throbbed and rang eerily under that glass roof.

"Good or bad, good or bad: what do these words mean? Listen, now."

Georgette, still clutching the handkerchief, sprang up

from the bench. Her expression altered, like that of an actress going into a part. Even while she laughed, her face grew intent and worldly wise. Even while she spoke someone else's words, she felt them with savage depth and sincerity.

" 'Is it the Lord Mayor going in state to mince-pies and the Mansion House? Is it poor Jack of Newgate's procession, with the sheriff and javelin-men, conducting him on his last journey to Tyburn?' "

"Mrs. Damon! Stop this!"

Georgette swept him a mocking curtsey.

" 'I look into my heart, and think that I am as good as my Lord Mayor, and know I am as bad as Tyburn Jack.' "

Clive's protest was checked on his lips.

" 'Give me a chain and a red gown and a pudding before me, and I could play the part of Alderman very well, and sentence Jack before dinner.' " Georgette's tone changed. " 'Starve me, keep me from books and honest people, educate me to love dice, gin, and pleasure, and put me on Hounslow Heath with a purse before me, and I will take it. And I shall be deservedly hanged, say you, wishing to put an end to this prosing! I don't say no. I can't but accept the world as I find it, including a rope's-end, as long as it is in fashion.' "

Georgette laughed again, and swept him another mocking curtsey at the end of the speech.

"A wise man wrote that, Mr. Strickland. He is dead these two years, but he spoke the truth. Say to me: can you deny it?"

"No. And you need not quote *Esmond*. I understand."

"You understand? You, the son of a well-to-do barrister, as Matthew himself was?"

"Yet I understand all the same. I have been thinking the same thing. But this murderer—"

"Oh, yes. The murderer!" Georgette threw back her shoulders. "Pray remember *I* was not the woman who repeated and repeated the story of Constance Kent over and over, never ceasing, to Kate and to Celia too. It was their precious Mrs. Cavanagh."

"So it was Mrs. Cavanagh who killed your husband? Was it?"

A silence, except for the wind blowing shrill and shrewd across the roof of the conservatory as dusk closed in, held the damp warmth of the foliage.

"Was it Mrs. Cavanagh?"

"I won't tell you. It would shock you too much."

"But you say you are going to tell the police!"

"So I am. You may hear it from Superintendent Muswell;

93

not from me! I am going upstairs to bathe my face and change my gown. And then . . ."

A sharp rustle, distinctly that of one moving past plants or ferns, approached closer to the cleared space round the bench and the table.

"Mrs. Damon, for God's sake, stop where you are! The murderer's here."

"Absurd! He would not dare attack *me!*"

" 'He?' "

Georgette's laughter was now that of a woman near hysterics.

"Did I say 'he'? Perhaps I was mistaken. You must ask Kate; she guesses as well as I guess. Let go my arm!"

"If you go upstairs in the dark, I go with you."

"Really, sir! Even if I entertained no objection to having you watch me undress, I am sure Dr. Thompson Bland would object and the servants would be positively horrified. Let go my arm! Must I scream for help and accuse you of molesting me twice in the same day?"

Clive did not let go her arm.

But, on the opposite side of a bedevilled ledger, he couldn't search the conservatory while she strained to wrench from him and run away. Still holding her, he picked up the lamp with his left hand. A brief, locked contest of wills carried them to the glass door of the conservatory, out across the back-parlor and to the door leading into the hall. Georgette seized the knob.

"I will argue no more, Mr. Strickland. I have done my best for Kate; I have tried to protect her as much, it would seem, as the good doctor has tried to protect Celia. *Now* will you release me?"

The door to the hall banged open. Most noises were unnoticed; the wind sang up amid the chimney-stacks as though in the shrouds of a ship.

"Miss Burbage!" said Clive.

Penelope Burbage, a small lamp in her hand, had just come out of the hall-entrance to the library. Georgette ceased struggling, with her intense feeling for keeping up the outward proprieties; Clive himself had gone past any care or concern for appearances.

"Miss Burbage," he continued, "will you be kind enough to accompany Mrs. Damon upstairs? When Mrs. Damon is safely in the care of her maid . . ."

"Hortense is not here," interposed Georgette. Anguish filled her throat again. "I was supposed to have run away last night (run away)! Mrs. Cavanagh gave Hortense leave of absence to—"

"Mrs. Cavanagh did, eh?"

"Mr. Strickland, you are hurting me. Stop!"

"Will you escort Mrs. Damon upstairs," Clive went on, fixing his gaze on Penelope, "and not leave her?"

"Oh, yes, sir!" breathed Penelope.

"Let me make this clear," Clive insisted. "Mrs. Damon has a matter of some moment to discuss with Superintendent Muswell when she returns. You won't leave her side until she goes to the study there? You promise?"

"Indeed I do promise!"

Clive released Georgette's arm.

"If you possessed the knowledge I have," Georgette flung at him, trying for immense dignity while she nursed the arm, "you would see how ridiculous this is. I—I have mislaid something. What have I mislaid? No matter! I shall think of it presently."

Penelope murmured soothing words. Gentle and self-effacing, her fine eyes studying Georgette as she moved ahead of the other woman towards the oak staircase at the front of the hall, Penelope spoke past her shoulder.

"I will attend to all, sir. You may trust me."

Wind whooped and swirled. Clive, reassured, watched them go. He could hear Superintendent Muswell's hoarse voice speaking behind the closed door, but he paid no attention to the words. Another thought coiled into his mind.

"Miss Burbage!" he called after the two women, and held his lamp high.

"S-sir?"

"When you have escorted Mrs. Damon to the study, will you oblige me further by joining me in the conservatory?"

"If you distinctly wish it, sir."

"I do wish it. You and I are the only living witnesses who have seen the murderer face to face. And yet neither of us can identify that face or even describe it."

"Oh, for pity's sake!" cried Georgette.

"If you and I compared notes, Miss Burbage, and understood why we were unable to see it even at close range . . ."

Penelope had held up her own lamp, so that the light of the two clashed in an unsteady shadow-play, slow and yet wild, across the walls and ceiling. But Georgette, nearly at the end of her nervous energy, cried out in a way that made the hall ring.

"*I* can tell you. Because of a woman's black silk stocking, cut off near the top with slits for eyes, and fitted over the head like a mask. I found it hidden where the other clothes were hidden: in Kate's bedroom. Is that all you wish to know?"

"No. Will you come and see me, Miss Burbage?"

"Yes, sir."

Abruptly, behind the closed door of the study, Superintend-ent Muswell's voice stopped speaking as though he had over-heard. Clive retreated into the back-parlour. He had been keeping watch from the corner of his eye; no person could have left the conservatory and slipped out by way of the arch-entrance to the dining-room.

But then no person had attempted to slip out.

Clive returned to the conservatory, closing the glass doors behind him. The glow of his lamp moved steadily through greenery, catching another black dress. When he emerged into the cleared space by the Indian azalea, Mrs. Mary Jane Cavanagh was waiting for him.

Slyness, triumph, pleasure? What was the look on Mrs. Cavanagh's face?

She stood beside the iron table, her strong hands folded. But her tone remained respectful, her bearing all unctuous-ness, as she lowered one shoulder in greeting.

"Good evening, sir," she said. Then her voice poured with reproach. "I'm sure I'm the last person, sir, that would want to alarm you or the madam. But you should have called out, sir, really you should, when you heard me walking here!"

The warm damp air seemed choking in Clive's lungs.

"It *was* you, was it?"

"Oh, deary me," cried Mrs. Cavanagh, shivering, "but I often walk in here. I love the dear plants. It wasn't my place to call out and announce myself, truly it wasn't, when you and the madam were having a private conversation."

"I see."

"Such a private conversation, too! If poor Mr. Damon had known——"

"He knew many things, Mrs. Cavanagh."

"Indeed and I'm afraid he did, sir! Poor Miss Kate wants to get away from this house (her own home, too); and I daresay she'd have done anything to be quit of her pa and all the people who are so good to her.—Did you say something, sir?"

"No."

"But it's a wicked world. Miss Kate's not the only one, even if she's the worst. Would you believe me, sir, if I told you Mr. Damon wanted to bring a detective-officer here be-cause of the madam's carryings-on with a certain noble lord?"

Once more Clive put down the lamp on the iron table and spoke clearly.

"Oh, no, he didn't!"

"Sir?"

"It was not because of Mrs. Damon that he wished to bring a detective-officer here. It was because he thought himself in danger. Over three months ago, Mrs. Cavanagh, Jonathan Whicher learned the full truth about Harriet Pyke."

"Lawk, sir, and who might Harriet Pyke be?"

"Don't you know?"

Mrs. Cavanagh's expression hardly changed. Yet it was as though malice, palpable if unspoken, slashed out at him like a cat's claws.

'My impulse to carry Kate away from here,' he was thinking, 'is more than passion for her or a wish to have her to myself. Kate is in as great danger from plots as Mr. Damon ever was from a bullet. I thought so before; now I know it. The murderer hid those clothes in Kate's bedroom. This woman here, who ought to cherish the child she once nursed, for some reason hates Kate as it seems scarcely possible to hate anyone.

'If I dared risk public opinion and abduct Kate this very night . . .'

Clive flung the vision away.

"Don't you know who Harriet Pyke was, Mrs. Cavanagh?"

"Lawk, now, but is poor old Cavvy a mind-reader?"

"Then I had better tell you what Whicher told me this afternoon."

"I've got no wish to hear what's none of my business, thanking you very much! If you'll permit me to go . . ."

"No. Stay where you are."

The close air seemed to grow damper and warmer. Mrs. Cavanagh, shivering, suddenly unfolded her hands before clasping them hard.

"Nineteen years ago," said Clive, "Harriet Pyke was hanged for the murder of her lover and of a maidservant. Whicher (yes, you've heard of him!) assisted at her arrest. But he was only a young sergeant under Detective-Inspector Charles Field. Even if Mr. Damon had questioned him then, Whicher knew very little.

"He knew she was the daughter of a very respectable poor family. Respectable mother and father, respectable brothers and sisters: none of these were in the courtroom when Mr. Damon prosecuted her. What else did Whicher know at the time? Only that Harriet Pyke, a brilliant dark-haired beauty with an overfondness for men, had borne a child by a former lover. This former lover (do you follow me, madam?) was a wealthy young idler named Ivor Rich.

"Whicher had not heard the name of the child or its age or birthplace. He knew only that such a child existed; Mr.

Damon, suffering a change of heart towards Harriet Pyke when she was in the condemned cell, attempted to obtain a pardon or a new trial—and failed. Harriet Pyke was hanged."

Mrs. Cavanagh started forward.

"And that was an end to it! What's more to be said? That was the end!"

"No. That was not the end."

"I'll not hear—!"

"You will hear. Early in August of this year Ivor Rich, now a middle-aged man who had dissipated two fortunes, poisoned himself at a shabby-genteel lodging-house in Pimlico. Whicher's a private detective now, I might remind you. The owner of the lodging-house, a friend of Whicher, sent word to him in a desperate hope of hushing up a suicide.

"The suicide couldn't be hushed up; you may depend on that. But the notoriety could be stifled, and the notoriety was stifled, when the lodging-house-keeper and Whicher found a packet of old letters from Harriet Pyke to Ivor Rich: one of those letters, madam, written in the condemned cell and smuggled out.

"She must have been fond of that man, I think. She admitted she was guilty; she had shot her latest protector in a fit of rage. But she prayed Rich to be silent, to keep all things dark; hope was not lost yet. She knew much about the man who had prosecuted her, since one of her sisters was the nursemaid in Matthew Damon's family—"

Clive stopped.

Mrs. Cavanagh, cracking the knuckle-joints of her fingers but not speaking, made a little swoop and dart to run out of the conservatory. Clive jumped in front of her.

"Don't go, Mrs. Cavanagh. If Harriet Pyke could persuade Mr. Damon she was innocent, and make him prove his earnest by promising to adopt her child, she thought he would move heaven and earth to save her neck. So he did. And the child—"

Mary Jane Cavanagh did not speak loudly.

"There's no proof of this, Mr. Clever! There's no bit o' proof!"

"Why do you think there's not? Because you destroyed Mr. Damon's will?"

"I destroyed nothing."

"Not even Mr. Damon's peace of mind? For nineteen years? Did you know your sister was guilty?"

"That poor lamb was innocent. Innocent, innocent, innocent!"

"Oh, no. That was what I meant by saying the notoriety

98

could be stifled but Rich's suicide could not be hushed up. Your sister committed two murders; the proof remains in a letter she herself wrote. That letter is now held by a lodging-house-keeper in New Elm Road. And your part in the deception—"

"*Deception?*"

"Yes."

For an instant, as Mary Jane Cavanagh breathed thinly, Clive thought that the colour had drained from her eyes as well as from her face. She raised her right arm stiffly, with an effort, as though taking an oath.

"A good action," she said. "A good, pious, Christian deed, maybe the best of me life! To take and cherish a motherless waif, to bring up an innocent child of an innocent mother, with the snares of the wicked far away! To hold sacred the memory of a sister I didn't hardly know! You call it deception?"

"Yes. Let's hear the truth."

"May the Lord strike me dead—!"

"Perhaps He will. Why did you never disclose your relationship to Harriet Pyke? If you scarcely knew your sister, how could you have told her so much about Mr. Damon? Above all, what's the reason for your hatred of Kate?"

Mrs. Cavanagh, square-shouldered, now threw up both arms with a yammering kind of noise as though bidding the Almighty to strike Clive instead of her.

"You do hate her, Mrs. Cavanagh. The very first time I saw you two together, in the morning-room about this time last night, you were taunting her or threatening her in some way I couldn't quite understand. Why were you taunting her?"

"Me? Poor old Cavvy? And it's lies! You can't prove who the child is; now can you?"

"No," admitted Clive—and lost the battle.

"Well!" said Mrs. Cavanagh. "Well, well, well, well."

White-faced but triumphant, drawing an unctuousness of mock-respect round her, she straightened up and folded her hands.

"Begging your pardon, sir, but I don't think I'll say any more. I'm not obliged to say more; and I won't. Will that be all, sir?"

Smoothing her crinoline, daring him to stop her, she moved past him as though without a care in the world. But she could not resist turning round, on the gravel path towards the glass door, for a sly little last word.

"When the great Whicher discovered this letter from Harriet Pyke, or said he discovered it, I daresay he'd have told Mr. Damon?"

"That's exactly what he did. It was after the beginning of the Long Vacation—"

"Sir?"

"The law vacation, I mean. Whicher made a special journey down to High Chimneys. Didn't you see him here?"

"I was at Weston the first week in August, that's what I was—"

"Or you'd have stopped him from speaking?"

The invisible claws slashed again.

"Don't you put words into my mouth, sir, or you'll wish you hadn't. Lawks! Whicher went to a deal of trouble, though!"

"Naturally. For nineteen years Mr. Damon believed he had sent an innocent woman to the gallows. Whicher told him a different story. Mr. Damon did not mention this to you, I take it?"

"Maybe he did, or maybe he didn't."

"Mrs. Cavanagh, why do you hate Kate? Why did you plan to blame her for her father's murder?"

"If I were you, sir, I wouldn't talk soft! I wouldn't; no! Blame Miss Kate? Why, there's nobody would blame Miss Kate or harm her in any way. She's in no more danger here at High Chimneys than if she lived in the blessed heaven itself."

Mrs. Cavanagh broke off, twitching her head in the other direction.

Last night Clive had heard Celia Damon scream from upstairs, presumably when Celia was told of Matthew Damon's death. He heard another cry from upstairs now.

Despite the shrill tumult of the wind, despite the closed glass door of the conservatory, he thought he could distinguish the words, 'Who's that? What do you want?' followed by a scream for help. This time it was Kate's voice.

Snatching up the lamp from the table, Clive plunged past Mrs. Cavanagh.

He flung open the glass door and raced across the back-parlour into the hall. Even as he ran, with all dreads astir, he wondered at the utter silence of the rooms on the ground floor. He had expected that Superintendent Muswell, at least, would have come charging out from behind the closed door of the study.

But nobody moved or spoke.

The downstairs rooms seemed deserted, with their curtains drawn together and their fires made up. The only noise, except for the wind, was the thud of his own footsteps when he ran towards the stairs.

"Kate!" he shouted, and took the staircase two steps at a time.

XIII. HOW A DEAD WOMAN WAITED FOR AN ELOPE- MENT

Still nothing. Nobody.

The upstairs hall, crossed by a transverse passage which turned it into two passages, was carpeted with coconut matting. A grandfather clock ticked at the back of the hall. Lines of closed doors gave on small bedrooms and dressing-rooms; they stretched away into what had been darkness before Clive brought the lamp.

"Kate!"

On his right, not far from the head of the stairs, someone scratched a match inside a partly open door. The reflection of a match-light, wobbling, grew larger into that of a candle-flame.

Kate, her mouth distorted, ran towards him. The brass candleholder slipped and fell on the floor, extinguishing its light. He could feel fear trembling through her whole body as he put one arm round her.

"I can't endure this," she said. "I believed anything was possible if I refused to be frightened, but it's not possible. I've seen him. He's—wearing the same clothes. He's here."

The steady ticking of the grandfather clock beat against silence. Though it was a good distance away, Clive could just make out that the hands pointed to fifteen minutes past six o'clock.

At this time last night . . .

"What happened, Kate? What did you see?"

"Georgette . . ."

"Where *is* Georgette?"

"No, no; she's all right!"

"Are you sure? Where is she?"

"That's the dressing-room I share with Celia." Kate nodded

101

towards the doorway from which she had run to him. She paused, tightening her face muscles in a desperate attempt at calmness. "I was—I was dressing for dinner in there. Celia's asleep; the doctor gave her more laudanum, and she's asleep in the bedroom next door."

"Where's Dr. Bland, for instance?"

"I don't know! Anyway, I had nearly finished dressing a few minutes ago when I heard Georgette and Penelope Burbage go past on their way downstairs."

"On their way *down*stairs?"

"Yes! Georgette was saying that she needn't change her gown; it was enough to bathe her eyes; and asking Penelope please to leave her because she was going to the police. Penelope said, 'I'll take you to the study, ma'am; I promised.'"

"Go on."

"That's all there is," cried Kate, staring at him. "I only tell you because you seem so awfully concerned about my stepmother."

"Not nearly so much as I am about you. And you're right; she can't come to any harm now. What happened then? What made you scream like that?"

"I had finished dressing and I—I put on some rice-powder. I took up the candleholder (the candle was burning then) to light my way downstairs. When I opened the door, I was holding the light in front of me. And that door doesn't make much noise.

"The man, the person, I don't know what to call it, was standing at the head of the stairs in the dark, looking down. For about half a second I was only startled. I never really expected to see it, because I thought. . . .

"Anyway, I saw the red-and-white pattern of the trousers. I cried out before I realized what I was doing. I said, 'Who's that?' and 'What do you want?' and then I could have bitten my tongue off for speaking at all. It turned round. It seemed to have no head. That was the worst: it seemed to have no head.

"I screamed for help. I dodged back into the dressing-room. The candle fell and went out. In the dark I was too frightened or bewildered; I couldn't even find the knob of the door to close it, and I thought the—I thought it was going to run at me, and I couldn't keep it out. Next I heard someone running upstairs; that was you. When I heard your voice I struck a match and lit the candle. But I dropped it again. I'm a fool. I'm awfully sorry."

Kate's voice trailed off in a shudder. She pressed her fingers up under her eyes, and Clive held her gently.

"You're not a fool," he said, "and there's nothing to be ashamed of. Did he run at you?"

"No."

"Where did he go?"

"I don't know. It was all dark. He made no noise. Where are *you* going?"

"I had better search—"

"No! Please! Don't leave me."

Holding the lamp high above his head, Clive looked round narrowly at the passages, at the lines of closed doors, at the steel engravings hanging in the wall-spaces between. Somewhere the wind was rattling a loose window-frame.

"This is madness," said Clive, and heard Kate draw in her breath. "You won't understand me; the subject was not mentioned in your presence. But it seems inconceivable that there are two sets of murderer's clothes here, when one set is now hidden at the Princess's Theatre. Tell me: when you saw this man (or woman, whichever it was!), you say he was standing at the top of the stairs, looking down?"

"Yes."

"As though following your stepmother and Penelope Burbage?"

"I—I don't know. That never occurred to me."

"How long was it after the first two had gone down?"

"A minute or two, maybe. I can't say exactly. It's so very hard to estimate time. Why is it important?"

Clive himself was growing desperate.

"Kate," he said abruptly, "won't you trust me? Won't anyone trust me?"

Love and amazement and alarmed tenderness were all to be seen plainly in Kate's face.

"Of course I trust you! What do you mean?"

"Come with me."

Holding her arm as he had held Georgette's, but in a somewhat different way, he guided her into the dressing-room.

The dressing-room, its pink wallpaper in the latest flower-design and a Turkey carpet underfoot, served two bedrooms: there was a bedroom door on each side. An identical gilt-painted bowl and pitcher stood on an identical marble-topped wash-hand-stand beside each bedroom door. According to the old-fashioned views of Matthew Damon, whose body now lay at an undertaker's in Reading, there would be no lamp here; there would have been no gaslight even if gas were obtainable so far out in the country.

A faint dampness clung to the room. The lamp Clive carried illumined drawn curtains, identical dressing-tables, and an empty hip-bath in front of the fire.

"Kate—"

"Sh-h! Don't speak too loudly," begged Kate, and nodded towards the left-hand bedroom door. "Celia's asleep in there." Then passionate sincerity made her speak loudly too. "Clive, my dear, why do you say I won't trust you?"

"You won't, you know. Let me repeat that nobody will."

"Clive, that's not true!"

"Two persons, Whicher and your stepmother, claim they can guess who the murderer is. I am certain that two more persons, Mrs. Cavanagh and yourself, really know who it is. And not one person will say a word."

Kate's eye shifted at mention of Mrs. Cavanagh.

"Darling, I can't! I daren't!"

"Yes; that's what I mean." Clive's desperation grew greater. "I've done my best, Kate; but I'm not a detective and I can't pretend to be one. If you were frank with me—"

"Have you been completely frank with me? Wasn't there something my father told you, last night in the study, that you haven't told me or even mentioned to anyone? Wasn't there?"

"Well—yes."

"And he told you, I suppose, as Uncle Rollo hinted this afternoon, that there might be insanity in our family?"

"Insanity? Great Scott, no! If I haven't been frank with you, it was only to spare you unnecessary worry and give you peace of mind."

"But that's it!" said Kate, her gaze moving towards a bedroom door. "That's why I haven't been frank with *you!*"

On the marble-topped centre-table was a copy of a recent novel by Anthony Trollope, called *Can You Forgive Her?* and dealing with a question much under debate. Clive eyed it with some bitterness before banging down the lamp there.

"Kate, the proprieties and the social customs be damned! This is murder. I'm not in danger, and you are. For instance: Georgette is with Superintendent Muswell now, telling him what she knows or suspects. And yet that's no good at all if she has no proof against the murderer, and I don't believe she has. I'm beginning to think the best course might be to kidnap you out of this house and take you to London."

There was a brief pause. Then Kate looked up into his eyes with a meaning he could not mistake.

"Take me!" she said. "Dear God, if only you would! Take me! Tonight!"

The wind whistled past the windows, tapping a branch there. Clive made a fierce gesture.

"You don't understand what you're saying!"

"Oh, yes, I do! You live in Brook Street, don't you?"

"Yes. Near Mivart's Hotel. I could—"

"No matter for Mivart's Hotel. Take me! Don't you want me?"

"You know I do."

"Then take me. As you say yourself, the proprieties be damned!"

"My dear, that was not my meaning. You're not in danger as Georgette is in danger: that the murderer may think she knows too much, and try to kill her. You're being kept very much alive to take the blame for this; that's now certain. You haven't been told, have you, that someone hid a set of the murderer's clothes in your bedroom for the police to find? And Georgette took them away and hid them elsewhere?"

A dusting of rice-powder emphasized the pallor of Kate's face, but brought out the vivid pink of her open mouth.

"That's the truth," said Clive. "So far as I know, the police haven't been told that piece of information. Superintendent Muswell won't believe this is a woman's crime, at least up to now, because he can't imagine a woman firing a revolver. But if—"

"Oh, I can fire a revolver," said Kate.

Again the wind whistled past while they looked at each other.

"At least," cried Kate, "I can fire the old-style kind with percussion caps. I can't hit anything. My arm's not strong enough to hold it steady." Terror showed in her eyes. "But I've been taught to fire a pistol as I've been taught to ride horseback without using a ladylike side-saddle."

"Then it would be madness to run away. Muswell's already suspicious enough of me. If he learns I'm in love with you—"

"*Are you?* You haven't said so."

"Do you want me to demonstrate?"

"Yes. I do. In every way." Tears of intensity came into Kate's eyes. "And do you trust Mr. Whicher? Do you believe he can discover the murderer, without my having to speak?"

"I think so. But the world . . ."

"Who cares what the world says or thinks?" Kate bit her lip. "Since you—since you force me to say this, I want to be with you and I've dreamed of it for a long time. Take me away! Or, if you don't want me . . ."

"Listen!"

"To what? What was it?"

It might only have been a tree-branch tapping the window-pane. Or it might have been someone stealthily moving in an adjoining room. Picking up the lamp, Clive went softly towards the door of the bedroom on the left. Very quietly, so that there should be no creak, he turned the knob.

Nothing!

In Celia's bedroom, its windows fast-closed and shuttered against night-air, the flame of a candle burned straight and steady in its holder on a chest of drawers. Shadows draped the room like its heavy curtains. Celia, her fleecy light-brown hair spread out on the pillow, breathing gently in sleep, lay pale and waxen-lidded in a great feather-bed from which the bolster had been removed.

Nothing!

Clive shut the door and turned back, meeting Kate's eyes.

"Kate, how long would it take you to pack a portmanteau?"

Kate, looking towards Celia's room and suddenly stricken with remorse, cried out and pressed her hands over her eyes.

"What am I saying? Dear God, what am I saying? I can't! With Celia in there, alone and unprotected—"

"Don't be a fool!" Clive went back to the table, set down the lamp, and took her in his arms. "How long would it take you to pack?"

"I . . ."

"How long, my dear?"

An intoxication of the senses gripped them both. Though Kate attempted to draw away from him, he held her and she yielded.

"Fifteen minutes, Kate? Half an hour?"

"Half an hour? Five minutes, and I mean no more! But—"

"We must slip away from here." Clive took his watch from his waistcoat pocket, opened it, and replaced it. "It's twenty minutes past six. The servants will be having their dinner until at least six-thirty. But we can't lose the time for a carriage to be made ready. Could you contrive to walk four miles, as I did last night?"

"What do you take me for? I could walk fifteen, if need be!"

"Good. My portmanteau is still in my bedroom here. I'll get it. Meanwhile, lock the door and admit no one until you hear my voice outside. Five minutes: I'll take you at your word."

He kissed her with a violence he did not try to conceal. Leaving the lamp, since there were matches in his pocket, he went out into the passage. After him the key turned in the lock of the dressing-room door.

In the passage darkness had shut down like an extinguisher-cap. High Chimneys, in a high wind, creaked and cracked as though at the stirring of Matthew Damon's ghost.

Groping his way along to the transverse passage, and then to the bedroom assigned him yesterday afternoon, Clive struck a match and found a spare candle. His evening-clothes he had worn back to London last night. A matter of seconds sufficed to fling back into the bag the clothes that had been unpacked here.

In a few more seconds, in hat and greatcoat, carrying the portmanteau, he had returned to the front of the upstairs hall. He could hear Kate moving about, with quick lithe steps, in the locked dressing-room.

Does your conscience bother you, my lad? Well, yes. But to the devil with it!

Do the police bother you? No!

All the same, he thought, the excitable Superintendent Muswell and the equally excitable Georgette Damon were being infernally quiet back in that study. Putting down his portmanteau at the head of the stairs, he went quietly down that uncarpeted oak staircase.

Still nothing!

At the back of the downstairs hall the paraffin lamp burned in its wall-bracket beside the green-baize door to the servants' quarters. Mrs. Cavanagh and Penelope Burbage too, presumably, would be at the table with the others.

He and Kate could leave by the front door. They need not pass the study. That left only . . .

Whereupon Clive had, or thought he had, one of those sheer illusions of sight which had occurred to him before.

He thought he saw Tress.

Standing in the downstairs hall, between the open doors of the drawing-room and the morning-room, Clive looked towards the drawing-room. For a split-second's lunacy he imagined he saw Tress, Dundreary whiskers and greatcoat and all, dodge back out of sight in the dull glow of a lamp painted in blue forget-me-nots against red and white.

A coal in the drawing-room fire spat and crackled. He heard no other noise except the wind. And there was no time to sponge away this illusion. A door opened and closed upstairs. Kate's footsteps crossed coconut matting towards the top of the stairs.

'I must be going completely—' he thought, and then quietly hurried up to meet her. Kate's was the image which swallowed up all other thoughts or feelings. When he saw her at the head of the staircase, touched dimly by light from below, the illusion had gone.

Kate, gloved and in the boat-shaped hat, with a short

sortie-de-bal jacket over a low-cut evening-gown of scarlet and yellow, did not speak. She only looked at him, and that was enough.

He took the portmanteau from her hand, and picked up his own. Together they descended the stairs towards the front door.

"Clive, do you think—"

"Quiet! We don't want Muswell to. . . ."

"What's the matter?"

He had turned the knob of the front door, and turned it again.

"The door's locked," he whispered. "It's not barred, as you can see, but it's locked. —Did you hear somebody laugh?"

"No."

The quick little furtive whispers struck at each other as they glanced over their shoulders.

"It's locked, and there's no key here. Does Burbage usually lock the front door at this time?"

"No. Never. Last night it was a special precaution to—"

"To what?"

"Nothing." Kate was deathly pale. "Superstitious people would say the omens were against us."

"To blazes with the omens! Are you with me?"

"Yes! I love you."

"We can go out by any full-length window; that's easy."

"No; it's not so easy." Kate moistened her lips. "Those windows are seldom if ever opened, and the—the catches are badly stuck. You could wrench one open, but it would take time and make a dreadful lot of noise. There *is* one way, though. The conservatory."

Again Clive glanced over his shoulder.

"There's—there's a full-length window there," said Kate, "as well as the little ones under the roof. The catches have to be kept in good order, or the temperature can't be controlled. But if those policemen are still in the study . . ."

"Does it matter?"

"No! I *won't* be stopped now."

Every step seemed of inhuman loudness as this time they ran towards the back of the hall. The quiet, dim-lit rooms moved past. They were just between the door of the study and the back-parlour, turning left towards the back-parlour and the conservatory, when the door of the study abruptly opened.

That, however, was not what caused both Clive and Kate to stop.

The person who opened the door was only Penelope Burbage. Clive could see past her; he could see nearly the whole

108

study; and, except for Penelope as she came out, it seemed otherwise empty.

Clive's whisper stopped her too, and forced a whisper in reply.

"Where are they, Penelope? Superintendent Muswell and the constable?"

"I know, sir!" Penelope wrung her hands.

"You know?"

"That is to say, sir, I am aware they are gone. That was why I returned."

"What do you mean?"

"Oh, sir! I escorted Mrs. Damon here, as I promised you. Afterwards, when I went in to supper, I wondered—"

"Speak quietly, please!"

"I wondered why no one had said, 'Come in,'" Penelope whispered, "after Mrs. Damon tapped at the door. No one did speak. Mrs. Damon opened the door and entered. So I returned. Was it so very improper of me to return?"

Small and dumpy, with worry behind her fine eyes, Penelope seemed for the first time really to see Kate and Clive. She looked at the two portmanteaux Clive was carrying. His low voice cut across even her thoughts.

"Penelope, you have not met us. Do you understand?"

"Oh, yes, sir! All too well!"

"You haven't even seen us, have you?"

"No, sir. I had best go back now."

"Wait!" said Clive, as she curtseyed. "Last night, when Miss Kate and Miss Celia questioned you about the figure you had seen on the stairs on Monday night, they asked you if it could have been a woman. You said no. That was not true, was it?"

His whisper, harsh as it was, could barely be heard above the ticking of the black marble clock on the bookcase in the study.

"Sir—"

"It was a woman you saw, was it not? But you feared you might implicate either Miss Celia or Miss Kate?"

"Yes, sir," Penelope answered, and shut her eyes.

"While you were being questioned, you saw Dr. Bland before you. You lost your head, said whatever words first occurred to you, and blurted out that you had seen a man with a beard?"

"Yes, sir."

"But the woman you saw," Clive stated rather than asked, "was Mrs. Cavanagh. Was it not?"

"I'll not tell them I've seen you, sir," replied Penelope, and turned and ran for the green-baize door.

109

Kate, gloved hand clenched at her breast, stared after her with steadily shining eyes.

"I knew it!" whispered Kate, all a glow and intensity. "Clive, we're safe; it's what I had believed and believed, except that Cavvy isn't . . . oh, no matter! Celia's safe. Why do you say you're no detective? We're free!"

"Are we?"

"What do you mean?"

Clive shut up his thoughts and turned a metaphorical key.

"Nothing at all!" he lied, looking at the back-parlour and the glass room beyond it. "But I left the lamp upstairs, and that conservatory will be a maze in the dark."

"Is that all? Give me your hand. I could lead you through the conservatory blindfolded. Give me your hand, my dear!"

Shifting both portmanteaux to his right hand as Kate extended her left, he followed her.

In darkness they went through the parlour, beyond the glass door, and along a gravel path amid tendrils that brushed their sides or even their faces. To Clive the place seemed distinctly less warm, as though—

"Stop here," whispered Kate, as they reached the clearing in the middle. Glass or iron creaked under the whoop of the wind. By this time her voice had an uneasy, unsteady note. "Stop here! The door to the south lawn isn't far behind the bench. But I—I'm not quite sure of the direction after all."

"Here: let me strike a match!"

"No; wait. I can find it. There's a path to it, and it's not ten feet from the beginning of the path to the door."

Clammy darkness pressed round him; it was not a time to use the imagination. He could hear the rustle of Kate's skirts, her footsteps on gravel, and then a low-breathed cry.

"Yes, here it is!" she called softly out of the dark. "Take two steps forward until you reach the bench. Then strike a match and follow me."

He took the two steps, but he went no further.

"Clive! What's the matter?"

There was no reply.

"Clive! What's the matter?"

Clive put down the portmanteaux, clearing his throat. He could hear Kate's quick, light steps approaching.

"Stay where you are," he said very clearly. "I am going to strike that match; but don't come any closer and don't look. There's someone sitting or lying on the bench, and she doesn't move."

The first thing he saw, after he had whisked the match along the edge of the iron table and the flame curled up, was

110

a wink of gold on a bottle of smelling-salts. But that was not what drew his attention. That was not what swam up at him to the exclusion of all else.

Georgette Damon had been strangled to death.

She lay face upwards on the bench, twisted there in the black gown and crinoline she had not changed, with the black marks of fingers on her throat and her head hanging down over the arm of the bench. The auburn hair, loosened, also hung down. And more than life had gone from her: warmth, vivacity, good-nature, soul. The pretty lady was not pretty now.

In the midst of a silence more unnatural still, except for the creak as of another glass door a hairline open, Clive pointed to the gold-stoppered bottle of smelling-salts on the gravel below the bench.

"That's what she left here," he said. "That's what she forgot. That's why she came back. That's how she died."

XIV. BEWILDERMENT IN AN OYSTER-SHOP

In London, towards mid-afternoon of the following day, when the events in a murder case ran fast towards the snare at their end, a four-wheeler drove at a spanking pace down Regent Street, past Regent's Quadrant and the top of the Haymarket, and along Coventry Street into Leicester Square.

It was Thursday, October 19.

Hidden by the semi-darkness of the four-wheeler sat Kate Damon and Clive Strickland, in another emotional state. Clive, who held a morning newspaper and a second crumpled telegram from Whicher, had real troubles aside from this. He looked out of the window as the cab stopped on the north side of the square.

The cabman, after hesitating, climbed down from the box and doubtfully opened the door.

"Sure this is the right address, sir?"

"Yes; I think this is it."

"But it's a oyster-shop!" protested the cabman. "You can't take the lady in there."

"I don't purpose to do so. The lady will remain in the cab. Wait here."

"Clive—" began Kate.

"You will remain in the cab!"

The cabman discreetly climbed back up on the box while the other two indulged in a series of farewells as though the gentleman were leaving for a ten years' stay in India. This lady, the cabman observed, was much upset and had been weeping.

"Clive, you'll not be long?"

"No; not if Whicher's there. I don't want to keep you in this neighbourhood any longer than is necessary."

"Clive, I don't mind! I—I rather like it."

"You wouldn't like it if you saw the square after nightfall."

And he repeated this to himself mentally as he climbed down to the pavement.

Except for one fantastic and would-be magnificent building on the east side, Leicester Square was so slatternly as to draw much public comment. In the centre of the square, amid rubble, the battered equestrian statue of King George the First had been covered with whitewash by some joker insisting that the place should be cleaned up.

Few people were abroad here at this hour. A pale sun tried to struggle out through smoke. Nor had the square's appearance been improved when Saville House, on the north side, was destroyed by fire in February of this year, and its cellars converted into a brawling night-haunt called a wine 'Shades.'

On the east side, grotesquely, the Alhambra Theatre and Music-Hall raised its gaudy arches and its four Moorish pinnacles in a lifeless splendour by day. But the oyster-shop, a dim cavern with tables bearing cruets of vinegar and red pepper, was beside the wine 'Shades.'

Clive's heart sank as he entered. Jonathan Whicher, very grave-faced, sat at a table and studied him.

"Where have you been all day?" demanded Clive.

"At High Chimneys. Talking to people. I've just got back."

Here the former Inspector, despite his gravity, whistled on a note of reluctant admiration as he shook his head.

"You've done it this time," he said. "Thunderation! You've really gone and done it this time!"

"Yes. I daresay."

"Have a plate of oysters, sir? Very cheap."

"I don't need any oysters, thanks. That's to say, I mean—!"

"Oh, ah. I think I know what you mean."

"You don't know, damn it!"

"Sit down, anyway."

112

Clive gritted his teeth and sat down.

"Look here, sir!" continued the bedevilled Whicher. "Having met the young lady, I can understand why you should want to kidnap her and bring her to London. But why must you do it after you'd discovered Mrs. Damon's body? As they tell it me, you and Miss Damon must have discovered the body. Why must you go on and do it *after?* Whose idea was that?"

"It was my idea, of course."

Though this was only partial truth, it would have to serve. The uncertainty, the irony of the past twenty hours, made him swear under his breath. Despite horror and shock at the death of Georgette Damon, whom he liked and for whom he sincerely grieved, he had been slam-bang determined to carry out an elopement according to plan.

And so was Kate: until, in the train, she had been seized by another fit of conscience. She cried out and called herself a monster of callousness. Kate said she could not understand herself. She compared herself unfavourably with Messalina, Lucrezia Borgia, and others of hard heart or doubtful morals.

By the time they were in London Kate had worked herself into such a state that he was compelled to leave her at Mivart's Hotel in the care of a maid.

And that was only right, as Clive knew.

Moreover, human nature being what it is, he had been prepared for what happened when he called on her this morning. In the luxurious atmosphere of Mivart's, on what would have been a fine day without the smoke, he found a different woman.

Now Kate called herself foolish and stupid for her state of mind last night; she asked him if he had ceased to love her; she asked him . . .

Oh, never mind!

Though Clive told Whicher not one word of this, he summed up his own state of mind when he banged his fist on the table.

"It was idiotic, if you like. Very well! But Kate says she doesn't regret it; quite to the contrary; and I'm very certain *I* don't regret it."

"You really mean that, don't you?"

"Yes!" Clive said honestly.

"Sir, listen to me! Superintendent Muswell . . ."

"He's got a warrant out for Kate's arrest, has he? Or for both of us?"

"Well . . ."

"On a charge of murder?"

"Come, now!" Whicher made a satiric face and clucked his tongue. "And you a lawyer, too! Coppers don't need a warrant to arrest for murder. For most felonies, yes. Not for murder."

"Then what is happening?"

"You'll have to lie low, both of you, and keep out of sight. . . ."

"Admirable!" said Clive, and meant that too. "We can take tomorrow's harbour-train for Folkestone, and be in Paris late tomorrow afternoon. Kate is delighted."

Whicher jumped up from the table.

"Thunderation!" he said in a voice of awe. Then, thick-set and pock-marked, his gravity increasing, he paced beside the table before wheeling round.

"I was afraid I'd failed you, sir," he went on. "But I haven't failed you, maybe. No! If you're prepared to help me through some ugly awkward moments with maybe danger in 'em, you needn't keep out of Muswell's clutches much later than late tonight. You and Miss Damon weren't the only ones who ran away from High Chimneys."

"Oh? Who else did?"

"The murderer did."

"You say you've guessed who the murderer is?"

"I *know* who it is. So does your young lady."

Again Whicher paced, jingling coins in his pocket.

"Hark'ee!" he added. "That's been on my mind too. It may be, yesterday, I misled you a bit. It wasn't as much as Mr. Damon misled you; not by a jugful. But what he said wasn't intentional. And what I said was deliberate. See?"

Clive drew himself up.

"Mr. Whicher," he announced, spacing the words with a kind of violent politeness, "let us have no more mystification. Should the earth cease to spin, should grass turn red and the Nelson Column grow a full set of Dundreary whiskers, I beg you to draw it mild and spare me more of your blasted mystification."

"Now, now, sir! You're in a bit of an excited state, what with one thing and another."

"I concede it. All the same——"

"Now, now, sir!"

"Last night," said Clive, and struck the table again, "I came to the conclusion that the murderer must be Mrs. Cavanagh. In addition to the other evidence, she has a straight-backed and rather mannish figure. She has strong hands. She wears her hair bound tightly round her head. If she also wore a part of a cut-off stocking over the head to hide her face, the hair-style could not be distinguished from a man's."

Here Whicher looked at him oddly, pursing up his lips.

"This notion, right or wrong," Clive continued, "would seem to be confirmed by what Penelope Burbage said. Or, rather, by what Penelope didn't say. I'll tell you about that." He did so, briefly. "Have you any observation to make?"

"We-el! Your notion's quite right, as far as it goes."

"As far as it goes? Either Mrs. Cavanagh is the murderer, or she isn't."

"Oh, ah," agreed the other, with an air of great profundity. "That's true too."

"Mr. Whicher—"

Suddenly the former Inspector bellowed at him, with savage worry and a surprising power of voice.

"Nix-my-doll! Stow it, sir! This murderer's the nastiest one in my experience, and I've seen 'em aplenty. There's awkward times ahead. Just you sit here while I have a word with a pal of mine at the back of the oyster-shop, and then . . ."

"You won't be a long time, I hope? Kate's in that four-wheeler you can see out there."

Whoever sits in a four-wheeler is as invisible as though spirited away. Under the bowler hat Whicher's eyes opened in something like consternation.

"Your young lady's here?"

"Yes. Why not?"

"Hum! We'll see. Nothing to be fretted about: no. I'll have a word with my friend, and then . . . trouble, maybe. We'll see."

Clive sprang up from his chair, but sat down again.

Few vehicles rumbled in Leicester Square. The grimy pink paint and fretwork of the Alhambra, beyond almost deserted cobblestones, loomed up like mosque-minarets summoning the faithful to a lascivious ballet under the management of Frederick Strange.

Clive, sitting there with the newspaper and the telegram summoning him into the oyster-shop, found death wherever he looked.

When he thought of Georgette Damon, it was first of all in life. He saw her in the conservatory, vivid and blue-eyed, sweeping him a curtsey.

" 'I think I am as good as my Lord Mayor, and know I am as bad as Tyburn Jack. Give me a chain and a red gown and a pudding before me, and I could play the part of Alderman very well, and sentence Jack before dinner.' " The voice changed. " 'Starve me, keep me from books and honest people—!' "

Georgette had not really laughed when she said that.

Whereupon you thought of her afterwards, swollen and black of face, motionless on the bench under the Indian azalea.

And Matthew Damon . . .

Clive thrust the pictures away from his memory. Looking down at the newspaper, he encountered only smudged and heavy black type announcing the death of Lord Palmerston at Brocket Hall on the previous day.

That was no stark tragedy, of course. Yet drums beat back through old years and times of crisis. Foreign Secretary under Lord John Russell, Prime Minister during the Crimea and Prime Minister still, towards the end of '61, when it seemed England might intervene in the late war in America.

Most people knew Pam had secretly sent troops to Canada. But it would have been a bad day for English-speaking peoples if Her Britannic Majesty's battle-fleet, with fifteen new ironclads, had sailed westwards to free the Confederacy's waters from the Union blockade.

Even here, three thousand miles away, men had been bitter partisans one way or the other. Probably there had not been as much favour for the South as the press liked to pretend; it was too convenient for agitators. Outside the Alhambra there was still an occasional uproar, with trouble-making rowdies shouting songs for South or for North.

Crimea, Indian Mutiny, Civil War; newspaper tales of revolving pistols used in all three, and a strangler's hands moving in a conservatory where . . .

Stop!

Clive sat up straight, as Jonathan Whicher, with a clouded brow, returned to the front of the shop.

"Mr. Whicher," Clive asked, "who found her?"

"Eh?"

"You sent this telegram," Clive held it up, "from Reading to my address in Brook Street. You say you've been at High Chimneys all day, and talked to everybody?"

"Got some ideas?" asked Whicher, eyeing him sharply.

"No, not very useful ones. But . . . after Kate and I left, who found Mrs. Damon's body? And why weren't the police there? And why was the front door locked?"

"If you'll excuse my saying so," the other spoke with dry politeness, "aren't you the one to give a few explanations about what happened?"

Clive did so, while the former Inspector whistled through his teeth.

"Ah! That's what we thought, more or less. Though Mus-

116

well and I don't get on any too well, as you might say. Now, sir: your young lady. Where's she staying?"

"At Mivart's Hotel. But she'd better not go back there, had she, if we're likely to be arrested? And I'd better not go back to my rooms."

"I said lie low, that's all. 'King' Mayne owes one one favour; it's gospel truth he does! To tell you the truth, I don't think either of you is going to be arrested."

"What's that?"

Whicher's eye had a wicked glitter.

"Unless I fail, that is. Look sharp if I fail. Meanwhile . . ."

"Yes?"

"You shook me, and I'll admit it, when you said you'd got Miss Damon out there. You and I are going on a bit of an errand. The young lady can't go with us; with your permission, we'll send her back to Mivart's in the cab. Still and all, I *would* like a word with her first."

Here Whicher hesitated, with all his old mildness and delicacy. He nodded towards the grimy windows, beyond which the four-wheeler stood at the kerb.

"But I wouldn't want to embarrass her, you know. After what's happened, an' all. D'ye think she'd mind if I went out and spoke to her?"

The question was answered by Kate herself.

Clive swore, and Whicher raised his head, as the door of the four-wheeler opened. Kate, staring at the oyster-shop, edged her crinoline through and lowered herself gingerly on the carriage-step.

Instantly Clive and Whicher were out of the shop and across the mud of the cobblestones, their eyes alert right and left.

No fights broke out in the square except after nightfall, when arrogant swells sought the night-haunts roundabout or, towards eleven o'clock, poured out of the Alhambra following displays of ballet-girls on the stage and of night-women who exhibited their charms in its promenade. But it was an uneasy neighborhood all the same.

Kate, startled, paused with one foot on the step.

"Really—!" she began.

"Now, ma'am," Whicher said heartily. "Now, now, now!"

Kate looked appealingly at Clive as he and Whicher stood in front of her.

"I've been telling Mr. Strickland, ma'am, that you two have got no call to fear the Peelers just yet. But you stop where you are, ma'am, like a well-conducted lady."

"Good heavens, whatever is the matter?"

117

Whicher did not seem to hear the question.

"About last night, ma'am," he went on, and Kate flushed as he spoke, "we've pretty well put together what must have happened at High Chimneys."

"Oh?"

"About your poor stepmother, that is. Mr. Strickland talked to her in the conservatory beginning at about fifteen minutes to six o'clock, say, and ending maybe at a few minutes past six. Sir," and Whicher turned to Clive, "would you say that's right?"

"Approximately, yes."

"What does she do then?" inquired Whicher, addressing Kate. "She goes upstairs with Penelope Burbage to shift her dress and wash herself. Muswell and the police-constable are still in the study then; Mr. Strickland heard the Superintendent talking.

"What you don't know, ma'am, and what Mr. Strickland don't know, and what Mrs. Damon herself don't know either, is that the Superintendent gets to the end of his temper not much after that. 'Blow this business!' says he; 'I want food.' Out he stamps with the constable, out of the house with Police-Constable Peters, while Mr. Strickland is talking to Mrs. Cavanagh in the conservatory. Out of the house he goes, mind you, without a word to anybody except Dr. Bland."

Kate began to speak, but checked herself.

"Dr. Bland?" said Clive.

"That's right, sir. He meets Dr. Bland in the hall. And the doctor, being an inquisitive sort of gentleman, walks down the drive with 'em to the lodge-gates where they've got a horse-and-trap waiting. That's when Dr. Bland locked the front door after him when he went out."

"It was Dr. Bland who locked the front door?"

"Right again. Borrowed Burbage's key much earlier than that. 'Burbage,' says he, 'there's somebody it's much better to keep in the house.' "

"But why?" demanded Clive. "Why should he lock the door at all?"

"Ah!" murmured Whicher.

Now look here—!

"Meantimes," said the inperturbable detective, "where's Mrs. Damon? She's gone upstairs, ay. But she hasn't shifted her gown. That takes ladies a long time, even if they don't change stays and knickerbockers and the rest of it too. She has a sob or two, bathes her eyes, and down she goes again to tell the police who the murderer is.

"Mrs. Damon's been shouting in the conservatory, she's

even been shouting in the hall, that she knows everything. It won't take her anything like a minute, much less two, only to walk downstairs to the study with Penelope Burbage. She taps at the study door and goes in. Follow me, sir?"

Clive made a gesture.

"Yes, I follow you. The question is: why did Mrs. Damon say nothing when she found the study was empty? And why stay there, for however long or short a time she did stay there, with the door closed?"

"We don't know, sir. The lady's dead."

"But—!"

"After she goes downstairs, the murderer's a-tracking her." Whicher looked at Kate. "The murderer scares you, ma'am, when you look out of your dressing-room. You scream. Mr. Strickland runs upstairs. It'd be dead easy for the murderer to dodge Mr. Strickland, with all those empty rooms."

Kate, still motionless on the carriage-step, cleared her throat but remained silent.

"It would have been easy, I agree," admitted Clive. "However! Mrs. Damon in the study must have heard Kate cry out. Why didn't she open the study door then?"

"Come, sir! How do we know she didn't? You were a bit quick off the mark in running upstairs. I say we don't 'know' what Mrs. Damon did, but she couldn't have been in that study for a long time. No! Not even long enough to make us puzzle our heads about it. Let's say she does come out, just after you've run past—"

"And meets the murderer?"

"That's right."

"Mrs. Cavanagh?" demanded Clive. "Mrs. Cavanagh stayed in the conservatory when I went upstairs. Was it Mrs. Cavanagh?"

"Well, no," answered Whicher.

"But Cavvy's bound to have been—" began Kate.

"Mind you," argued Whicher, biting his forefinger, "I'll not swear it's impossible. The servants didn't hear Miss Damon cry out; there was a thick green-baize door between. Still and all, sir, from what you tell me about the time it happened, Mrs. Cavanagh must have been having her supper with the others when the dead woman was strangled.

"Mind you something else! Mrs. Damon didn't fear the murderer. Not a scrap; you tell me so. She didn't fear the dark either. And she'd mislaid her bottle of smelling-salts. If she met this person in the murderer's clothes—"

"This person," said Clive.

"Oh, ah. If she'd met the murderer, if she'd been invited or even compelled into that conservatory, Mrs. Damon would have laughed. She'd have gone out of bravado on the excuse she wanted her smelling-salts. But that wasn't wise."

And he made the gesture of one who strangles.

Kate cried out a protest.

"Who did find her body?" asked Clive. "After we left, I mean?"

"Dr. Bland."

"How did that happen?"

"Back comes the doctor," said Whicher, "from saying good-bye to Superintendent Muswell at the porter's lodge. He looks for somebody, anybody, in what's pretty much a deserted house. The temperature in the conservatory's down, because a door to the south lawn has been not quite closed. As for Mrs. Damon, you might say her temperature's lower still."

"Stop this!" exclaimed Kate.

"Miss Damon, ma'am, I'm only too happy to stop. But you do see, don't you, Mr. Strickland's made it uncommon hard for me to help either of you? And you haven't made it easier, yourself, by playing Bess-o'-Bedlam with a gentleman Mrs. Cavanagh says you've been in love with for years?"

"Cavvy said that?"

"She did, ma'am. She's not fond of you. But then," and Whicher studied her, "I expect you knew that already?"

"Yes. I knew it."

"Shall we forget Mrs. Cavanagh?" suggested Clive. "Dr. Bland borrowed a key from Burbage and kept the front door locked. Very well: what explanation did he give for locking the door?"

"He didn't give any."

"He didn't give . . . ?"

"No! And that does help all of us. When Superintendent Muswell was fetched back from Reading, not too sweet-tempered either, the doctor wouldn't answer any questions and finally went off to London in a huff. Didn't I say you two weren't the only ones who ran away from High Chimneys last night?"

Kate and Clive looked at each other.

"I ask your pardon, both of you," Whicher continued, with a new kind of tensity in his voice, "for speaking sharply. It'll be all right, I'm certain; just trust me and don't upset my plans any further. Now, then, Miss Damon! Mr. Strickland is going with me on a very important bit of an errand. If you'll be good enough to get back in that bird-cage and let the cabby drive you to your hotel . . . ?"

Kate turned on the step. "Without Clive?"

"Yes, ma'am! You can't accompany us where we're going;

'twouldn't be fitting if you could. Mr. Strickland won't be long away. He'll be with you by tea-time. But I'm bound to add something else, which is the reason why I wanted a word with you."

"What do you wish to add?"

"There's like to be trouble tonight, ma'am," Whicher told her gently. "Mr. Strickland can't be with you at all this evening. At least, not after eight o'clock he can't. D'ye take my meaning?"

XV. CHERRY RIPE

Kate, with a beaded reticule pressed against her side and the front of the crinoline pressed out over silk petticoats, regarded him in dismay.

"No, I do not take your meaning. If you must know, Mr. Strickland and I eloped from High Chimneys just to—just to—"

"To be together? Ah! So you did. But you'd like to know who killed your father, ma'am. *I* think you would."

"Where are you going?"

"That's part of the secret, Miss Damon."

"Tea-time," said Kate. "Tea-time!" She bit her lip. "Clive, have you a key to your rooms? Give it me, will you? Please, my dear! And don't return to the hotel; come to your rooms, and tea will be waiting for you."

In silence, torn by several emotions but not knowing what to say, Clive handed her the key and gave money to the cabman.

"Mivart's Hotel," he said.

"Yes, I trust you," Kate said to Whicher, before drawing back inside the four-wheeler. "But I'm afraid of you. Dear God, I'm afraid of you!"

Clive closed the door. In a day that had begun to turn dull and chilly under the smoke, the four-wheeler rattled round the square and turned westwards by way of Panton Street. There was no reason for Clive to feel he was losing Kate forever; that the slam of the cab-door made a final parting; but he did feel this with a sense of doubt and dread.

"What's the game?" he demanded. "Where *are* we going?"

121

"Sir, why do you think I asked you to meet me at that oyster-shop? Come along. I'll show you."

And, jamming his bowler hat down on his head, Whicher led the way across the square to the Alhambra Theatre.

Its main entrance, a Moorish arch like a gigantic keyhole with long lines of smaller arches on either side, towered above them in a bleakness that would not soften until the gas was lighted. The management of Mr. Strange, announced bills inside the arches, would celebrate their first anniversary with a revival of that "Oriental musical spectacle" *L'Enfant Prodigue,* based on the comic opera *Azael* by the French composer Auber.

"Yes, here!" said Whicher, striking his hand against the side of the arch. "You're familiar with the fashion o' doing things at the Alhambra?"

"Who isn't?"

"That's to say, you've been here any number of times?"

"More times," Clive retorted, "than most of us would care to admit. The place is very nearly as disruptable," and he nodded towards another building on the east side, "as that 'Plastic Poses' exhibition in the cellar there."

"Well, sir, you be grateful! It was your telling me about going into the Princess's Theatre, slap-bang at the wrong time, that gave me idea for this dodge."

"What dodge? What do you expect to find at three o'clock in the afternoon?"

"A magsman," replied Whicher. "Or to say you fair, though there's no such word, a magswoman. She'll be waiting for us."

Clive glanced round him.

No drunken gallants capered here now. No willing dames were fumbled under archways, or in alleys, or amid the ruins round King George the First's statue. A gritty wind blew across the furtiveness of the square.

"Yes, three o'clock," agreed Whicher, consulting his watch. "It's just time. Follow me."

So different did the inside of the theatre appear, in pitch darkness, that Clive would hardly have known where he was. Mostly you thought how vast it was; before the present management remodelled it into a music-hall, Clive had seen Howe's and Cushing's American Circus go through its paces in the amphitheatre. A different kind of wild-beast atmosphere haunted the Alhambra today.

Whicher, striking a Lucifer, led the way upstairs to the promenade between the pit below and the Grand Circle above.

"I've got all sorts of friends, you see," he explained from

the corner of his mouth. "And they're a rum lot, as the devil said of the Ten Commandments. But I need 'em. Sir, is it worth ten pounds to you to find proof of who killed Mr. and Mrs. Damon?"

"Yes. A good deal more than that."

"No! Not more!" Suddenly Whicher turned round, with his pock-marked face ugly in the match-light. "Never let a fancy-woman gammon you; and I'd advise you that in more ways than one."

"What the hell are you talking about?"

They were in the painted promenade, whose long and narrow length ran south to north, supported by a low line of Moorish pillars. The front, on the east side, faced out towards the great stage. When the deliberately dim gas-jets were kindled, you bought a promenade ticket to stroll here in gloom, amid others who strolled and made assignations. Its thick close air was flavoured with a scent of dead cigars, spirituous liquors, and stale perfume.

"Is it worth ten pounds, say, as a special fee to the magsman who helps?"

"Yes. But I still want to know what you're talking about!"

Whicher's match went out. Somebody laughed. And, as though extinguishing the match had been a signal, faint light bloomed from one dim gas-globe.

At the north end of the promenade, behind what looked like a semi-circular bar-counter, stood a handsome young woman of seventeen or so, with bright eyes and an assured air. She wore an outdoor costume, semi-fashionable, including a flat oval hat on fair hair.

Whicher hurried towards the counter.

"Ah! Hope I'm not late. A very good afternoon to you, Cherry."

"And a very good afternoon to *you*, Mr. Whicher.—Not half it ain't!"

The young woman laughed again.

It was a loud laugh, though not unpleasant. It rolled and rang and echoed back in this hollow shell, making nerves jump, while the young woman did a little dance-step. Whicher stopped short, his manner altering from that of an indulgent uncle.

"Cherry, my girl . . ."

"Hear ye, hear ye, hear ye!"

"Have you been at the gin again?"

Cherry's manner altered too.

"Bale up, grandpa! What's a yard o' white satin among friends?"

"Four bars in this promenade," said Whicher, tapping the counter, "and they put you at selling oranges and sweets so they could keep you off the drink, that's why."

"And what do they pay me, I should like to know?"

"They don't have to pay you. It brings you clients, my girl. More'n you'd ever get for yourself. And it brings you the kind of work *I* give." Whicher raised his voice a little. "The coppers will be here tonight, Cherry. This is murder."

The word "murder," though not loudly spoken, emerged with clear ugliness among other echoes.

"This is murder, my girl. And if you fail me . . ."

The bright-eyed seventeen-year-old, going into a rage behind a counter displaying heavy glass jars and bottles of coloured sweets, reached towards one as a weapon before altering her mind.

"Have I ever failed yer? Answer me! Have I ever failed yer?"

"Then be a good girl and see you don't. Did you arrange it?"

" 'Course I did!"

"What time?"

"Nine sharp. There's a near-naked do on the stage and they'll all be watching it. Most of 'em, anyways."

"Well! That'll do. Now then: Cherry, this is Mr. Strickland. Take a good look at him and make sure you'll recognize him again."

"Oo-er!" said Cherry with interest, running her gaze up and down Clive and then striking a languishing pose which was far from being ineffective. "Most pleased to make yer acquaintance and happily charmed, I'm sure. Oo-er! And if *you* ain't doing nothing after nine o'clock, nothing that can't be postponed for a better—"

"None o' that, now!" snapped Whicher.

Again the echoes thundered and rang. Under the dim spark of gas, with Cherry posturing sensual allure in the background, Whicher swung round from the counter. He had lost his usual meditative air; he was nervous-looking and pale.

"Listen to me, sir. I don't like drawing you into this. . . ."

"Into what?" demanded Clive. "What am I supposed to do?"

Whicher stroked his chin.

"At nine o'clock tonight, as I've planned it, somebody's going to walk into this promenade and come up to the counter here. Cherry'll be on duty then, selling sweets. The person who comes in may be a man or it may be a woman. . . ."

"Hold on! It can't be somebody from High Chimneys?"

"Oh, yes, it can," Whicher said sharply.

"In a place like this? At the Alhambra?"

"In a place like this," agreed Whicher. "At the Alhambra."

Cherry laughed.

Clive glanced behind him, at the thin Moorish pillars and the fretting shadows on a mosaic-tiled floor that glittered vari-coloured where the light touched it.

"But I've got no choice," said Whicher, biting his forefinger. "You'll see how it is. One day the Detective Branch may have officers that don't look like coppers. As it is the nearest thing they've ever had is me; there's not a man-jack at Scotland Yard who wouldn't be known as a copper ten yards away. I've got to hide 'em; I've got to hide myself, even. You're the only one I can trust, if you'll do it."

"I'll do it, right enough."

"Promise, sir?"

"You may count on me, I swear, for anything from pitch-and-toss to manslaughter. What is it you want me to do?"

"Ah! Brighten up that gas, Cherry!"

Uttering another loud laugh, Cherry waved her arm and complied. The gas-jet, in its frosted globe above a lustre of glass prisms, was still very dim. But it threw a little more colour into the heavy bottles of sweets, together with piles of oranges and prawns.

Whicher looked along the line of pillars. He stalked past Clive and selected the third pillar away from the semi-circular counter.

"Here," he announced. "At nine o'clock you'll be standing against this pillar. Smoking a cigar or whatnot. Buy a ticket for the promenade only. Come here whenever you like, but for God's sake don't make it later than a quarter to nine. There'll be other people about, but that's all to the good as long as it's not heavily crowded."

"Does it matter whether I'm seen?"

"No. Not a bit. Stand where I'm standing, and . . . ah! That's it."

"But I can't see the middle of the counter from here. The other pillars are in the way!"

"No matter for that either. At nine o'clock, maybe a little before or maybe a little later, a certain person will walk up to the counter and ask for something."

"Ask for what?"

Whicher did not seem to hear the question. He consulted his watch, on a wire of nerves, and kept glancing past Clive towards the darkness of the stairs by which they had ascended.

"Next!" he went on. "As soon as this something is asked for, Cherry will move to one side so you'll be able to see who's speaking to her. You won't be able to hear much, what with the orchestra-music and voices and all, but Cherry will give you a signal it's the right person. Like this. Show the gentleman, my girl!"

"Hear ye, hear ye, hear ye! It's a pleasure."

Drawing on all her histrionic powers, bright-eyed, tipsiness all but conquered, the handsome young woman moved to one side. She lifted her right arm in an exaggerated gesture with her elbow almost vertical, and patted her back curls.

"Stop!" said Whicher.

Cherry screamed at him.

"Stop, I tell you!" said Whicher. "Don't overdo it."

"Gord's bloody truth, Mr. Acting-manager—!"

"If you're drunk, my girl, and you dish us: so help me—!"

Cherry picked up an orange to throw at him, but his eye conquered her. Again Whicher consulted his watch, peering towards the dark staircase.

"When you see that, Mr. Strickland, *you* go to one side (it won't matter which side), and take off your hat. Just take off your hat as though you were too warm. It'll be hot enough, what with the gas and the boozing and the rest of it, so that'll look natural. You're tall; you can be seen anywhere. Got it, sir?"

"Yes. What do I do then?"

"Nothing. That's all. Take off your hat and watch what happens."

"But I don't understand . . . !"

"I don't want you to understand. Not everything. Not yet. See?"

Here, trying to draw round him his usual mild and thoughtful air, Whicher swung back to the counter.

"You've heard what I've got to say. You've done your part so far, my girl; just see you do the rest and I'll have no complaint to make. If it's all straight and understood, I won't detain you. That's all."

"Oh, no, it ain't!" said Cherry.

She lifted the flap of the counter and came sweeping round. In a semi-fashionable grey crinoline and black mantle, Cherry assumed another dramatic pose.

"Oh, no, it ain't all. There's a little matter o' ten pounds, Mr. Detective Police; it's been spoke for; I'll thank you for payment in advance."

"And have you go straight to the nearest public-house?"

"Ten quid, grandpa. Stump up! Pay it over handsome, and pay it over like what you promised, or I can get boozed a-plenty on tick and something-me but I will. And *that* ain't all either. If yer puts me (me, mind yer!) in the position where I've got to stand behind that counter and be nice to a woman—"

Clive, who had taken a note-case out of his inside pocket, stopped dead.

"What woman?"

Cherry laughed with shattering effect. Whicher spoke quickly.

"Pay no attention, sir. Howsoever! You'd best give her a five on account, and I'll have a word to say when this business is finished."

"Here you are, then. But I want to know . . . !"

"Hah!" said Cherry.

Instantly her manner changed again. Genteelly lifting her crinoline and her one petticoat to tuck the five-pound note in the top of her stocking, Cherry made it clear in the most ladylike way that she wore neither pantalettes nor knicker-bockers.

"Now you're a gentleman," she breathed, looking up sideways. "Crikey-blimey- and so-and-so me," cried Cherry, wriggling herself at the back of seductive eyes, "but you're a gentleman and no mistake. And I can give you a better time—"

Up swept Whicher's hand as though for a blow.

"You clear out, my girl. I've warned you for the last time."

Cherry said he was not going to knock her about. Jeeringly, as she pirouetted towards the staircase, her voice was upraised in a song.

> Hit him on the boko!
> Dot him on the snitch!
> Wot a lovely fighter—!
> Was there ever sich?

It woke more echoes at the Alhambra. It had once celebrated Tom Sayers, retired former Champion of England. Sung with joyous sarcasm in Cherry's loud if not untuneful voice, while the hat joggled on her fair hair, it carried her pirouetting into the shadow beyond gaslight and still warbling down the stairs.

"Thunderation!" said Whicher.

He drew his coat-sleeve across his forehead.

"You wouldn't believe, now would you, that girl's one of the cleverest sharpers that ever worked a game to help the Peelers and not flummox 'em? She's already done most of her part, and it's a good deal. She'll be sober tonight, I promise you. And—"

Here he stopped, since Clive was still staring at him.

"Don't think that, sir! Not what you're thinking!"

"How do you know what I'm thinking?"

"Even if it is a woman, that needn't necessarily mean anything!"

"I don't suppose," observed Clive, at once coldly courteous and violently driving the note-case back into his pocket, "you could bear to indicate what it does mean?"

"Yes," said Whicher after a pause, "I owe you that much."

It was the mosaic-tile floor, under a low roof with the pillars, which threw back so many noises. Whicher took a turn back and forth by the counter.

Heat, too, with the stuffiness of dead cigars and stale perfume, closed in round Clive's throat. After muttering to himself, Whicher again consulted his watch.

"The fact is, sir, I'm waiting for somebody. You'll recall I spoke to a pal o' mine at the oyster-stop?"

"Yes. Well?"

"It was to leave a message. I'm not even sure my game's to be allowed, and even if it is . . . anyway! You know I'm setting a trap. But it's not what I had a mind to do yesterday. No! Or, to say truer than that, what I had in mind yesterday was only a beginning of what might 'a' been good if I'd had time. Got it?"

"No."

"Then I'll tell you. Nineteen years ago, when Harriet Pyke was in the condemned cell, she wrote a letter to the father of her child. And, three months ago, that man—Ivor Rich, remember?—killed himself at a lodging-house in Pimlico. When the keeper of the lodging-house called me in to see if we could hush up the scandal of a suicide, we found Harriet Pyke's letter. Got *that?*"

"Of course. You told me so yesterday."

Whicher pointed a finger with some intentness.

"Now, then! In Harriet Pyke's letter, d'ye see, there are a lot of references to her sister, Mary Jane Pyke Cavanagh, and also to the child. . . ."

"Wait!" interrupted Clive. "You told me you didn't know the name of the child!"

"I didn't, sir, and in a manner of speaking I still don't. Howsoever, the trap's been set and that letter is the bait. Cherry, posing as a blackmailer, has offered to sell that letter to a certain person who'll walk in here tonight. Cherry says she won't hand over the letter except in a public place where there's no danger of trying any shooting or strangling games. So it'll be handed over in the sight of witnesses: including you. So, if the Peelers turn up on the spot too . . . follow me?"

"No, I don't follow you. Simply because someone buys a letter about a child's parentage, it won't prove that person killed Mr. and Mrs. Damon!"

"Quite right," agreed Whicher, with a sardonic look. "It won't prove anything at all."

"Well, then?"

"Howsoever!" said Whicher, raising his forefinger impressively. "If a self-confident copper, who's dead certain he's right, thinks that's the proper moment to step in and take the guilty party off balance and force a confession—eh? What do you say?"

And he raised his eyebrows.

"I say," retorted Clive, "it's too damned risky and too much of a long shot. Do *you* want to try that?"

"No," said Whicher, rounding the syllable.

This time it was irony which stamped satiric puckers round his eyes and mouth.

"You see, sir, that's what I did in the Constance Kent case. There was evidence all over the place, evidence that told me certain-sure the girl was guilty. But there wasn't a scrap of evidence I could show a jury. Thinks I to myself, 'Aha! I'll put that girl under arrest straightaway, with what we call the shock o' surprise, and I'll have a confession before she's got time to think.'

"Well, I was wrong. That's the mistake I made. That's one mistake I swore I'd never make again. I swore it to you as late as yesterday afternoon. But now, if Sir Richard Mayne lets me have a tack at it, I'll risk it and glad of the chance to do it. Because, if I don't get the authority from Scotland Yard, as sure as guns Superintendent Muswell will walk in tomorrow and arrest you or somebody else who's not guilty. Now do you see?"

It was a rhetorical question. For a moment Whicher stared into vacancy.

"Tonight, sir," he added, "I'll be arresting that girl all over again."

XVI. THE SHADOWS OF
SCOTLAND YARD

"That girl?" echoed Clive.

"In a manner of speaking, yes."

"But you said—"

"Stop!" interrupted Whicher. "Let's have this fair-said. Whatever else may be, nothing's going to happen to your young lady. I promise you that. Or, at least," and he hesitated in bad worry, "I think I can promise that; it's the part I like least. Still and all! If nothing happens to your young lady, do you care who's arrested?"

"No, I do not."

"Then never mind what my original scheme was. It had to be altered when you and Miss Damon ran away. But the clothes still fit the very same customer."

"When you use the term 'clothes,' you refer to—?"

"The murderer. Oh, ah! Maybe it's what they call poetic justice that there's more than one likeness at High Chimneys to the matter of Constance Kent. Evidence, evidence all over the shop! But not one scrap you can show a jury here either."

"Where did you get this evidence?"

"Mostly from you. But also from talking to the lot of them today. And a bit of it, too," Whicher stared at the past, "from visiting Mr. Damon last August, and finding all of the family except Mrs. Cavanagh were gathered round a table for Miss Celia's birthday. Have you thought about motive, sir?"

"Well, unless there's insanity in the family after all, as Dr. Bland seems to fear . . ."

Whicher made no comment.

"Unless there's insanity, I say," repeated Clive, "the great problem is simply the motive. The great problem is why in Satan's name the murderer behaved like that."

Whicher uttered a noise between a snort and a breath of triumph.

"Now you're getting warm!" he declared, to a man getting warm in the physical sense as well. "Now you're using your wits, thank'ee. I'll ask you one last question, Mr. Strickland, and I'll say no more."

"What question?"

"In all the times you've seen men's parts played by women on the stage, and there must have been lots of 'em. . . ."

"There have been. Admittedly!" Clive attempted to sweep this aside. "I've seen women play every part from Rosalind and Viola to the boy-apprentice in *Sweeney Todd*. What does it mean if I have?"

"What does it mean? Thunderation! Did you ever see one that deceived you into thinking she was a man? Or was meant to deceive you? That's the secret. That's the answer. It means—"

Clive started as though a revolving pistol had been fired behind his ear.

His companion broke off, also jumping a little, as someone began to bellow Whicher's name downstairs in the foyer of the Alhambra. Exasperation, doubt, even nervousness poured out of that voice, together with a stumbling and groping on bare boards in the dark.

"Up here, Hackney," called Whicher, clearing his throat. Again he addressed Clive. "Just you keep your eyes skinned tonight, that's all; and be ready to testify (in court, if needs be) to anything you see or hear."

Whicher consulted his watch for the last time.

Slow footfalls, a wheezing of breath from someone carrying too much weight, clumped up the staircase and across towards them on mosaic tiles.

The newcomer, a burly man with a moustache flowing into fan-shaped side-whiskers, and a beaverskin hat above an open greatcoat, must ordinarily have been jovial and knowing, carrying a wink at one corner of his eye.

But he was not merry now.

"Afternoon, Hackney," said Whicher. "You're late, aren't you?"

"Late, eh?" said the newcomer. "That's a good 'un, that is!"

"Didn't George tell you at the oyster-shop?"

"He said the Alhambra. He didn't say where in the blooming Alhambra. He didn't say you was as mad as a March hare."

"Mr. Strickland," observed Whicher, who had become his old imperturbable self, "this is Inspector Hackney of the Detective Branch. Old friend of mine. Hackney, this is the gentleman I spoke of."

Inspector Hackney touched two fingers of his hat towards Clive, but did not look at him. Inspector Hackney only wheezed.

"What's the word, Hackney? Did you see Sir Richard?"

"I saw him."

"And what did he say? What luck?"

"Bad luck. We got the news you wanted from Yorkshire by police-telegraph; but bad luck all the same."

"Won't he let me use the Detective Branch?"

"Yes. He'll let you. That's the bad luck."

"Ah! I rather thought he would."

"Jonathan," burst out Inspector Hackney, "what's become o' you? Are you simple? Don't be took in! 'King' Mayne didn't stand by you when he ought to have done, in '60; and he's never forgiven you because he didn't stand by you. He'd like you to see trouble again."

"Maybe."

"You telegraph me from Reading," said Inspector Hackney, taking a grimy if bright-spotted handkerchief from the tail-pocket of his coat, and mopping his face with it. "You ask me to meet you at the Great Western depot here in town—"

"*And* Cherry White too."

"All right. Cherry White too. You ask me to see the 'King' and get his permission for this do, and that might be well enough if the scheme had reason in it. But it ain't and it hasn't. Don't you see that? There's no sense in it!"

"Oh, I don't know," said Whicher.

While Inspector Hackney made noises, Whicher went thoughtfully round to the side of the semi-circular counter. Raising the flap, he strolled inside the counter. There, with a rather terrifying little smile, he faced Hackney between pyramids of oranges.

"It's not what I'd have chosen, mind you," he pointed out, "if I'd been given more time. Still and all, it's got a good chance. Have an orange?"

Inspector Hackney condemned oranges to complete spiritual ruin.

"Jonathan, my lad, it's got no chance at all! That's what I'm a-complaining of!"

"Not even," inquired Whicher, "with Cherry's testimony too?"

Inspector Hackney peered past the handkerchief.

"Cherry hasn't—?" he demanded.

"Yes. Cherry has."

"Then why can't we make it a dummy arrest? You always used to be a rare one for dummy arrests. I could 'a' helped

132

you out with a dummy arrest, and no bones broken. Why has it got to be a real arrest?"

"Because I've seen the guilty person,"_ answered Whicher, picking up an orange. "And I'll lay you ten to one the guilty person won't give way except under a formal charge at a real police-station. That's not the danger of failure. The danger of failure is with us, don't think it's not!—Mr. Strickland," Whicher added abruptly, "I thank you very much. But hadn't you best go home now?"

There are times when too much mystery, too many statements which will not fit into a comprehensible pattern, produce the effect of a physical fear. Clive felt it now. The whole atmosphere of the promenade had grown poisoned.

"Your young lady will have tea ready for you, won't she?" asked Whicher.

"That's what Kate said, yes."

"Ah! Then you'd best go," Whicher told him in a persuasive voice. "You'll have a servant at your rooms too, I imagine?"

"I have a housekeeper. She—"

"Good. Very good, sir! Well! When you take your leave of Miss Damon tonight, sir, just be sure she's at Mivart's Hotel. And tell her not to admit anybody to her room. Not anybody, no matter who it is!"

"Mr. Whicher, are you suggesting Kate's in danger?"

"Not in any danger of being killed, if that's what you mean." Whicher gave him another of those indecipherable glances. "There's probably nothing in a notion that did enter my head. It's just in case, sir. It's just in case."

Just in case.

The fuming face of Inspector Hackney, the impassive blandness of Whicher, faded behind Clive as he hastened downstairs through the echoing shell. When he emerged into the street, his watch told him it was nearly four o'clock.

He could find no cab in the scabrous emptiness of Leicester Square. He did not find one until he had walked to lower Regent Street, through spattering mud. With the leisureliness of wheeled traffic, it was nearer five when the hansom jingled into Brook Street. He could have walked in far less time.

In this part of town, where the bows and the raising of hats became a very stately process for those few who were on foot, a tinge of darkness had crept into the smoke. Gaslight was glowing, curtains were being drawn across stately windows, in Mivart's Hotel at the south-western corner of Brook Street and Davies Street.

Clive had started up the stairs, to his apartments on the first floor at number 23, before he remembered that this was a Thursday. Mrs. Quint, his superior and modern-minded housekeeper, would have taken the afternoon off.

Nonsense! It made no difference.

Nevertheless, Kate was not there.

The outer door, fastened with a Chubb lock, had been left on the latch. In his sitting-room the gas-jet in a glass dish burned beside the mantelpiece; it had acquired its usual faint whistle against an emptiness of silence.

Rows of calf-bound books looked down at him. The tea-service had been set out on a table near the fire, with tea in the pot; a filled kettle was on the hob. In an easy chair near the fire he found a handkerchief with Kate's initials.

It reminded him of her presence, as such small things can, with an almost unbearable vividness. It caused him to see her face and hear her voice.

But Kate wasn't there.

Now why, he wondered, should the image of Kate in some fashion suggest the image of Tress?

Tress, supercilious and ever-triumphant, seemed to stand (only in imagination, as he must have appeared at High Chimneys last night) over beside the velvet curtain covering the archway to Clive's bedroom. Tress's wide mouth moved, his eyes jeered.

'Make an end of this!' Clive said to himself.

'Make an end,' he insisted, holding Kate's handkerchief. 'Or it will become a hallucination. There's an easy explanation of why Kate is not here. She has returned briefly to Mivart's Hotel, that is all. That fire has been made up in the past ten minutes. Kate will return at any moment.'

Rat-tat went the heavy knocker on the outer door; first hesitantly, then with a firmer *rat-tat-tat*.

Fool! He had closed the Chubb lock on the inside. Kate, instead of using the latch-key, must be summoning him with a knock. Clive went over and opened the door, beginning to speak her name.

Outside stood Celia Damon.

Of all the persons he had least expected to see, here was the most astonishing.

"Celia!"

"You are somewhat familiar, Mr. Strickland," said Celia, with a gentle but firm flash of rebuke. Strained grey eyes regarded him from under a black pork-pie hat. She was all in black, including sealskin mantle and muff.

"I—I beg your pardon, Miss Damon. Will you come in?"

"Under the circumstances, I think I might. And I am properly chaperoned."

Celia nodded towards Penelope Burbage, hovering near

134

her. Celia, her colour a little high and apparently holding herself calm by force of will, swept across the threshold.

"It is rather surprising to find you in London, Miss Damon."

"Not at all surprising, sir. I am staying with Aunt Abigail in Devonshire Place. Aunt Abigail is Uncle Rollo's wife; it is my custom to stay there."

Here Celia caught sight of Kate's handkerchief, which Clive made no attempt to conceal. Her gaze moved to the tea-service on the table, and beyond that to the velvet curtain which so obviously covered the entrance to the bedroom. Quickly looking away from that, she glanced at another closed door across the sitting-room.

"May I ask, Mr. Strickland, where that door leads?"

"To the dining-room."

"Thank you. Will you be good enough, Penelope, to wait in the dining-room?"

"There is no gas lighted in there," Clive began, but Celia's curt little gesture silenced him.

"Sir—" began Penelope, in an almost rebellious tone.

"Penelope wishes to tell you, Mr. Strickland," Celia interrupted, "that she did her best to shield you and Kate. When you and my unfortunately headstrong sister ran away from High Chimneys, with—with luggage, and left by way of a conservatory where our stepmother had been killed, Penelope would have said nothing but that Uncle Rollo compelled her to speak. Penelope, not a word. Wait in the dining-room, if you please."

With not a little dignity Penelope crossed to the dining-room. Celia waited until she had gone.

"Mr. Strickland, for shame!"

"If you are here to find Kate, Miss Damon," said Clive, "I would beg you to have a care. You speak of my future wife."

"Oh. That alters matters, I daresay. None the less, where is Kate? Is she," and Celia's colour went higher as she nodded towards the curtained arch, "in there?"

"No. Kate, so far as I know, has stepped out for a moment to Mivart's Hotel. She is staying at Mivart's, though I must tell you I did my best to persuade her to remain here with me."

"Mr. Strickland, for shame!"

"Madam, I see no reason for feeling shame. However, Kate has a room at Mivart's—"

"I am aware of that, sir. But she is not at Mivart's Hotel now. I have only just come from there."

"Then she must have gone to see Victor. Victor has rooms in Gloucester Place, Portman Square—"

"The place where my brother lodges," said Celia, her soft lips beginning to tremble, "is already known to me. His rooms are empty and not even locked. A note for his house-keeper, left in the sitting-room, tells us that he has gone to High Chimneys with (oh, gracious heaven!) his new mourning clothes. Kate is not there either."

Alarm cried its warning through Clive's brain as well as his heart, the more so as both Celia and Penelope brought with them the sense of dread and suffocation from High Chimneys.

"However, if it were only a question of Kate," Celia continued, "I should not have come here at all. It was *wicked*, Mr. Strickland; I should have left it to Victor or to Uncle Rollo. A sister's lot is to blush for her or weep for her; not, I do assure you, to persue her in any fashion."

"Miss Damon, we must find Kate!"

"*You* must find Kate. I love her, Mr. Strickland, and I—I," tears rose into Celia's eyes, "I can only trust that you love her too. No, thank you; I will not sit down."

"Where the devil is Kate?"

"Strong language, sir, is neither fitting nor proper at this time. Kate must look out for herself. She has made her b—— that is to say, she has chosen her course. It was not love which drove her. It was lust."

"Oh, be damned to such talk!"

"Mr. Strickland!"

"I said be damned to such nonsense, and I mean it. There speaks your father."

"Mr. Strickland, *you* cannot be expected to honour my late father. . . ."

"On the contrary, madam. I honour and esteem him more than anyone can possibly know. He had only one great fault: he was impossibly idealistic; he lived and died by those ideals."

"Amen to that, at least." Celia faltered a little. "It is the true reason why I am here. If only I thought I could trust you . . ."

Her voice trailed away. Clive's conscience awoke to trouble him.

"You can trust me," he assured her. "Forgive me for saying what I said. Are you sure you will not sit down?"

"For a moment, perhaps. No; I will keep my mantle."

As Clive set out a chair for her by the fire, Celia had become rather pale. She cast little glances at him, as though reluctant to speak and yet impelled by a determination more than would seem possible to her fragile nature.

"Mr. Strickland, I—"

"Yes?"

"There are those, including Uncle Rollo, who say a woman should not trouble herself with such matters as the question of who is guilty, who is guilty, who is guilty. I am sorry, but I can't help myself. The person who died was my father."

"And your stepmother too."

"Yes, I know. On Tuesday night, at High Chimneys, no doubt I behaved very badly. I was sure the—the murderer," Celia forced out the word, "must have been Georgette Damon. It was no secret (Cavvy hinted often enough!) that my stepmother had been behaving very indiscreetly, to say the least, with Lord Albert Tressider."

Clive picked up the tea-kettle from the hob, and set it forward on the fire. Instantly the kettle began to simmer; it must have been near boiling before, when someone—Kate, no doubt—had taken it off the fire before leaving.

Even in the midst of wondering about Kate, desperately trying to think where she might be, Clive was caught by his companion's words.

"Indiscreetly? Yes," he said.

"Often enough, as I told you," continued Celia, "Mrs. Damon had laughed when she spoke of Kate dressing in men's clothes. I said, and truly I thought, that woman must be laying a plan whereby she would kill my dear father to put the blame on Kate. And then—"

"Yes?"

"Last night Mrs. Damon herself was killed." Celia shuddered. "She was strangled. I wondered if I might not have been doing her some measure of justice."

"You have been, let me assure you. But what—?"

"Often and often," said Celia, "I have been called fanciful. Perhaps I am. There is no harm in it. It may even be of assistance. Mrs. Damon told the story of Kate in boy's clothes no oftener than Cavvy herself told it."

Clive straightened up from the fire.

"Good old Mrs. Cavanagh!" he said through his teeth. "Kind, loyal old Cavvy!"

"I beg your pardon?"

"No matter. Continue."

"Cavvy *is* loyal! Never doubt it. But Cavvy has sometimes strange notions of humour, as all our elders have. Cavvy seemed to mock me with that story no less than ever she mocked Kate. Or so I had thought for a long time, when

Cavvy spoke so much of the girl called Constance Kent. It has occurred to me to wonder . . ."

The kettle was simmering hard again, with a tap and rattle at its lid.

With a spasmodic gesture Celia rose to her feet.

"Oh, I should not have come here! I should not have evaded Uncle Rollo; I should have done as he advised, and taken more rest!"

"Miss Damon," said Clive, "what occurred to you? What did you wonder? What are you attempting to tell me?"

"Nothing at all! If I hurt you . . ."

"How can you hurt me?"

"It occurred to me, then," and Celia swept out a gloved hand, "that both Cavvy and Georgette might have been trying to warn me. To warn me, and in a certain fashion to warn Kate too, lest she encompass her own destruction."

"Miss Damon, I understand not one word of all this!"

"Nor do I, really. Thoughts go through the mind, and are with us in the dark hours. 'Hell is murky. Fie—!' Unless it becomes necessary, I pledge you my honour I will never mention to another person what I ask you now. Mr. Strickland, what did my father tell you in the study on Tuesday night?"

"I am not at liberty to say."

"Then am I at liberty to suggest?"

"By all means."

Celia drew a deep breath.

"May God pardon me if I do wrong in word or thought. But could these murders have been committed by Lord Albert Tressider? And could the one who planned my father's murder and helped him carry it out have been my own sister? Kate?"

XVII. THE HANDS OF
CELIA DAMON

"Kate? Are you mad?"

"Mad?" cried Celia.

The kettle boiled over.

As though from far away, Clive heard the splash and hiss as the bubbling water burst its confines and spurted out on the fire. Steam eddied up round him. Again the water hissed viciously on burning coals before Clive swung round, seized the handle of the kettle, and banged it back on the hob.

To one watching this, it might have seemed a threat from which Celia shrank back.

"Forbear!" she said, and stood rigid. "I tell you this only because you love Kate; or at least, in your man's way, you must have some fondness for her. *You* visited High Chimneys with that—that ridiculous proposal for my hand in marriage. How much did it mean? Kate has been wanton of thought since she was a child. Have you not good reason to know it now? You have heard Kate speak with intense dislike of Lord Albert Tressider. Did it not seem to you she protested too much?"

"Miss Damon . . ."

"Forbear!" said Celia. "When you and Kate ran away from High Chimneys, did you persuade her? Or did she persuade you?"

"Does it matter?"

"I hope not. But it might."

"How?"

"Will you listen to me," pleaded Celia, "and not strike me, if I tell you what is in my mind?"

"I have no intention of striking you, Miss Damon."

But Celia retreated, though she still faced him. Clive, his throat dry with rage and fear, stood at one side of the chimneypiece. Celia slipped behind the easy-chair, behind the table with its gleaming tea-service and its wooden paper-knife painted to resemble a heavy steel dagger.

Dusk had begun to gather in the sitting-room. Celia's back was turned to a wall of bookshelves; one door, to the entry on the landing, and another door to the dining-room, were both in that same wall.

Celia cleared her throat.

"My father's murder was carried out by two persons, a girl and a tall man, who planned it between them. No! Pray don't interrupt!"

Clive said nothing.

"Each person, the man and the girl, had his and her different part to play on different nights. Each wore the same kind of clothes, and we thought it was the same person. Each shielded the other from suspicion. That's why it was so horribly clever; that's why you couldn't suspect anything until you saw everything."

Here Celia lifted her voice.

"Penelope!" she called.

It was fully ten seconds, which can seem a long time, before the door to the dining-room opened. Penelope Burbage must have been sitting there in twilight. Her jowly, unpretty face appeared round the edge of the door.

"Penelope, dear!" cried Celia, still without looking round. "On Monday night, when you returned from the lecture at half-past eleven, you saw a figure on the stairs. Everyone else was abed. You told Superintendent Muswell yesterday, did you not, that it was really a woman in man's clothes?"

"And if Miss Burbage saw that," interposed Clive, before Penelope could speak, "what does it prove? She told me as much yesterday evening. I know all this! What does it prove?"

"Penelope!"

"Yes, Miss Celia?"

"Was it my sister you saw?"

"I don't know, Miss Celia. Before God I—"

"But you think it was?"

"I . . ."

"Go back into the dining-room, Penelope! Close the door."

Penelope fled. The door jarred and scraped against a warped frame as it slammed shut.

"Then it was a woman in man's clothes," said Celia, "who did nothing except stand there and show herself to Penelope. Why, why, *why* was that done? It was to make everyone think the prowler must be a man, a man from inside the house, because no person could have got in from outside that night.

"Oh Tuesday evening my father was murdered. Mr. Strickland, you saw the person who fired the shot; you saw him face to face; he let you see him. And you say, they all tell me, this person was a man. Is that true?"

"I said so, yes! I thought so at the time."

"Of course you did," cried Celia. "There were two of them."

Her eyes brimmed over.

"On Monday night, when no outsider could have entered High Chimneys, Kate played the part of a tall man. She stood on the staircase, high up, and seemed tall to Penelope standing below with a lighted candle. On Tuesday evening, when Kate was with me and had what they call an alibi for the time my father was shot, she had admitted a stranger to the house and locked a door or a window after he had gone. Did this never occur to you, Mr. Strickland?"

No reply.

140

"Please! Did it never occur to you?"

"It occurred to me that there might have been an accomplice. But—!"

"You know, you must know, Kate could never, never, never have fired a revolving pistol and hoped to shoot someone as my father was shot. She is not strong enough to hold a pistol steady. She needed a man to fire and kill. If any witness had ever seen that man inside the house, ever once glimpsed his face without a mask . . ."

Clive blundered back against the side of the chimney-piece.

"What is the matter, Mr. Strickland? Did *you* see him?"

"No!"

"Not at any time? Are you sure? Kate's lover, Lord Albert Tressider—"

It would be far from true to think that Celia did not or could not use cold reason. But this outpouring of words, as she stood white-faced on the far side of the table, seemed to come less from reason than from an inspired guess flying to the heart of truth. She hated it; she feared what she said; yet she screamed it aloud.

"Kate's lover, Lord Albert Tressider—"

"Miss Damon, stop! No more of this! Are you mad?"

"You shall not call me mad," and now Celia was paler yet in the black costume, "until you can say what else could have happened, or explain the how and the why. Kate's lover, Lord Albert Tressider—"

Abruptly Clive turned away.

Towards the front of the sitting-room, looking out over Brook Street from the parlour-floor above it, there were two large windows with many rectangular panes. Clive had not drawn the curtains, though he now saw the lamplighter must have come and gone unperceived.

A yellow glow of street-lamps shone up from outside. A four-wheeler rattled past towards Grosvenor Square. The red, blue, and yellow glass vats in an apothecary's window kindled spectral colours against the dusk.

Presently London would wake up at nightfall. Presently there would be crowds and a roar of noise towards Evans's, towards Astley's, towards the Alhambra. . . .

Clive, still in his greatcoat and sweating, went over blindly to draw the curtains.

The sight of the street was blotted out as wooden rings swung together. Clive remained there for a moment, his face turned to the curtains. Celia continued to talk, but he did not hear her.

141

The image of Tress, the ever-triumphant, being triumphant with Kate too . . .

Clive turned back.

"Miss Damon."

Celia ceased to speak, gloved fingers at her lips, grey eyes enormous. Only the thin singing of the gas-jet broke a hot silence.

"Miss Damon, you have accused your sister of conspiring in the murder of your father. There can be no denying that you present a case to be answered. Do you *wish* to believe this accusation?"

"No! No! No!"

"Then will you answer questions concerning it? Will you answer them calmly and rationally?"

"Yes! Yes!"

"How many times, to the best of your knowledge, has Kate so much as met Tress?"

"How can I say? Six times, eight times, when I was there. But how can I say what may not be within my knowledge?"

"Six times. Eight times. No more?"

"Mr. Strickland, you shall not bully me!"

"I will do what is necessary, madam. Have you any reason for thinking Kate is even interested in Tress, except for the somewhat curious reason that she says she is not?"

"I can only tell you—"

"Can you name one occasion when she has been alone with him?"

"No."

"Then why do you state so positively that he is her lover?"

Trembling, and yet with a firmness and strength of will belying her delicate appearance, Celia put down the sealskin muff on the table and straightened up. The wooden paper-knife in the shape of a steel dagger lay beside the tea-tray. Celia saw it. She caught it up, holding it longways in both hands.

"Miss Damon, be good enough to answer me. You state in so many words that Tress, Tress of all people, is your sister's lover." So much did this thought affect Clive that he stressed it and hammered it all the more. "If you were to testify under oath—"

"I don't testify under oath!"

"Then how can you say such a thing? Why?"

"I know what I feel. *Here.* That is all."

"Has Penelope Burbage identified your sister as being the woman on the stairs? Has she? Shall we bring Penelope back and ask her?"

Celia's fingers twisted on the paper-knife, which was long

and heavy despite its flatness. Clive took a step forward.

"You accuse—"

"I do not accuse. Never think it. I wish to be reassured; no more!"

"You accuse Kate and Tress of a masquerade. Each, at different times, wears the same type of clothes, so that each may have an alibi for the murder of your father. Why should Kate want to kill your father?"

"I don't know."

"Suppose Tress had made an offer for Kate's hand in marriage instead of yours? Would your father have objected or prevented that?"

Now Clive had gone too far.

He knew it.

Celia's eyes, bright in the fluttery gaslight, were fixed on him unwaveringly.

"You know my father would have prevented it, Mr. Strickland," she answered in a clear voice. "At High Chimneys, just before you went to speak with him in the study, you told Kate and me he had something to tell you concerning one of us. Which one? Mr. Strickland, what did he have to tell you?"

Silence.

"You taunt me again and again," said Celia in a loud but steady voice, "and say I will not answer your questions. Will you answer mine? Did you at any time, either on Tuesday or Wednesday night, see Lord Albert Tressider at High Chimneys?"

"No."

"That is a lie, is it not?" inquired Celia, gripping the paper-knife. "I see it in your face."

"Miss Damon . . ."

Celia's voice went up.

"Unless you believe my poor sister conspired with that man to kill my father, and perhaps destroyed his last will so that she might inherit money not due to her and leave High Chimneys forever, how else can you explain all that happened?"

Beyond the still-unlocked outer door of the rooms, past the dark little entry now on Clive's right, a board creaked and a footstep stirred. Somebody was listening.

Kate?

It could not be Kate. The footstep had been that of a man, and of a large and heavy man as well. From the corner of his eye Clive glanced towards the outer door. Celia neither heard nor saw.

"I ask for reassurance," she cried. "And I ask on more counts than those. Inspector Whicher—"

The footstep creaked again.

"What did you say of Inspector Whicher?"

"I have seen him twice," replied Celia, gripping the paper-knife harder and blinking back tears. "I saw him this morning at High Chimneys. But I saw him last August, when all of us except Cavvy were gathered there for my twentieth birthday. Mr. Strickland, has Kate never told you her childhood's ambition?"

"No, she has not. How could she? I had scarcely exchanged twenty words with Kate before I met her again on Tuesday evening. . . ."

"And carried her away on Wednesday. Poor man!"

"You were saying?"

"Her ambition was to be a dancer, like that woman Lola Montez. Until Cavvy slapped her so hard, when she mentioned it, Kate never spoke of the wish afterwards. But she was to be a dancer, and Victor was to be a general covered with decorations and leading cavalry-charges, and I was only to be a good wife and mother, as indeed I still wish. Why shouldn't I be? Why shouldn't I be?"

"There is no reason why you should not be, Miss Damon. But you were saying? Of Inspector Whicher?"

Outside in the passage, a floorboard squeaked sharply. There was no noise, however, when the outer door opened.

Dr. Rollo Thompson Bland, cat-footed despite his weight, stepped into the narrow entry. He was watching Celia, head turned partly sideways, his bright blue eyes fixed on her face.

Celia did not even notice him. But in just such a manner, Clive vividly remembered, Dr. Bland had looked at Matthew Damon from the doorway at the study not long before the murder; and at a time, according to Whicher, when Mr. Damon had been half out of his mind and not very clear about what he was saying.

A pang of dread touched Clive Strickland now. Dr. Bland remained motionless, and so did Celia.

"Inspector Whicher? Oh!" She drew her thoughts back. "He—he was announced when we were all at table for my birthday dinner."

"And what happened at the birthday dinner?" Clive asked in what seemed to him a very loud voice.

"Well! Georgette had been going on, as usual, about one of us getting married. All of a sudden my father got up and said none of us was going to get married without 'the truth being known first.' I don't know what he meant; he spoke in

144

the middle of simply a—a general discussion, that's all.

"At that very second, as though by a kind of dreadful stage-signal, Burbage came into the dining-room and said there was a Mr. Whicher, an Inspector of the Detective Branch at Great Scotland Yard, calling to see him. My father put his knuckles on the table and told Burbage to show Mr. Whicher into the dining-room. That astonished everyone still more."

Celia, her gloved hands twisting at the wooden dagger, swallowed hard.

"Inspector Whicher came into the dining-room. He said, 'Sir, I've brought you a letter from a dead woman, written nearly nineteen years ago; but I think you'll find it's good news.' Then he looked round at all of us. My father swayed as though he might faint. All he said was, 'Let us go into my study.' He spoiled my birthday dinner. It was hard to forgive him for spoiling my birthday dinner."

Once more Celia's voice rose piercingly.

"That's what happened. I can't say what it means; I don't know. But that's what happened. Don't you believe me? Ask Uncle Rollo! He was there. Ask—"

Dr. Bland took one step into the room.

"Celia," he said gently.

Except for Celia's gasp, as her large eyes turned sideways and she saw the doctor, a hush held the curtain-muffled room. Dr. Bland's brown moustache and beard stood out against a face far less florid.

"At Mivart's Hotel, my dear, they said you had inquired after Kate. They also said you had inquired after Mr. Strickland." The doctor's gaze moved round. "Ah. Mr. Strickland. May I ask, sir, whether you will be at home this evening after dinner?"

"No! That is to say, I shall not be at home."

"It is vitally necessary, sir, that I see you this evening."

"That's impossible. I am going to the Alhambra—"

"To the Alhambra?" repeated the startled Dr. Bland. He did not speak loudly, but there was a jump in his voice. "I tell you, sir, that I am obliged to see you. By your leave, then, I must meet you even there."

"And I tell *you*, sir, it is quite impossible. Don't come there! Don't try! In the meanwhile," and Clive still watched Celia's face, "did you hear what Miss Damon was saying?"

"Yes," replied Dr. Bland.

"What part of it?"

The doctor's rich voice, full and hypnotic, took on rounded utterance.

"If you refer to a murder-plot conceived and executed by Kate Damon and Lord Albert Tressider, I heard all of it."

"Is her explanation the true one?"

"Alas!" smiled Dr. Bland. "Or, rather, the word should be 'happily.' Celia is the best and dearest girl on earth. But she is sometimes fanciful. Happily (I say happily!) she was utterly mistaken from beginning to end."

Celia's expression changed. Dr. Bland stretched out his hand.

"You should not have left Devonshire Place, my dear," he said gently. "Come home now. Come home to your aunt and uncle. You are weary, Celia; come home."

What happened then, as Celia's expression changed still more and her grip tightened on the painted dagger, toppled Clive into a realm of nightmare.

"Celia!"

The girl did not reply. There was a splintering crack of wood, like the cracking of a neck, as she broke the paper-knife in two pieces and flung them across the room. Then, dodging under the doctor's arm, she ran out through the entry. Clive had a last glimpse of her face, wistful and tragic, before she ran out into the passage and frantically down the stairs into the dark.

XVIII. NIGHT-LIFE:
THE ALHAMBRA

Into the dark.

But it was light now, with the lines of misty gas-lamps stretching down towards the Regent's Quadrant and beyond to Leicester Square, as a hansom took Clive to a rendezvous that might mean everything or nothing.

He was late. Not too late, he hoped, but late all the same.

"No, sir," the liveried hall-porter at Mivart's had assured him for the sixth time. "Miss Kate Damon has not yet returned."

Nearly all theatrical performances commenced at a quarter to eight, or with a curtain-raiser which began at that time. The customary dinner-hour was at seven; but it was wiser to dine far earlier if you meant to be punctual.

Clive, taking dinner at Mivart's after hastily donning evening-clothes, could no more hurry the waiters than he could hurry the seven courses. He declined three of the courses. He declined four different wines so as to keep his head. But the steam of cooking rose, in the stately dining-room with the looped curtains of blue and canary silk. When he hailed a hansom in Brook Street, it was twenty-five minutes to nine.

Fortunately, the roar and crush of crowds had partly dwindled away into theatres or music-halls or public-houses. There would not be much yelling or carousing until nearly eleven; the streets lay reasonably clear. Even so . . .

"Cabby!"

The roof-trap flew open.

"Make haste! Twice your fare if we're at the Alhambra by a quarter to nine."

"Dunno, governor. 'Tain't easy. I'll try."

The long whip cracked as the hansom tried a less crowded approach by way of Piccadilly instead of Regent Street. The danger of delay was caused by omnibuses, which pulled up wherever a passenger elected to call out to the conductor and get down. If you were caught behind one of those, you could be infuriated and lost.

Furthermore, Clive decided as they passed the Burlington Arcade with its vast amount of female flesh, the West End seemed to be preparing for a large night. A new law, attempting somewhat to purify the night-haunts by forbidding the sale of spirituous liquors after midnight, could not be enforced; it only delighted robust souls by providing opportunities for breaking it.

Twenty minutes to nine.

"Cabby!"

"Doing me best, governor."

There was more delay in the approach to the Quadrant. Some few figures capered in silhouette outside the misted lights of the Argyll Rooms in Windmill Street. One or two pleasure-seekers, who had begun the evening's drinking too early or with too much enthusiasm, were being sick in the gutter. Clive's hansom jingled past the top of the Haymarket, followed by a mirror-glitter and a burst of song from the Sweet Daisy.

And he was going towards . . . what?

Celia had gone long ago. Dr. Bland had gone, without a word of explanation. Assuredly, he told himself, he would not meet Celia Damon in the promenade at the Alhambra. But then he would not meet Kate either.

The sickening shock he had felt, when Celia began her ex-

147

planation about how the first murder must have been committed, was in some degree passing off. He could laugh at it now, or thought he could.

How to understand, now, in what fashion he had been duped towards half-belief?

'If one thing may be accounted certain,' he said to himself, 'it is that the first murder was designed to throw the blame on Kate. Kate herself, even supposing her capable of it, which I do not for a moment—'

'Are you sure?' whispered a horned and devilish doubt.

'I am sure. Kate herself would never have dressed in a man's clothes and thereby done what she was bound to be accused of doing. Celia, at the beginning, knew Kate would be accused. Georgette Damon knew Kate would be accused. Whicher knew it too and bases his course of action on that belief.'

Once more Clive looked at his watch.

It was a bitter experience, he reflected, that in defending Kate against Celia's fancies he had been compelled to defend Tress. Tress, of all people! If only Tress could be the murderer, without in any way involving Kate, Clive felt he could die happy for one blow at that sneering face.

Tress could not be the murderer. Fulfilment of hopes is not granted so easily in this world. And yet Tress (now Clive felt sure of it) *had* been at High Chimneys on the night Georgette Damon was strangled. If only as one who had suavely blackmailed Georgette for her favours of love, Tress fitted somewhere into the pattern.

If only—

"Cabby!"

"Haven't yer got no eyes, governor?" demanded an injured voice, as the trap flew up. "Look where we are."

The hansom stopped. Music, even though muffled by the gaudy shell of the theatre, smote out into Leicester Square. It shook the twinkle of so many gas-jets, up there amid Moorish arches and minarets against the sky.

Clive paid the driver. An angry curiosity and beat of excitement, like the pulse of the "Oriental" music itself, carried him up through the red-and-white arch into the outer foyer. And Inspector Hackney of the Detective Branch tapped his arm as he passed.

Inspector Hackney, a face of uneasiness behind moustache and fan-shaped whiskers, spoke in a low hoarse voice.

"Sir, where in God's name have you been?"

"It's Miss Damon, Miss Kate Damon. She's disappeared—"

"Oh, ah. We know she has," agreed Inspector Hackney.

148

"But I'd rather you'd not question me, sir, or say aught about Miss Damon."

There had recently been an interval in that "Oriental musical spectacle," *L'Enfant Prodigue,* whose chief attraction was its large corps of ballet-girls kept by the management for purposes in addition to dancing.

Distantly in the shell, a female voice was singing above the music. Here in the foyer, under gaslight, the bare and muddy floorboards were strewn with orange-peel, prawn-shells, drifts of paper, and discarded cigar-ends.

Clive stared at Inspector Hackney.

"Where is Miss Damon? Do you know that too?"

"No, we're not sure. But don't worry."

"Don't worry, eh?"

"It's ten minutes to nine." The other's voice grew loud. "Buy a promenade-ticket, sir, and cut along upstairs. I'm here now, at risk of being seen, to give you an extra word from Whicher."

"Oh? What's that?"

"Stand by the third pillar from the oranges-and-sweets counter," said Inspector Hackney, sweating. "When Cherry gives you the signal, move to one side and take off your hat. But, whatever you see," and here the Inspector cleared his throat powerfully, "don't speak and don't interfere. Mum's the word, and don't move. That's all."

Then he had slipped out into the quiet square. Thirty seconds afterwards, with a promenade ticket, Clive went upstairs into noise, smoke, and confusion.

'This place,' he thought, 'is going to lose its dancing-license one day. And why should the police trouble about being recognized or even seen in such a mob?'

In the promenade, under dim gas-globes with glass prisms, about a hundred low-pitched voices seemed to be murmuring and laughing at once. A dampness of beer and brandy tinged the layers of tobacco-smoke. The women, more than half of them in evening-gowns with bared shoulders, posed on their best behaviour; when they could not wheedle a bottle of champagne from gallants in silk hats, they spoke refinedly for a tall gin and remembered not to call it a yard o' white satin.

"So I am too a clergyman's daughter! Don't you believe that?"

"Ho!"

"Stand up, Elvira! You're as drunk as Davy's sow. Stand up!"

"Thirty bob, madam? Come, now. I'd not pay thirty bob for—"

"Same again. Damn that barmaid. Same again."

" 'Swelp me, sir, and no bloody chaff! What I say—"

Heat flowed over Clive in a dizzy wave. Feet shuffled on mosaic tiles. The ballet-girls, in costume, hurried here when a particular turn was finished. Oriental draperies fluttered as one of them leaped, landed in front of Clive, and suggested that he was lonely.

"Fizz, ducky? I loves fizz. Buy us a bottle of fizz?"

"Another time, perhaps."

"Not now? Ducky!"

"No; not now."

He could not even see the counter at which Cherry sold oranges, prawns, and sweets. Pushing forward, he found the third pillar and established himself there while the low-voiced tumult swirled round him and the minutes ticked past.

Nobody paid the least attention to the stage. Seen as though through tunnels at the front of the promenade, operatic shadows swayed against a vast back-drop to the swell of music and cries from rowdy spectators on the bare benches in pit and galleries.

The crowd in the promenade shifted. Briefly Clive caught a glimpse of the bright-eyed Cherry behind the counter: no longer tipsy, it seemed, wearing a scarlet gown with a very low bodice, serving no one.

The gas-globe, somewhat brighter than this afternoon, shone above her head. It lighted Cherry's fair hair; it kindled colours in the great pyramids of oranges and in the heavy bottles of sweets. Then the movement of the throng blotted out the sight.

If he stayed by that third pillar, how could he see anything at all?

Mysteriously, the ballet-girls in their tights and draperies had begun to disappear. One of them laughed soundlessly amid the buffeting of noise and dodged away.

Clive backed away, moving first left and then right. Except by accident, the counter at the end of the promenade remained out of sight.

And it was nearly nine o'clock.

The music rose to crescendo and stopped amid spatters of applause mingled with jeering calls. Somebody whistled between his teeth.

Already Clive had removed his gloves to gain easier access to the watch in his waistcoat pocket. His greatcoat he also removed, draping it over one arm. He was about to remove his silk hat when he remembered the signal in time, and stopped. Not anywhere in the crowd was there a face he recognized.

"Walk-*er!*" yelled a voice.

"What is it?"

"Stage. Dance of the What-d'ye-call-'ems. Eh?"

A strolling lady in a swaying striped crinoline flicked her cigarette into the air. Another cursed as the glowing cigarette landed in the flowers of her hat. There seemed to be a fight or at least a scuffle on the edge of the tunnels overlooking the stage.

Once more Clive groped for his watch and opened the lid. It was just nine o'clock.

And, as he did so, a hand fell on his shoulder from behind.

Clive stood still.

Many times afterwards he tried to analyze his feelings in the second or two before he turned round to see who was standing there. But the attempt always failed, as it failed before he turned now.

"Dr. Bland," he said, getting a grip on his nerves, "I have no wish to be discourteous. But some hours ago, when I told you it would be impossible for me to speak to you here at the Alhambra, I meant exactly that."

The physician, in evening clothes and greatcoat, with white gloves and silk hat, wore an expression Clive could not read. It was a disturbing look none the less.

"No doubt you did," returned Dr. Bland, breathing noisily. "Under any other circumstances, I might have accepted your refusal. Now I can't. Believe me, sir! I can't. I have been searching all over the theatre for you, Mr. Strickland. If you will accompany me downstairs, where we may have some privacy . . ."

"For the last time, Doctor, that's impossible!"

"Sir, you must. The situation has changed."

"How?" Clive drew back. "Nothing has changed! If you guessed why I am here—"

"Sir, I think I know why you are here."

They were keeping their voices studiously lowered, though Clive could have yelled aloud.

"Doctor, trust my discretion. I won't betray you."

"About what?"

"About Celia Damon. You think, perhaps you've thought since the beginning, that Celia may be . . . how shall I say this? . . . a little disturbed in the balance of her mind. Whether that's true or not I can't presume to say. But that's what you have come to tell me, I suppose."

"*No*," retorted Dr. Bland, his eyes opening as he rounded the syllable firmly. "That is not what I have come to tell you. A few hours ago it might have been. Not now."

Suddenly Clive realized that he had turned his back to the counter at the far end, from which Cherry might have given a signal while he was not looking. He whipped back again, to find a transformation.

The crowd, for the most part, had begun to clear away. They were shuffling, pushing, edging shoulders and elbows towards the front of the promenade towards the stage, so that they could watch what was going to happen there. Their expressions were eager, perhaps a little furtive.

Very clearly, now, Clive could see straight towards the counter over which Cherry White presided. But Cherry herself, at the moment, was invisible. As Clive had noted that afternoon, two thin wooden pillars were in the way. Painted a dingy red and white, supporting the roof of the promenade, they loomed as obstacles in gloom.

In the orchestra-pit, distantly, the orchestra-leader lifted a baton. Cymbals smote in brassy clang on the opening bar of new music; the dreaming violins took it up with a wave of melody. And, as Clive ran to the right to look towards the counter, his companion seized his arm. At the same moment, he saw Cherry—alone.

"Doctor, for God's sake!"

"Mr. Strickland, understand me—"

"Understand *me*. I can't accompany you anywhere."

"Then I must stay here."

"This is a public place," Clive snapped. "Nobody can prevent you from staying. But you will have to address the side of my head while I watch that counter there. I tell you, I can't discuss anything with you now! I am waiting . . ."

"Exactly," said Dr. Bland. "You are waiting for the murderer, I fancy. That was what I wished to discuss." He drew a harsh breath, with something of bitterness mingled with defiance. "Very well!" added the doctor. "Shall I explain my guilt?"

XIX. NIGHT-LIFE:
AT THE THIRD PILLAR

Still Clive did not look round, though he felt Dr. Bland's eyes on him as he felt those of Cherry.

Under a swell of sensuous music from the direction of of stage, the promenade had gone almost silent. Two or three persons leaned against a bar-counter towards Clive's left, whispering and muttering together.

"You see, Mr. Strickland, I have always accounted myself an honourable man. You may well ask if it was the act of an honourable man to direct suspicion towards yourself, as confessedly I did when poor Damon was shot on Tuesday night. I had good reason, then and afterwards, to think you were not guilty. . . ."

"Thanks very much."

"Young man, this is not a time for sarcasm."

"Neither, apparently, is it a time for truth-telling."

"I tell you the truth," cried Dr. Bland. "Or I attempt to do so. You may remember when you were in the study with Damon on Tuesday evening, shortly before the murder? And I somewhat unceremoniously interrupted?"

"Yes. You interrupted with a question about Mrs. Damon's whereabouts."

"Tut, now! I was not in the least troubled concerning Mrs. Damon's whereabouts. Usually Damon sat there alone before dinner. Since I had not expected to find a stranger there, meaning yourself, when I had entered for another purpose . . ."

"What purpose? To kill Mr. Damon?"

The doctor's hand went up to his beard.

"Good God, sir, can you seriously think I would have killed my old friend? *I*, who have protected his family beyond all the limits of professional etiquette?"

"You said 'confess,' Doctor."

"But not to murder. Manalive! That is the very last—"

"Come, then!" said Clive. "Have you gone to all these lengths in order to confess you are innocent?"

"Of ill or evil intent, entirely so! When I was summoned to High Chimneys on the report that Damon's health gave cause for alarm, I was not happy. I did not think him mentally ill in any dangerous degree, any more than I believed it of Celia. Yet let me repeat that I was not happy. He had been brooding for three months, over what cause I did not know and have not learned even yet. Celia has always shared his tendency to brood. This past week it seemed at its worst in both of them."

"And so, when Mr. Damon was shot, you felt Celia must be guilty?"

"Believe me, sir: in my heart I never credited such a possibility!"

"But it *was* a possibility?"

"I—"

"It *was* a possibility?" demanded Clive, his own bitterness welling up. "You found it easier to protect Celia by blaming me?"

"That puts it too strongly."

"Strongly or not, that's what you meant?"

"In effect, perhaps it is. If you examine my every word and action in the light of what I say now, you will understand."

"Oh, I understand. That's not difficult. Still! You never really believed Celia was either guilty, or in any way out of her mind?"

"Never."

"In that case, Doctor, why did you lock the door?"

The exotic beat of the music took on a tempest of strength and passion. Dr. Bland's manner seemed to be affected by it.

"Door? What door?"

"The front door at High Chimneys. Kate and I, as we've been reminded so often, ran away from there last night. When we tried to leave by the front door, it was locked. According to Whicher—"

"Ah. Yes. Whicher!"

"According to Whicher," pursued Clive, staring at the counter behind which Cherry made an elaborate pretence of not seeing him, "you borrowed Burbage's key. You said there was one person you had better keep locked in the house. When you walked down the drive with Superintendent Muswell and Police-Constable Peters, you locked the front door behind you. Was it Celia you meant to keep in the house?"

"Alas! It was."

"If you never really thought Celia might be unbalanced and dangerous, why should you lock her in?"

"My dear young man, it was only to prevent her from wandering out of the house and perhaps doing herself a mischief when she had been given an opiate. The night before, you may recall, she wandered downstairs as soon as Kate left her alone and unattended? If I had fancied the poor girl dangerous to anyone at High Chimneys, do you imagine I should have locked her *in?*"

Clive opened his mouth, and shut it again.

"Well, do you?" asked Dr. Bland.

The watch was still in Clive's hand. It was three minutes past nine o'clock, and still no person had approached that counter at the far end.

"Listen to me, Doctor!" said Clive, still without turning his head. "Late this afternoon Celia escaped from your house in Devonshire Place. . . ."

"You will favour me, sir," interrupted Dr. Bland, "by not using the word 'escape.' The girl is not under restraint."

"Her own word," retorted Clive, "was 'evade.' She said she had evaded you. She came to my rooms, with Penelope Burbage, and you followed her trail. No, don't interrupt again! Whether Celia visited me in the hope of finding Kate, or only to tell me the story she did tell, the fact remains that she told me. She accused Kate and Lord Albert Tressider of conspiring to commit these murders. Kate's, she said, was the mind and strength of will which inspired the killings; and Tress, her so-called lover, was the man who carried them out. You heard that, Doctor?"

"I heard it. Agreed!"

"Can you deny you still believed Celia might be unbalanced?"

"No, heaven help me! I can't deny it."

"You admitted to me, in Celia's presence, that this theory was all nonsense from beginning to end?"

"I did."

"Then in what way has the situation changed? What are you doing here at the Alhambra? Why should you now believe Celia's sanity can't possibly be doubted?"

Dr. Bland's voice took on richness and power.

"Because I have seen your friend Whicher," he replied. "I have learned that Celia's theory of the murders, in all its essentials, was perfectly correct. We were wrong, Mr. Strickland, and that 'unbalanced' girl was right."

Clive thrust his watch into his pocket and spun round.

"That's a lie," he said.

"Oh, no. I pardon your offensive language, Mr. Strickland, in consideration of the overwrought feelings which give rise to such words—"

"It's a lie, I tell you!"

"Look at me, young man. Look into my eyes! Then be

satisfied as to whether I am in any way hoaxing or deluding you."

The dance on the stage, observed here only as the shadows of ballet-girls writhing against the background of a palace-hall, had grown faster and more abandoned. Cymbals smote hard. The presence of the audience could be sensed by its breathing; not from any sound or movement it made.

Cymbals smote again as Dr. Bland spoke.

"My professional experience," he declared, "should have given me wiser counsel. Neither poor Damon nor his daughter Celia was ever afflicted by the slightest mental instability. We slow-coaches, I suppose, are inclined to distrust keen minds when they are accompanied by nervous temperaments. They show us intelligence, and we call it lunacy."

Clive seized the lapel of the doctor's greatcoat.

"It's a lie, I say! You are not going to tell me that Kate—"

"I am going to tell you," said Dr. Bland, "precisely what Inspector Whicher told me not long ago. No more, sir, and no less. Will you hear it?"

"No!"

"Ah. Then you don't dare to hear it? You are so besotted with a pretty face and an immodest nature that you would close your ears to truth? And you welcome the excuse to attack a man far older than yourself? Release my coat, sir!"

"I welcome the excuse to attack someone, yes. I will release your coat when I'm ready. Meanwhile—"

"Mr. Strickland—!"

"Meanwhile," said Clive, "tell me what you have to tell me."

"Release my coat, sir! Will you make a public spectacle of yourself?"

"Yes. Say what you have to say, Dr. Bland, or I'll wring your God-damned neck too."

"This is intolerable!"

"So *I* feel. Now speak!"

"Inspector Whicher," retorted Dr. Bland, managing to keep some air of dignity even when he was held nearly up on tiptoe, "appeared to enjoy the prospect of an arrest no more than you do. But he, at least, can face truth."

"*Will* you speak?"

"Very well. I met him here when I was searching for you, and Whicher was also searching for you. It seemed you were late. He asked me if I had seen you. I said I had seen you towards six o'clock in your rooms. I told him Celia had visited you, with Penelope Burbage; that Celia had left your rooms, and that I had followed with Penelope.

"Mr. Whicher asked me whether any incident had oc-

156

curred to upset or delay you. I replied that Kate Damon appeared to have absented herself; otherwise, I said by way of jocularity, I could not think you had been upset or delayed by a mistaken theory of Miss Celia Damon.

"To my astonishment he wished to know what this theory was. Though I had no intention of telling him, he grew so strange of manner and even so threatening (there were three police-officers with him) that . . . well! In short, I was obliged to speak of it. His exact words afterwards were, 'Why, sir, there was never any doubt that Mr. Damon was killed by a man and a woman working together.'—Now will you let me go?"

Dr. Bland jerked back, but Clive held him.

"No! What else did Whicher say?"

"I was astounded enough, as you may imagine. . . ."

"Doctor, we'll take your feelings for granted. What did Whicher *say?*"

"He said—"

"Yes?"

" 'Miss Celia Damon's an uncommon clever young lady. She was dead right, you know, except about two things. It wasn't the woman who planned this scheme of murder; the woman was only a kind of assistant. She idolized the man, and was entirely under his influence, and couldn't help herself. . . .' "

The ballet-music throbbed and soared towards its end. Clive's grip, fastening more tightly, suddenly wrenched the doctor forward towards the third pillar.

" 'Idolized the man . . . entirely under his influence . . .' "

"Mr. Strickland," said Dr. Bland, in a cool and panting voice of fury, "I will say no more."

"By God, you will!"

"I will say no more," continued Dr. Bland, looking him in the eyes, "because it will not be necessary. I should like to think you have not entirely taken leave of your senses. If you care to look behind you at this moment, you can need no further proof of my truthfulness. You might even be constrained to apologize."

"What else did Whicher say?"

"Look!" said Dr. Bland.

There was something so utterly compelling about the doctor's voice that Clive glanced round.

It was only for an instant, but it was enough.

A woman had come into the promenade from the direction of the stairs. Though the gas-globes shone dimly enough above their glass prisms, there were so many of them that

Clive could distinguish her features without difficulty even at a distance.

She, on the other hand, did not see him. Frightened, repelled, seeming almost in a trance, the woman moved like a sleepwalker towards the northern end of the promenade. White-faced in the malodorous air, stepping as though gingerly over dirty mosaic tiles, she wore a boat-shaped hat and a short *sortie-de-bal* jacket over a low-cut evening-gown of scarlet and yellow.

And the woman was Kate Damon.

Kate, on her way towards the counter over which Cherry presided, passed the line of red and white pillars within half a dozen feet of where Clive stood.

"Well, young man?" said Dr. Bland.

Clive could no longer see Kate; the pillars obscured the view again. But his hand dropped from Dr. Bland's lapel.

He darted to the right; it was as well he did. Kate had gone in that direction too, her back to him. Cherry, casual and bright-eyed, seemed to be talking in an animated way to Kate. She was recommending some sweets, it appeared, in a heavy glass jar on the counter.

Removing the lid from the jar, Cherry made a gesture of invitation. Kate's own movement implied assent if only the other would make haste. Cherry smiled and was all eagerness. While Kate opened her reticule as though looking for small change, Cherry took up a piece of paper which she curved into a fairly large cone-shape, twisting its lower end together for a sweet-container.

Lifting the jar, Cherry poured it nearly full of loose sweets. She replaced the lid. Clive, some distance back, would never have seen the letter Cherry slipped in beside the sweets if he had not been on the alert for it. Nor would he have seen the packet of bank-notes Kate pushed across the counter.

Smiling, Cherry extended the improvised bag of sweets in her left hand. With her right hand, arm behind an elbow lifted so that it seemed almost vertical, she carefully patted her back curls.

The bait had been taken. It was the signal.

Clive, already well to the right, was supposed to remove his hat and signal someone else. But he did not do so. He stood motionless.

It was rather dark on the right of the counter, though not dark enough to hide the shape of a man lounging there. As Kate received the bag from Cherry, making sure the letter was there, the shape on the right moved with tigerish swiftness.

Round the side of the counter, in a plum-blue greatcoat

158

trimmed with strips of astrakhan, swept Lord Albert Tressider.

Tress, with a broad and cruel smile, his eyelids drooping, towered up over Kate. He extended his hand, inviting her to give him something. Kate jerked back, whirling round so that Clive could see her in profile.

Still he could not hear what Tress said, but the words were clearly spaced:

"I'll have that, my girl."

A scream froze in Kate's throat. She shrank back, whirling the paper cone away from him so that sweets flew out of it.

"No!" she cried very distinctly. Whereupon Tress, seizing her right wrist in his left hand, slapped her full across the face with his right.

Then it happened.

"*You so and so,*" said Clive Strickland.

He did not merely say this; he shouted it. The words tore through the thick and murky air, ringing above the last loud bars of music. There was not a man or a woman in the promenade who failed to hear; several spun round.

Tress heard it too. Momentarily he loosened his grip on Kate's wrist; he straightened up, turned to his left, and saw Clive coming at him.

Kate, still clutching the paper cone with the letter inside, may or may not have seen Clive. She had wrenched free, and was running towards the western side of the promenade. Tress, silk hat on the back of his head and greatcoat open, seemed in one triumphant instant to make up his mind.

Already Clive had dropped his own greatcoat. Sinuous, sneering, Tress slipped out of his. He flung it back over his shoulder and waited with his back to the counter.

"Well, well!" he jeered, in savage contempt. "The feller wants to fight, does he? He wants to *fight!* Let's see what he gets, then! Let's see—"

That was when Clive hit him.

The music of the dance ended in a shattering cymbal-crash as Clive hit him twice, with a left to the body and a right to the head.

Tress didn't or couldn't guard. The first blow landed in his stomach, cutting off breath and speech; the second, crossing with full body-weight behind it, caught him on the left side of the jaw and sent him spinning along the counter into a pyramid of oranges.

A yell of delight went up from spectators. Glass jars of sweets toppled and crashed amid falling oranges as Tress's weight struck the floor.

"Hoo-roar!"

"Go it, Jem Mace!"

"Make a ring! Make a ring!"

Tress, corpse-pale with wrath, shaken and winded but not much hurt, scrambled up to his knees. Clive waited. For a moment Tress breathed noisily; afterwards he screamed and charged. Clive took two flailing blows in the face. Then he broke Tress's nose with a straight left, doubled him up again with a right to the stomach, and sent him reeling into more oranges with a second left.

A stupefying roar shook the gas-flames in their globes.

> "Hit him on the boko!
> Dot him on the snitch!
> Wot a lovely fighter—!
> Was there ever sich?"

It was not Cherry who sang or chanted that. Cherry wasn't there; mysteriously, she seemed to have disappeared. The tearing noise of a policeman's rattle, which somebody had sprung across the room, pierced through the din.

Clive, panting and waiting, could not watch what was happening on the north side of the promenade. Shouts blattered round the counter.

"Mind yer eye, Jem Mace!"

"Got a bottle, he has!"

Tress gripped a heavy bottle of sweets by the neck, shifting it. The blood from his nose stained his mouth, which gaped wide as he charged for a second time. The bottle, swung up for a blow on Clive's skull, stopped in mid-air. Clive landed again on the smashed nose, and nearly broke his right hand when he brought the fist up under Tress's chin.

The bottle flew in a coloured arc and broke to pieces against a pillar, showering sweets.

"Mr. Strickland!" shouted a voice Clive knew.

Clive, with murder in his heart, paid no attention. Tress pitched face forward, unconscious on his feet, and dropped amid rolling oranges.

"Mr. Strickland!"

It was Whicher's voice. Clive tore his arm free of the detective's grasp and jumped back.

"Sir, for God's sake!"

"There's your murderer," yelled Clive, just stopping himself from a vicious kick in the unconscious man's ribs. "Pick him up. Get him to the station-house where he belongs. What in hell's name is the matter with you?"

"And what in hell's name," shouted Whicher, "is the matter with *you?* That's not the murderer."

160

Clive, his swelling and painful right hand cocked back, panted and stared for a long moment before he dropped both hands.

"That's not the murderer, I say," blurted Whicher. "We've got the murderer, sir, but it's no thanks to you we have. If he hadn't broken to pieces when Cherry faced him—"

" 'He'? Who is *he*?"

Across the promenade, someone was struggling and screaming in the grip of two plainclothes-officers.

"Come and see," said Whicher. "Stand back, the rest of you! Stand back!"

Clive plunged after him. The first person he saw, in the grasp of a uniformed constable, was Kate. The gaslights seemed to splinter and dissolve before Clive's eyes.

"No, no," groaned Whicher. "Your young lady had nothing to do with all this, as I kept telling you all the time. There! Look there!"

Someone screamed again. Clive saw the rumpled shirt, the staring grey eyes, the heavy light-brown moustache against a terrified and twisted face. . . .

"Victor Damon?" shouted Clive. "Victor Damon is the murderer? He killed his own father?"

Whicher snorted.

"He's the murderer, right enough," Whicher said. "But he didn't kill his own father. Easy does it, now! The lad you know as Victor Damon is Harriet Pyke's son."

XX. NIGHT-LIFE:
THE GAS BURNS HIGH

At two o'clock in the morning, in the dimness and hush of the house at number 23 Brook Street, a footstep sounded on the stairs.

Clive Strickland, pacing up and down the sitting-room, had just finished his fourth cigar. He threw it into the fire and opened the outer door to Jonathan Whicher.

"Where," Clive began, "is—"

"Stop!" Whicher said firmly, and pointed to a chair by the hearth. "Sit down, sir. Your young lady will be here at any minute. They had to have her testimony at Scotland Yard. After what happened at the Alhambra, you know, you can understand why they didn't care to have you there too. By your leave, now: sit down."

Both gas-jets, one on either side of the chimneypiece, were burning with low flames. Clive turned up both, so that they flared with broad high light. Then he did sit down.

"Victor Damon!" he said.

"Come, now!" Whicher's face looked old and ugly. "Can you tell me you never suspected him?"

Clive groped for words.

"I suspected him, yes, in the sense that I thought of him. But—"

"Ah! That's interesting! Why did you think of him?"

"In the first place, Victor spent two years at Sandhurst preparing to become an officer in the cavalry. But he never went into the Army; it was easier to lead a social life with plenty of money and any number of titled friends."

"Ah! That young gentleman's rather a painful kind o' snob, isn't he?"

"The most painful."

"And the one thing that would have fetched out the worst in him," inquired Whicher, "would be to have his position in life threatened? Eh?"

"Agreed. But—!"

"You thought of him, you were saying. Why?"

"When I was thinking of Lord Palmerston's death this afternoon," replied Clive, staring at the fire, "I remembered hundreds of press reports about Army officers using revolving pistols in the Crimea and the Mutiny and the American war. Victor could hardly have spent two years at Sandhurst without learning to shoot and ride.

"Well, somebody taught Kate to use a revolver and ride horseback without a side-saddle. Her father wouldn't have taught her that; and Dr. Bland, with his strait-laced ideas of how women should behave, certainly wouldn't have taught her. Victor was the only one left. Then, again . . ."

"Yes, sir?" prompted Whicher, as Clive hesitated.

"You weren't here this afternoon, of course, when Celia Damon outlined a certain theory about the murder of her father—"

"That theory! Oh, ah!" interrupted Whicher, nodding sagely. "Very clever young lady, Miss Celia. She hit the truth slap-bang in the middle, blow me if she didn't, except for two things. The man was the leading spirit in the game, not his woman accomplice. And Miss Celia applied it to the wrong two people. Otherwise," and Whicher looked awed, "blow me if she didn't hit truth slap in the middle!"

"Mr. Whicher, who *was* Victor's woman accomplice?"

"Come! You can guess that, can't you?"

"Perhaps I can. But—"

"Ah!"

"But I've been looking all the time for a *daughter* of Harriet Pyke! Damn it, Mr. Damon told me in so many words the unofficially adopted child was a daughter!"

"Sir," Whicher asked gently, "are you sure that's what he told you?"

"That's how I understood it, yes!"

"While we're waiting for your young lady, Mr. Strickland, suppose we go back over what you've already told me? Eh? And suppose we see if that's what the gentleman did tell you?"

"Well?"

Whicher was silent for a moment, his bowler hat in his lap, looking at the fire.

"At just before one o'clock on Tuesday afternoon," he continued, "you met Mr. and Mrs. Damon at the railway station on your way to High Chimneys. Who'd begged you to go there? Who'd begged and prayed and wouldn't take no for an answer? It was young Victor, wasn't it?"

"Yes. But—"

"Half a moment, sir. Now, then! At High Chimneys, the night before, there'd been a goblin or a prowler apparently doing nothing except scaring Penelope Burbage with a senseless prank of masquerading on the staircase. Mr. Damon took that pretty hard, didn't he, when no harm had been done? And who was the very first person he suspected?"

"Victor. Admittedly."

"Ah! When you told him Victor had been with you until two o'clock in the morning, he wouldn't believe you. He'd gone to London specifically to find out if it wasn't Victor. He questioned you in the train; he hammered at you until finally, or so it seemed—I say it *seemed*—he accepted your word.

"But did he really accept it? Think! You were mulling it over in your own mind, while he asked you what explanation *you* would give of the prowler on the stairs. A certain notion came into your head; you smiled; that didn't please Mr. Damon; and he walloped out in a temper to insist on knowing what your notion was. Now, then! What was this notion o' yours?"

Clive shifted in the chair.

"I wondered," he said, "whether the prowler might not have been a woman in man's clothes."

163

"So you did." Whicher nodded. "And do you think that same fancy didn't occur to Mr. Damon too?"

Clive, remembering the scene in the train and its atmosphere, was compelled in his heart to agree. But he did not answer.

"You wouldn't tell him," continued Whicher. "And that nearly brought on a row. He snapped at you. You told him you weren't going to High Chimneys entirely of your own free will. You said you had a proposal of marriage for his daughter. That's all you said. 'I promised as an act of friendship,' you told him, 'to put before you a certain matter concerning your daughter.'

"Now, then! His expression changed when he said, 'My daughter?' You then added, 'The truth was bound to come out sooner or later, and it had better come out now.' That was where the poor gentleman crumpled up as though he'd seen a ghost. Correct?"

"Yes! And naturally I assumed—"

"Stop!" interposed Whicher.

Above their heads, as the former Inspector leaned forward, the two gas-jets sang with broad, high flames.

"Just you put yourself in Mr. Damon's place, sir. Suppose the world thinks you've got two daughters, but one of 'em is really the tainted child of Harriet Pyke? Along comes a man you know, and says he's got a proposal of marriage for 'your daughter.' What question would you ask, sir? What's the very first question you'd ask?"

Clive sat up straight.

"I should ask which daughter," he answered.

"Exactly! Just so. 'Which of the two is it?' But Mr. Damon didn't ask that, did he? It didn't even seem to concern him. And, if he was bowled clean over at that news, there must have been a reason why the name of the daughter didn't matter twopence.

"Howsoever!

"Let's try to remember what you saw and heard at High Chimneys that same night. When you first overheard Miss Kate Damon talking to Mary Jane Cavanagh, Mrs. Cavanagh was taunting and bedevilling Miss Kate, as you noticed. It didn't take you long to realize that for some reason that old witch hated Miss Kate.

"Next day you learned Mrs. Cavanagh hated Miss Celia almost as much as she hated Miss Kate. Hated the children she'd nursed? Why? Next day, too, I told you Mary Jane Cavanagh was Harriet Pyke's sister, and must have been almighty thick with Harriet in the old days for all her pretenses of terrible respectability.

164

"But you'd had the essential clue in that very first talk between Mrs. Cavanagh and Miss Kate. While Mrs. C. kept on taunting, Miss Kate flashed out at her with a question that told a whole lot. 'Victor has always been your favourite, has he not?' Didn't Miss Kate ask her that?"

Clive nodded. In memory he could see the two women standing in the morning-room: Mrs. Cavanagh looking sideways, sly and malicious; Kate holding up the lamp with one hand, her other hand clenched at her breast, under the shadows of High Chimneys.

"Let's see if we can decide," argued Whicher, "what was in Mr. Damon's mind on Tuesday evening. He was shot before he got the chance to tell you; we'll never know for certain, in spite of Victor's confession. But most of it's very plain.

"He said he was going to tell you everything, and be at peace before dinner. In August, at High Chimneys, I overheard him tell his family what was on his mind; I heard him tell it before ever I handed him a nineteen-year-old letter from Harriet Pyke. He told you the same thing in the study on Tuesday evening.

"When *any* of his supposed three children arranged to get married, any of 'em at all, he meant to tell the prospective groom or the prospective bride about the adopted child. Didn't he say that in the study?"

"Yes," admitted Clive. "He did."

"And that's the key to the lock. He didn't like telling it. Thunderation, no! It was his family skeleton. The skeleton flew out of the closet and caught him unprepared, sooner than he'd ever expected; he'd said that too. But he was too honest not to warn anyone who married into his family, especially since he guessed Harriet Pyke's child, working with an old nurse who was Harriet Pyke's sister, had got out of control and might commit murder to suppress the secret.

"Think, sir. At six-fifteen on Tuesday evening he called you into the study. You were in the drawing-room talking to Miss Kate and Miss Celia. You'd just told 'em he meant to make some startling revelation; and you said, in all good faith, it concerned one of *them*.

"Well, naturally they were both a bit staggered-like. Neither of 'em ever dreamed there was a changeling in the family, whatever else they might dream or suspect. But Miss Celia, she immediately up and asked the proper question—'Which one of us?'—that her father hadn't troubled to ask.

"In you went to the study. Mr. Damon began telling you the story. The Good Lord knows he never meant to mislead you for one moment, though I warned you he did mislead

165

you. That gentleman never thought you could possibly mis-understand. . . ."

"Wait! Why couldn't I misunderstand?"

"Because he believed you knew," answered Whicher.

The two gas-jets sang thinly against a brief silence.

"He'd already given you a broad enough indication in the train. He'd ordered Burbage to lock and bar the whole house on the inside. If he suspected somebody *in* the house might try to kill him, where in thunderation was the sense of that?

"He was afraid of his supposed 'son': living in London, but able to get to High Chimneys at any hour of the day or night because Reading's a big railway junction with several railway-lines and any number of trains.

"If Mary Jane Cavanagh had been playing the 'man' on the stairs on Monday night, to give sweet innocent Victor an alibi for Tuesday night when Victor might try to kill him—

"Follow me, sir?

"Mr. Damon, naturally, was upset and half out of his mind. He didn't make himself clear when he quoted an ex-ample, like all lawyers, to point his meaning. 'Would *you* care' to marry the daughter of a vicious murderess?' The light went out completely a little later when he was talking half to himself.

" 'A daughter of Harriet Pyke,' he said, 'would have been born to sin in any case.' The important words were 'would have been,' he didn't say 'is.' Next: 'As it was,' he said, 'I hoped to avoid the worse eventuality.' He hoped to avoid murder; but, with the child a man now, he was afraid he couldn't. Finally: 'There would have been problems in any case; as, for instance, the necessity of telling the truth when *any* of the three married.' Is that what he said?"

"Yes."

"As you told me, sir, he was surprised enough when you said you didn't follow him. 'Oh, come! Pray don't pretend you misunderstand.' Almost the very last words he spoke were: 'You have guessed, of course, who has inherited these criminal traits?' You said you hadn't.

"And he was exasperated, as you might say, with an intelli-gent man like you. He couldn't see why it wasn't plain, much as he disliked to make flat statements about a devilish distasteful subject—"

"I can understand all that," groaned Clive. "But there was one statement he made that misled me more than anything else, whatever he may have meant by it. I thought the child *must* have been either Celia or Kate. He was speaking of what he called tainted blood; and he said, 'This very evening

166

I have seen Harriet Pyke's eyes and Harriet Pyke's hands.' Where could he have seen them?"

"In a photograph," said Whicher.

"I beg your pardon?"

"Didn't Muswell tell you about the photographs in his desk?"

"Hold hard! I do seem to remember—"

"In the desk in the study, where that gentleman always sat alone and brooded before dinner as a rare-good murder-trap, he'd got three large full-length photographs: one of each child. Thunderation! You can bet he'd have had a look at 'em while he was waiting for you. Or, at least, he'd have studied the face of the conceited, spoiled, selfish lad who was going to put a bullet in his head if he spoke out with the truth.

"Now, then: considering all the facts everybody has told you, and considering we've got Victor Damon's confession—"

Clive rose to his feet. His swollen right hand throbbed painfully, and he moved its fingers with difficulty.

"Mr. Whicher," he said, "we can consider what you like. But how in blazes could you fit together all these details from the very beginning?"

Whicher coughed.

"Well, sir," he said in a tone of apology, " 'tisn't hard to fit together the details if somebody's already given you the answer."

"The answer?"

"That's right. In the letter Harriet Pyke wrote to Ivor Rich. I told you, quite truthfully, I didn't know the name of Harriet Pyke's child. I told you I didn't know how old it was or where it was born. What I failed to say, in case I was wrong about who killed Mr. Damon, was that I knew the child was a boy. If the letter kept talking about the child as *he,* you'd have to be denser than I am to make a mistake."

"But look here! You agreed that there is no such thing as 'tainted blood.' "

"I did, sir. And I still agree. If you'll just turn you mind to Victor Damon's scheme—"

Whicher paused.

Against a hush of early morning, in the sedate old street, they could hear a four-wheeler draw up at the kerb. The street-door opened. Only a few seconds afterwards, Inspector Hackney escorted Kate Damon into the sitting-room.

Kate was very pale, though composed and even half-smiling. Whicher rose to his feet.

"Ma'am," he said gently, "I hope you don't blame me too

much. We could keep the news from you that your brother wasn't really your brother until such time as we nabbed him; after that, I thought, it wouldn't matter. You already suspected he was a wrong 'un and a murderer, just as Mrs. Damon did. So if you feel strong enough to tell Mr. Strickland one or two things . . ."

"That's not necessary," Clive intervened. His heart smote him as he watched Kate. "It's very late, my dear. I'll take you to the hotel."

"No!" said Kate. "I've hated myself, Clive, for not being frank with you. But I *couldn't*. That's to say, about Victor . . ."

Whicher set out a chair for her.

"What she means, Mr. Strickland, is that you're a good friend. And you thought that young fellow was a friend of yours. So she couldn't tell you, and neither could Mrs. Damon. Besides, Miss Kate was what you might call horrified; it wasn't easy to believe a brother of hers would kill her father and arrange to put the blame on her."

"It's not easy," snapped Clive, "to believe anybody would do it. How did all this begin? What made Victor think of it?"

"I made him think of it," said Whicher, swallowing hard. "I told you I was partly responsible. And now I'll explain why."

He spoke again when the rest of them were seated.

"The answer to *that*," he continued, biting the side of his forefinger, "is that Mary Jane Cavanagh wasn't at High Chimneys when I went there in August. Up to August, this year, Mrs. Cavanagh never told her darling phenomenon he wasn't the real son of Matthew Damon. She'd hinted, mind you, in case a day came when the spoiled son got a nasty shock. Victor knew there was something wrong, and spent bad times wondering about himself; he says so now, with buckets of tears for his plight.

"At Miss Celia's birthday dinner, just after Mr. Damon had mentioned an ugly secret he'd be bound to tell when any of the children married, *I* turned up with a letter from a dead woman. The long and the short of it is that Master Victor managed to listen when I was explaining the letter to Mr. Damon in his study.

"And Master Victor learned everything.

"But Mary Jane Cavanagh wasn't there at the time. Follow that; you'll see its importance.

"Hark'ee, now: this lad didn't *want* to kill anybody, any more than his mother ever had. Not by a long chalk! It mightn't be needful, if Mr. Damon never opened his snitch:

though there was always the question of how Victor could ever inherit money if he wasn't a real son.

"All in all, he was in an uncommonly bad state of mind.

"And then, not long afterwards, one of the swellest of swells—Lord Albert Tressider—wants to marry Miss Celia for the money her father will settle on her.

"Whatever young Victor does, he's bound to do something. He can't risk having his noble friend, who's contemptuous even of men that demean 'emselves by marrying actresses, learn who *his* mother was.

"Master Victor has a friend (yourself, Mr. Strickland) who's got him out of fixes before this. He can always persuade you to go down to High Chimneys and offer the proposal of marriage: suggesting his sisters are in some terrible danger, probably from a father who's a little insane, in case Mr. Damon tells you the truth.

"It's possible, just remotely possible, Mr. Damon may be so impressed by an offer of marriage from the noble gentleman that he won't say anything. You'll be the man to test that. But Mr. Damon mustn't even tell you; he mustn't tell *anybody*. If he starts to, Victor's all ready for it. Mr. Damon's got to die."

Again Whicher contemplated the fire.

Then he snorted.

"Naturally, as you said, you'd never have accepted that errand if you hadn't seen Miss Kate's portrait in Victor's rooms. But Victor never doubted his charm. He was so sure he could persuade you that he got it arranged before then. He and his wily aunt had several days' notice of Penelope Burbage going to a lecture in Reading on Monday night, so Mrs. Cavanagh could play the prowler while Victor got drunk with you to prove he couldn't have been within forty miles of High Chimneys.

"Thunderation! When women play men's parts on the stage, they don't deceive anybody and they're not meant to; there wouldn't be any men-customers in the audience if they did. Penelope was never meant to think the prowler was a man. But her short sight . . . well, there it is. All hand-tailored to prove it was Miss Kate."

Kate, her eyes closed, hesitated before she spoke.

"Mr. Whicher," she cried, "does Victor hate me as much as all that?"

"Ma'am, he doesn't hate you at all."

"But you said—"

"No, ma'am. He's rather fond of you, as far as he can be fond of anybody. He didn't teach you to ride and shoot with

169

that notion. But your wearing boy's clothes on a well-known occasion, and Mrs. Damon's talking about it too much, gave him an uncommon neat idea. By the time *he* came to High Chimneys to kill his 'father' on Tuesday night, he and Mary Jane Cavanagh thought it'd be taken for gospel the goblin was a woman.

"Victor's short and slight. He would be taken for the same woman, he thought. Naturally there were two sets of clothes, Miss Kate! One for Mrs. C. to wear and then hide in your room with a cut-off stocking-top for a mask. And one for Victor, who could wear 'em when he went to High Chimneys, and was admitted through the conservatory door by Mrs. C.; they wouldn't make anybody suspicious anywhere; nearly every man in England's got a costume like that.

"Neither he nor his aunt wore shoes. That was partly to avoid noise, and partly so dirt wouldn't be tramped into the house if it happened to be a damp night. No outsider, d'ye see? *You.* As for Mary Jane Cavanagh . . ."

Whicher scowled and looked at Inspector Hackney.

"Hackney, my lad," he asked, "have they telegraphed from Reading yet? After they arrested Harriet Pyke's sister?"

"Ay; they've telegraphed," growled Hackney.

"But the woman hasn't confessed, I'll lay you a bender? No; I didn't think she would. She's a hard nail. Not like the young 'un who planned it all and then broke like a rotten board when the law tapped him."

"Why is it so important," demanded Clive, "that Mrs. Cavanagh wasn't at High Chimneys when you met the rest of the family?"

"Because Victor, who *was* there, didn't remember my name and never troubled to say who I was. I'd been announced as an Inspector of the Detective Branch. Mrs. Cavanagh, when he told her about it, thought I was an official detective. She never associated the official detective with the cove she'd heard of: me.

"Got that, sir? When household gossip said Mr. Damon was going to London to see me, she imagined it was about Mrs. Damon and the gentleman you call Tress. She never hesitated to threaten Miss Kate with my name, even before the murder'd been committed." Whicher glanced at Kate. "Begging your pardon, ma'am: but you knew it was about your so-called brother, didn't you?"

"Yes. I—I as good as told her so, when Mr. Strickland was listening. I told her there was a man in the house on Monday night, prowling up and down. Of course Victor wasn't there that night, but I thought he was."

170

"And so Master Victor killed the gentleman who'd done so much for him," said Whicher.

He was silent for a moment.

"We know now," he went on grimly, "he brought a pistol to High Chimneys. His aunt stole Mr. Damon's revolver, to make it seem more of Miss Kate's work. His aunt tore up Mr. Damon's will. That's another pointer. Under the law as it stands, a daughter can't inherit money unless it's specifically allowed her in a will; a son can. You're a lawyer, Mr. Strickland; didn't that occur to you?"

"It occurred to me when Celia mentioned it long afterwards, yes. Not until then."

"So he killed Mr. Damon; oh, ah! It would all 'a' gone according to plan except for two things. First, Victor's short and slight; but he's not effeminate; you saw him in the goblin's clothes, and knew it was a man. Second, Mrs. Damon was in the train to Reading that afternoon; she guessed the dirty work, whatever it was going to be, would incriminate Miss Kate. When Mrs. Damon nipped away from High Chimneys that evening, because a noble lord was blackmailing her and she had to meet him in London, she took the clothes that were meant to hang Miss Kate.

"Sorry, ma'am, but that's a fact! And then, next day, Victor saw her in Oxford Street.

"He did more than see her, you know.

"As he admitted in the rum and stupid note he left for Mr. Strickland at my office, he followed Mr. Strickland and Mrs. Damon. He met her. He told her Mr. Damon had been shot; up to then he never dreamed she'd twigged him.

"What she let fall, when she heard her husband was dead, his confession don't say. But Victor knew he might be a goner if he let her speak. In that tomfool's note he left at my office he said he was taking her to the train; he couldn't have taken her to the train if he nipped up and left a note for you.

"No! It was only to show he was staying in London, when he meant to go down to High Chimneys again. That's where *I'm* to blame again. Mr. Strickland, when you talked to Victor in London on Wednesday morning, didn't he do his best to throw suspicion on a woman?"

"He did."

"Also, as you told me from overhearing Mrs. Damon talk to the manager of the Princess's Theatre, Mrs. Damon knew the guilty party was a man. She said some person ought to be condemned to the treadmill, before she'd even heard about a murder; and we don't condemn women to the treadmill.

I couldn't have asked for many more clues about Victor. If I'd gone to High Chimneys on Wednesday afternoon, as I'd intended—"

Whicher stopped. He rose to his feet, all bitterness.

"But, oh, no!" he said. "That's not mysterious enough, or devious enough, for Johnny Whicher. I'm the dealer in short-cuts, and dummy arrests, and hocus-pocus to get a confession. Thinks I to myself, 'I'll borrow that letter of Harriet Pyke's from the lodginghouse-keeper in Pimlico. I'll send Cherry White to the young fellow's lodgings, offering to sell the letter; I'll let Cherry play on his nerves for a few days or a week; and then I'll have Peelers ready to step in when Cherry hands over the letter with a close friend of Victor's looking on.'

"It's the same scheme we did use, except that it had to be done next day and risk failure by acting too soon. And, mark you, it succeeded.

"Howsoever! I should have seen that Victor Damon, after he'd talked to Cherry on Wednesday afternoon, would hare off for High Chimneys that evening. But I didn't, and I let Mrs. Damon die. You can guess what Victor did, can't you?"

Clive made a savage gesture.

"In many ways, that may be . . ."

"Sir, sir! It was easy for him to get into the house by the front door. But he hadn't warned Mrs. Cavanagh he'd be there; he hadn't taken counsel with a wiser head. If he had any doubts about killing Georgette Damon, he forgot 'em when he heard Mrs. Damon saying what she did say.

"He could kill, but he couldn't leave the house again—what with the windows stuck, and the front door locked by Dr. Bland, and a mort o' people in the servants' hall watching the back door—unless he left by way of the conservatory and left that door unlocked.

"That's why you and Miss Kate found the temperature lowered in the conservatory when you two ran away; the door had been left partly open. I told you, among other things, your theory about Mrs. Cavanagh being guilty was right as far as it went. I told you the murderer had left High Chimneys last night.

"Mind, I couldn't possibly have known Lord Albert Tressider was there to get material for blackmailing Master Victor too. . . ."

"Blackmail? Tress?"

"Well, sir, didn't he blackmail Mrs. Damon in another way? That gentleman's a beauty. He wants everything he can get, in every way.

172

"According to Victor, he turned up at Victor's rooms when Cherry was there yesterday afternoon. At the time Victor didn't think he'd heard anything, but Mr. Tress is nobody's fool. He's not likely to tell us what he saw when he followed Victor to the country. If he could get his fives on that letter, to hold over the head of an unstable young 'un who presumably would now be a very wealthy young 'un, he needn't demean himself by marrying Celia Damon after all.

"In any event, you and Miss Kate here ran away to London. I had to set the trap immediately. And I thought it would catch the weasel. The danger—"

"Yes?" Clive prompted. "The danger?"

Whicher, standing by the chimneypiece, glanced round at Kate.

"The danger was that Victor mightn't go himself to get the letter. He might send a deputy. And Miss Kate was in London. What's more, she was alone in these rooms because there was nowhere else to send her except Mivart's Hotel, where she wouldn't go. If Victor *should* turn up there to see you, and throw himself on her mercy, and tell her the whole story, and ask her to get the letter for him . . . eh?"

Now it was Clive who sprang up.

"You thought he'd dare do that? To the girl he was trying to get hanged? And Victor thought he could persuade her?"

"He did persuade her. You write devilish good stories, Mr. Strickland, but you don't understand much about criminals. That's the answer."

"In what way is it the answer?"

Whicher looked down at the fire.

"The Victor Damons of this world, you know, think they can persuade anybody of anything. Most often they do manage it. They never think they're in any real danger, they never think *they* can hang from a gallows, until they feel the bracelets on their wrists. They've got too little imagination, and then too much. That's all."

Kate spoke out strongly.

"He didn't persuade me," she said. "It was only that I couldn't bear it any longer. When *he* told me he wasn't my brother, I was ready to help him because it wouldn't be helping him; I knew it would be leading him into a trap. Clive, can you forgive me?"

"For what?"

"For letting him be taken? And bribing the hall-porter at Mivart's to say I hadn't been there?"

"But there's nothing to forgive!"

"Isn't there?" Kate shivered. "When I went into that promenade, I was horribly frightened. I was afraid he wouldn't be following me to watch from a distance, though he said he would."

"Well, ma'am," observed Whicher, "it was a risk we took too. The betting was in favour of his following you; I thought he couldn't help himself. And by that time Hackney had an officer watching both of you.

"Nothing was certain. Mr. Strickland was supposed to take off his hat when Cherry gave the letter to somebody at the counter. That would give the signal to the Peelers; we were hidden where whoever got the letter couldn't see us. We couldn't ha' foretold his friend Tress would turn up.

"So it's almighty lucky Master Victor took up a position not far from the Peelers when you ran to him with the letter, and Cherry followed and denounced him as she was supposed to do. Without that confession . . ."

Whicher rubbed his jaw, disturbed at what he remembered.

"You see, sir," he added to Clive, "there was one other matter I didn't tell you, though Hackney mentioned it when we were at the Alhambra this afternoon.

"It was easy to remember that nineteen years ago Mr. Damon lived at a place called Fairacres, near Doncaster in Yorkshire. It was easy to go to Scotland Yard yesterday and ask 'em to telegraph to the Doncaster police.

"They got the news from Yorkshire, right enough. Mr. Damon's real children were Miss Celia, born in August, 1845, and Miss Kate, born in July, 1846; their births were registered in the parish. What's more, the clergyman who baptized 'em is still alive. He remembered how a Mrs. Mary Jane Cavanagh, a young widow, came there as nurse just over twenty years ago and not over twenty-one years ago, as she's claimed since.

"Harriet Pyke's child, that proved, was nearly two years old when Mrs. Cavanagh was put in charge of the boy. Mr. Damon didn't leave any record except an account in his will. If Mrs. Cavanagh destroyed the will, everybody was used to accepting Victor as a real son; it'd be done so quietly that nobody would have ever doubted. We could have shown he wasn't a real son, to be sure, but proving murder was a different matter if we didn't get a confession. Tell me, sir: if you thought the child was a daughter, which of the young ladies did you imagine was the one?"

"I thought it was Kate."

"Ah," murmured Whicher.

"Me?" cried Kate. "Why?"

"Because Celia and Victor both have brown hair and grey eyes. Harriet Pyke was described as dark, and you're dark."

174

The faintest shadow of a smile hovered round Whicher's mouth.

"You won't see very clearly, sir, if you maintain two people are brother and sister just because they have brown hair and grey eyes. Thunderation! You might as well prove Master Victor was Harriet Pyke's son because he's got a taste for booze too."

"Clive!" exclaimed Kate. "You thought. . . . But didn't it horrify you?"

"No. I can't say it did. What does rather horrify me," Clive spoke doggedly, "is this question of tainted blood. I could have sworn the murderer, whoever else it might be, wasn't Harriet Pyke's child at all. Are we reduced to believing that Victor shot one person and strangled another because he was the son of a woman who did the same?"

"No, by George!" Whicher said sharply. "But you *can* inherit an unstable temperament; we all know that. And then, if you've got solid motive enough, and you learn you're the son of a murderess and believe you're going to act like it anyway . . ."

The hush of the drugged hours, of suicides and bad dreams, held the town outside. Whicher went to one of the windows overlooking Brook Street. He threw back the curtains.

"It could apply to millions of people sleeping out there," he said. "I'm not what you'd call an educated man, sir, but a cove named Hamlet puzzled about that before any of us was born. It's all in what you think you are, sir. Thunderation, yes! It's all in what you think."

The End

NOTES FOR THE CURIOUS

This novel attempts to present, through the medium of the formal detective story, an accurate picture of life at several levels of society in the year 1865. It may vary from accounts with which the reader is familiar: chiefly from those of Victorian writers themselves, who were prevented by social taboos from telling the whole truth even when they wished to do so. Therefore I must beg leave to offer documentation.

With the obvious exception of High Chimneys and one other place, every scene in the novel is set at a real address in a real street. In some parts of London the topography has changed almost as much as the manners and customs. But these events are seen through the eyes of Clive Strickland, who is a man of his time and has not the gift of prophecy. He cannot be expected to read the future in any sense. It would be the height of clumsiness for the author to have intervened, explaining on every occasion what it was that Clive didn't know. That is another reason why I beg the reader's indulgence for these notes.

1 TOPOGRAPHY

With the aid of *Wyld's New Plan of London* (published by James, Wyld, Geographer to the Queen, 457 West Strand, June, 1866), and H. B. Wheatley's *London, Past and Present* (London: John Murray, 3 vols., 1891), we can reconstruct the background exactly as it was in 1865.

It must be remembered that Piccadilly Circus did not yet exist. Neither did Shaftesbury Avenue. A part of their site, between Oxford Circus and the top of the Haymarket, was occupied by a disreputable district known as the Regent's Quadrant. For remarks about the Quadrant, see Mr. Serjeant Ballantine's *Some Experiences of a Barrister's Life* (London: Richard Bentley & Son, eighth edition, 1882). The Argyll Rooms stood on the site of the Trocadero. Oxford Circus, at that time, was called the Regent Circus.

Only one other main change affects the novel. Charing Cross Road, which runs from Oxford Street south to Trafalgar Square, did not exist either. A part of its site was then occupied by the Crown Street mentioned in chapter eight.

The opening of Charing Cross Road and Shaftesbury Avenue, in the eighteen-eighties, was a desperate bid to abolish some of the worst slums in the world: the district of St. Giles's, which no longer exists as a separate entity. Today, if you stand at the top of Charing Cross Road and look down the little street bearing southwards to the left, you will see all that remains of St. Giles's High Street, with St. Giles's Church in the distance.

2 POVERTY, CRIME, PROSTITUTION

The nightmare squalor of St. Giles's is depicted in several novels by Charles Dickens. More particularly, for our own purposes in this story, Dickens wrote a factual article, *On Duty with Inspector Field*, in the issue of *Household Words* for June 14, 1850; it may be found in any edition of *Reprinted Pieces*. The account begins at St. Giles's police-station; it explores, with vivid detail, the night-scenes in the shadow of St. Giles's Church and on the slum-fringes of Oxford Street after dark.

Even Dickens, however, did not dare tell all the truth about economic conditions in the eighteen fifties and sixties; Mr. Podsnap and his kind said they did not exist. For the whole truth we must try Henry Mayhew's *London Labour and the London Poor* (London: Griffin, Bohn and Company, 4 vols., 1862).

Mayhew's four volumes, a compilation by various writers of which he was editor, will turn unsqueamish stomachs today. The first three were originally published in 1851; the last, the "extra" volume called *Those Who Will Not Work*, published in 1862, is the one which mainly concerns us. Since squalor and degradation are not necessarily interesting no matter how pitiable, and since night-life and prostitution are always interesting no matter how squalid, emphasis in this novel has been placed on the last two. They are presented exactly as they existed, without exaggeration or prettification.

When first published, it would appear, Mayhew's work did not blow up the polite roof because it would have a limited appeal to the casual reader. Even in our times, anyone except a student may well quail at the prospect of wading through four volumes of which each contains five hundred large pages of small print in double columns.

But a knowledge of the fourth volume is necessary for an understanding of Victorian night-life. The curious in such matters, who would learn without going blind over small print, are recommended to *Mayhew's Underworld* (London: William Kinder & Co., 1950), an abridgment admirably edited and arranged, with a pertinent introduction, by Peter Quennell.

3 NIGHT-LIFE, REPUTABLE AND OTHERWISE

Mayhew's accounts must be amplified by others which followed. In 1865 the authorities were growing seriously alarmed by a widespread and uproarious night-life which extended over an area stretching (on today's maps) from Oxford Circus to Piccadilly Circus, and from there to Leicester Square, with all the fringes round about.

In 1865, with the law forbidding the sale of liquor after midnight, began the clean-up campaign which culminated when the Alhambra Music-Hall lost its dancing-license in 1870. The excuse for revoking it was the dancing of the can-can in a musical extravaganza. One present-day writer has expressed wonder at this, pointing out that the Prince and Princess of Wales had watched the can-can at the Lyceum without interference or protest on anyone's part. But by 1870 the authorities were ready to seize at any excuse.

Engravings of the Alhambra as it looked then will be found in H. G. Hibbert's *Fifty Years of a Londoner's Life* (London: Grant Richards, Ltd., 1916), together with lore about the curious night-haunts in Leicester Square and a full list of all shows at the Alhambra from 1864, the beginning of Strange's management, to the outbreak of World War I.

Two sharp clarifications, however, must be made here. First, the Alhambra ballet then must not be confused with the decorous post-1870 Alhambra ballet of later years; and neither must be confused in any sense with the classic ballet of today.

Second, with one or two exceptions, all theatres offering stage-plays presented a drama so respectable and indeed so painfully moral that you could have taken your grandmother to see it.

Unless you occupied one of the boxes, it is true, your grandmother would have been infernally uncomfortable. In 1865 Mr. and Mrs. Bancroft took over the management of a little theatre in Tottenham Street (on the site where the Scala now stands) and rechristened it the Prince of Wales's. Only in subsequent years did the Bancrofts introduce such luxuries as carpets on the floor, orchestra stalls which threat-

179

ened to abolish the pit, and other refinements we find described in Marie and Squire Bancroft's *Recollections of Sixty Years* (London: John Murray, 1909). Even then the theatre was often a rowdy place.

For instance, Charles Reade's dramatization of his own novel, *It Is Never Too Late to Mend*, opened at the Princess's Theatre, in Oxford Street opposite the Pantheon, on October 4, 1865. Some account of the near-riot on the first night is given in Bernard Falk's *The Naked Lady* (London: Hutchinson & Co., 1934).

The last-named book has a misleading title. It is a biography of Ada Menken, who in October, 1865, was appearing at Astley's in *Child of the Sun;* and who, rumour to the contrary, did not appear naked or anything like it in *Mazeppa* earlier during the same year. Being a friend of Charles Reade, she was with him at the first night of *It Is Never Too Late to Mend*.

Despite protests from the audience at "too realistic" prison scenes in a rather naïve story, the play had the (for then) amazingly long run of 124 nights. It was what current slang called a "screamer," or success; had it failed, the world of fashion would have described it as a "gooser."

Please restrain the ribald comment which already has crossed your mind. When a singer was received with disfavour by the audience, a critic could write, "She was goosed last night," and mean only that the lady had failed to please. All slang terms in this novel have been verified against a contemporary authority, *The Slang Dictionary, or, The Vulgar Words, Street-Phrases, and 'Fast' Expression of High and Low Society* (London: John Camden Hotten, 1865). From this book comes the description of a FAST young lady quoted in chapter eight.

Let us return to the theatre, since there is a comparison here with Victorian life. In addition to being uncomfortable and rowdy, the stage had few good plays and no first-rate plays.

If the novelist laboured under many restrictions, the playwright was so much more fettered and even strait-jacketed by Mrs. Grundy that he had almost lost touch with human life. This was not so much the fault of Victorian life; it had been going on since the eighteenth century.

Consider what happened when *The Moonstone*, Wilkie Collins's inoffensive detective novel, was dramatized at the Olympic Theatre.

In the original story, centered round the theft of the great orange-yellow diamond, Franklin Blake is loved by two women: the heroine, Rachel Verinder, and the deformed

180

maid-servant, Rosanna Spearman. All are on an edge of nerves for fear the diamond will be stolen by a group of sinister Hindus. . . .

(Sorry; this was a new idea in 1868.)

. . . and Franklin Blake, who has been sleeping badly, angrily swears nothing can make him sleep. The doctor, to teach him a lesson, secretly puts opium in his coffee. Still alarmed in his secret mind, Franklin Blake walks in his sleep and removes the diamond to a different hiding-place. The two women, who see him, believe he has stolen it knowingly, and are concerned to protect him. But Blake doesn't know he is the thief and in all innocent fairness can tell his own story in the first person: thereby anticipating and bettering *The Murder of Roger Ackroyd* by nearly sixty years.

This wouldn't do for the stage.

The hero must not take opium, even when he doesn't know he is taking it. In the play he goes sleep-walking after an indigestible dinner, carrying things to the edge of farce. A servant-girl must not cherish an unholy passion which can never be crowned by marriage; and so Rosanna Spearman, the most moving and effective character in the book, is cut out of the play. These are not the only differences, but they will do.

If such a degree of "niceness" seems incredible, read Dutton Cook's *Nights at the Play* (London: Chatto & Windus, 2 vols., 1883), containing selected theatrical notices by a leading dramatic critic during the sixties and seventies.

The playwright, for the most part, was reduced to bombast and fustian. Though the script of *It Is Never Too Late to Mend* is not available, allow me to quote some speeches from *Masks and Faces,* a very popular play which Charles Reade wrote in collaboration with Tom Taylor.

The central character is Peg Woffington, Garrick's girlfriend, beloved of audiences because she could be shown as a noble-minded if abandoned actress destined for a no-good end. Here she speaks to Mabel Vane, the heroine:

"Such as you are the diamonds of this world! Angel of truth and goodness, you have conquered. The poor heart which we both overrate shall be yours again. In my hands 'tis but painted glass at best; but, set in the lustre of your love, it may become a priceless jewel."

Then, in a later speech, Peg really hits it for six:

"When, hereafter, in your home of peace, you hear harsh sentence passed on us, whose lot is admiration, rarely love; triumph, but never tranquillity, think sometimes of Margaret

181

Woffington, and say, 'Stage-masks may cover honest faces, and hearts beat true beneath a tinselled robe.' "

Thus the mid-Victorian stage—like mid-Victorian life—might be uncomfortable, at times rowdy, and hiding much that mustn't be seen; but at least it expressed the most high-flown sentiments in public.

4 KEEP ALL THINGS DARK

The above is not written to mock or deride those who in so very many ways were our betters.

On the contrary, with Dickens and Thackeray, this age produced the two greatest English novelists of all time; and its poets have not been matched since then. The triumph of the Titans lies not in what they said but how they said it.

When Thackeray cuts loose with a denunciation of George the Fourth, all he is really saying (as the Victorian lady observed at a performance of *Antony and Cleopatra*) amounts to: "How different from the home life of our own dear Queen!" But he says it with such effective rhetoric that we are swept away.

The Titans, who were realists and knew their audience, knew also that they must conform to the pressure of public opinion—outwardly, at least—in their lives as well as in their books.

In 1857, when Charles Dickens was over forty-five years old, he fell violently in love with an eighteen-year-old actress named Ellen Ternan. It played havoc; it wrecked his already tottering marriage; it was not a happy relationship even after she had become his mistress.

His family and his friends knew of this relationship. And yet it was never so much as mentioned by any biographer until 1936, or dealt with at length until 1939. For a full discussion of this point, see Gladys Storey's *Dickens and Daughter* (London: Frederick Muller, 1939) and Edgar Johnson's monumentally detailed biography, *Charles Dickens, His Tragedy and Triumph* (New York: Simon & Schuster, 2 vols., 1952).

Public gossip would have ruined him. The question is not what we think of this relationship, but the problem of a social organization which could smother all mention of it during Dickens's lifetime and for nearly seventy years after his death.

Though Thackeray had no secret of this kind, he railed frequently at his lack of freedom to write as he pleased. Lesser lights, including Wilkie Collins and Charles Reade, paid only perfunctory lip-service to Mrs. Grundy in their private lives. Not all people, of course, were would-be rebels. Indeed, it might be possible to argue that the irksomeness of writing under restrictions helped stimulate the creative *diablerie* which makes Victorian literature stand supreme.

5 FORMER INSPECTOR JONATHAN WHICHER

Whicher is the only real-life character in this novel; we reconstruct him from various sources.

The Constance Kent case is too well known to be discussed here, but there are many excellent accounts of it; those interested may be referred to John Rhode's *The Case of Constance Kent* (London: Geoffrey Bles, 1928).

Dickens, in another factual article called "The Detective Police" for two issues of *Household Words* on July 27 and August 10, 1850, introduces Whicher when he was a young Detective Sergeant. We are told his appearance and his manner.

"Sergeant Witchem, shorter and thick set, and marked with the small-pox, has something of a reserved and thoughtful air, as though he were engaged in deep arithmetical calculations. He is renowned for his acquaintance with the swell mob."

We are given his conversational style, when he talks for several pages about the capture of a magsman named Tally-ho Thompson. His style of talk is further quoted in a contemporary discussion of the Constance Kent case, *The Road Murder, a Complete Report and Analysis of the Various Examinations and Opinions of the Press in This Mysterious Tragedy, by a Barrister-at-Law* (London: published at 184 Fleet Street, 1860). From these it is possible to deduce and amplify his character.

Finally, an account of him is given in Douglas G. Browne's *The Story of Scotland Yard* (London: George C. Harrap & Co., 1956). It is generally believed that Whicher resigned because "King" Mayne refused to support him (see *The Story of Scotland Yard*, p. 160), though Whicher in a letter to the press attributed his retirement to ill-health. But he was still a private detective in 1872, investigating the Tichborne Claimant and making accurate discoveries for which he was again attacked.

6 SUMMING-UP

There are a few other points in the narrative on which the reader might care for clarification.

The description of the train and of Paddington Station in

chapter two is based on a contemporary train-model in the Science Museum, South Kensington, and on Frith's once-famous painting *The Railway Station* (1863), whose background is Paddington and which may be seen at the Tate Gallery.

In chapter eleven, when Clive Strickland is challenged to name any genteel woman who would not be afraid to pick up a pistol, he replies with three names of which only that of Florence Nightingale may be familiar. He himself would not have explained, since the other two names were much in the newspapers. Mrs. Garrett Anderson, in 1865, was the first woman permitted to qualify as a doctor. Mrs. John Stuart Mill might be called the female beginner of the woman suffrage movement.

It is hardly necessary to say that Lord Palmerston did die on October 18 in that year. For details of British naval strength, see the Ninth Edition of the *Encyclopedia Britannica,* published in 1884, vol. XVII, pp. 284-285. The first four British ironclads, *Warrior, Black Prince* (each of 9200 tons' burden), *Defiance,* and *Resistance,* were finished in 1860. Eleven more had been completed by the end of 1861. This hasty and enormously expensive shipbuilding activity was caused by the maritime rivalry with France, which in 1858 commissioned four ironclads in an ambitious programme never completed.

And what was formerly Mivart's Hotel is now Claridge's.